#famous

JILLY GAGNON

#famous

KATHERINE TEGEN BOOKS
An Imprint of HarperCollins Publishers

Katherine Tegen Books is an imprint of HarperCollins Publishers.

#famous

Library of Congress Control Number: 2016935932
ISBN 978-0-06-243003-8

Typography by Carla Weise
17 18 19 20 21   PC/LSCH   10 9 8 7 6 5 4 3 2 1
❖
First Edition

To Dad, for telling me to follow my dream;
Mom, for her endless support;
and my sisters, who have always been
my best friends in the entire world

#famous

chapter one

TUESDAY, 4:15 P.M.

Loving your mom can lead to some seriously bad decisions.

I'd agreed to tag along on her quest for face creams mainly out of boredom. But the mall with my mother on a Tuesday afternoon—as though I suddenly believed in the calming effects of retail therapy? We'd been here maybe ten minutes and already I was regretting it.

We were almost at the makeup counter that was our *raison de mall* when she grabbed a black, fluttery top with laces winding up and down the front.

"Ooh, Rachel, isn't this nice?" She held it out to me. It looked like batwings in a corset.

"Not my style." I pushed the shirt away, turning to a rack

of oversized sweatshirts in neon-bright colors. Where had she even found that thing?

"No, not for you, for me. I think it's cool. Edgy. Don't you?" She held the shirt at arm's length. One chunk of frizzy hair fell from behind her ear onto her cheek. She always cut it too short; at that length, hair as electrical-socket nutso as ours would not be contained behind mere ears.

"Sure, Mom." I'd be pretty shocked to see my mom commit to a shirt she had to lace herself into. Usually her style tended toward neutral-colored sacks, but if she really wanted to dress like a vampire, I wasn't going to tell her no. Besides, it's kind of awesome when parents try to be cool, like watching a baby sloth play the piano or something. Terrible on the execution, and therefore adorable.

"Hey, do you care if I go get something at the food court? I went straight to ceramics club after sixth period, so I didn't have a chance to get a snack." Things would move a lot faster if she didn't have me to bounce awful fashion ideas off of.

She glanced at her watch. "Meet me back here in fifteen minutes. I don't want to spend the whole evening at the mall."

"Sure," I said over my shoulder.

"And don't be drinking one of those gallon-sized sodas," she said. "They're poison."

Mom was always finding some new threat to my precious development. Too late: I'd topped out at five foot three years ago.

I felt my phone buzz against my hip bone as I passed by

Banana Republic, its faceless, elongated mannequins watching disdainfully as I rounded the Wet Seal, following the faint scent of tasty greases.

> **(From MO-MO):** Do you have a new draft of Twice Removed ready yet? I don't think I'll be able to look at it until the weekend, but we need to be on top of this.

> **(To MO-MO):** No, I had ceramics today. I'll work on it soon—we still have what, three months until the deadline?

> **(From MO-MO):** There's no point in putting it off.

Mo must be stressed about something; trying to micromanage someone else was always her go-to when she had too much on her plate. We were applying together to a summer playwriting program with *Twice Removed*, but the due date for applications was forever away, and I was doing more of the writing regardless—Mo was more into performing, which meant I usually just let her help with edits. There was no point in calling Mo on it though, unless you wanted to intensify her stress-crazies. The best thing was to divert her to whatever she really wanted to talk about, so you wouldn't start arguing about not-really-the-point.

(To MO-MO): Don't worry. I'll send you something by the time you're able to look at it. Why so busy?

(From MO-MO): Did I ever mention how much I hate Europeans?

(To MO-MO): That's racist.

(From MO-MO): You can't be racist against a continent.

(From MO-MO): Trying to absorb the entirety of their pointless history—which is all just wars and oppressing women, BTW—is making my head hurt. I am SO going to fail this test.

Doubtful. Monique never failed anything. We'd been best friends since we were in diapers, and I couldn't remember her ever even getting a B. In third grade, she made two entire projects for the science fair in case one was better than the other.

(To MO-MO): That's what you get for taking smart-kid classes EVEN FOR ELECTIVES.

(To MO-MO): Guess how hard my Art II test will be? Oh wait, we don't have one.

(From MO-MO): I hate you.

(From MO-MO): I take it back. Distract me. If my head explodes I at least want to die laughing.

I looked around for something I could send to Monique. We had this ongoing game where we'd send each other funny pictures on Flit (basically anything that got an out-loud reaction—from snort to guffaw—scored a point, honors system) and the mall was the perfect spot to play. Monique loved unintentional double entendres or grammar mistakes on store signs. I usually sent funny graffiti or dogs in clothes. There's something about a dog wearing pants that never gets old.

I glanced around as I made my way across the mall to the food court, but nothing jumped out at me. And now that I was getting close enough to really smell all the different kinds of grease in the air, there was no way I'd be able to focus on the game. I was too hungry to hunt down a costumed Pomeranian. Food would have to come first. I spun around slowly, trying to figure out what I was in the mood for.

There was the depressingly beige buffet of breaded meat bits at China House (pass), sushi that was probably fresh off the boat a week ago at Japan *EXPRESS* (side of food poisoning, please?), Mrs. Butterbun's Cookie Shoppe (even thinking about putting an inch of frosting on a cookie made my teeth hurt) . . .

That's when I saw him.

Kyle Bonham.

Instinctively, I ducked my head over my phone and half turned away, so he wouldn't think I was staring.

I was, obviously—you couldn't help but stare at Kyle. He was about a thousand miles away from my type—so clean-cut he could be in an ad for drinking enough milk—and still I went fricking googly-eyed whenever I saw him. Extra embarrassing since I had fifth period with him every single day—it was only a matter of time until he caught me drooling.

He was standing behind the register at the Burger Barn, solemnly counting out change for a little girl who couldn't be more than seven or eight. She had this dreamy, beaming look on her face, like she was so proud to be getting treated like a grown-up, or maybe like she was half in love with him.

You and me both, babe.

He placed a final coin in her palm and straightened up, his shaggy brown hair flopping over his forehead in perfect just-barely-curls. Somehow he looked even hotter here than he did at school. The burnt-orange Burger Barn T-shirt he was wearing made his eyes—a little too far apart on his face, which made them even more beautiful—look greener. He somehow managed to make his pointed paper uniform cap seem jaunty and alluring.

I looked down at myself. I was wearing a shapeless old oxford I'd stolen from my dad's Goodwill pile. It was so long it made me look like a little kid playing dress-up, and it had clay all over the hem from where my apron hadn't covered it up. Then of course there were the faded leggings, starting to go baggy at the knees, the Chuck Taylors that had gotten so scuffed over the summer I wasn't even sure anymore what color they'd started as, and the sloppy side braid that did approximately nothing to contain the bursts of dark-brown frizz I call my hair.

Great look, Rach. No wonder Monique was always asking to give me makeovers. I was a fricking disaster.

Not that it mattered; I was not the kind of girl guys like Kyle Bonham—or really, any guy—paid much attention to. I'd managed to stay pretty much invisible for my entire high school career by hiding out in the art room. Especially to the painfully adorable lacrosse-star seniors who go out of their way to make even eight-year-olds feel special.

An older couple shuffled up to the register, staring perplexedly at the dozen or so variations on meat and cheese the Burger Barn packaged as "specials." Kyle watched them blankly, looking like someone out of one of those catalogs where everyone is leaning against rustic wooden furniture just "being themselves."

I should totally send a picture of him to Mo. After all,

what could be a better distraction than a perfect-looking boy? Bonus: if I snapped a picture of Kyle I could look at it on my phone whenever. Yes, borderline pathetic, but it's not like anyone would know but me.

I walked up behind the old woman, trying to look casual by keeping my phone down by my waist.

I tilted the phone up so Kyle's face was in the frame. He was staring out over the rest of the food court while the older couple worked out their order. I couldn't believe I was doing this; he was only a few feet away. Even with my flash and sound off, it would be so easy for him to realize what was going on.

But it would be worth it. In fact, this might be my best entry yet. Not like it was hard to find something better than a misplaced apostrophe, but this was gold-star emoji material.

As soon as he turned his head back toward the couple, I could take the picture quick and head over to the Pretzel Hut, like I'd realized I didn't want anything Burger Barn had on the menu. At least, not on the food menu.

"Well I don't know, Fred, I don't think I want triple cheese. Can't we get regular cheese?"

"Ma'am, if you like, I can substitute the cheese," Kyle said, smiling easily at the older woman. She seemed startled that he was talking to her. Enough so that she shifted over into my frame right as I was clicking to take the picture.

Well, crap-sandwich. Great photo of old-lady shoulder, Rach.

I shifted my weight onto my left foot, easing over as

imperceptibly as I could. Just move your arm, Grandma . . .

That's when I saw her, sulking in the line for the Caribou kiosk about twenty feet past the entrance to the food court: Jessie Florenzano.

. . . and her mom, waving cheerily at me like I wasn't the last person Jessie wanted to see, especially with her mom in tow. Jessie had been embarrassed by her even *before* our friendship imploded.

Jessie raised an eyebrow as though she could smell what I was doing. I dropped the phone down to my side and waved back. Jessie rolled her eyes and turned her back on me. I could see her whispering sharply to her mom, who smiled apologetically, then turned to Jessie, frowning. There were very few people I'd rather see less than Jessie, anywhere, ever, but I kind of loved that her mom still automatically acted friendly, four years after Jessie had sliced me out of her life.

I turned back. Grandma was laughing and nudging her husband's arm.

"*You* know how I love pickles!"

Ew. Not the mental image I needed before eating.

Kyle smiled and tapped at the register. If I moved my arm a couple more inches . . . but not too far. He couldn't know what was happening, and Jessie couldn't guess; it would be way too mortifying. He tapped his fingers on the counter in a rat-a-tat rhythm as the old lady dug through her wallet.

He was perfectly lined up in the frame, the last traces of a smile lingering on his smooth cheeks.

I glanced over at Jessie. She was resolutely pretending I didn't exist. There was never going to be a better time.

Click.

He looked toward me for a second. Crap, I was totally caught. I could feel my cheeks burning, betraying me. My breath caught somewhere around my sternum and stopped there, trapped.

But then he smiled and turned back to the customer, taking her pile of ones and quarters.

I exhaled, trying not to grin. I cropped the photo, typing in Mo's Flit handle so she'd see it. This was even better than a German shepherd with a tie.

"It's Rachel, right?"

I looked up, startled. The old couple had moved away to wait for their order, and Kyle was staring at me expectantly. I checked over my shoulder to make sure he wasn't talking to someone else. Like the Burger Barn only served Rachels or something? But I was the only person in line.

"Um, yeah." I felt my face going hot again. "Rachel. That's me." Oh god, I sounded like the worst kind of stupid. Quickly, I clicked to make my screen go dark.

He pointed at himself.

"Kyle."

I just stared, totally incapable of forming words.

"We're in Creative Writing together? Fifth period?"

As though I hadn't spent every day of the three weeks

since school started thanking all the gods for that fact.

"Right," I said, trying to sound like a girl who didn't eye-assault him daily. "You sit in the back, right?"

"Yeah! So Jenkins won't call on me too much. I'm not as good as you are at that stuff."

"I'm not that good," I said automatically, looking down at the counter. Someone had made a ketchupy fingerprint to the right of the register. Like a cheeseburger crime scene. I couldn't believe he knew who I was. The semester had barely started, and I wasn't even his year. Not only that, he had an *opinion* about me. A nice one.

"No, you are. That story of yours that Jenkins read yesterday was . . . well it was really weird, but, like, in a cool way," he said.

"Oh. Um, thanks." All my words were melting, puddling around my feet in a big sloppy jumble, too liquid-slippery for me to get a grip on. The story had been about a computer that got a weird virus that convinced the machine it was actually the ghost of Queen Elizabeth I. He'd already summed it up: It was weird. I was weird. I could feel my armpits stinging with sweat.

"Anyway, what can I get you, Rachel from writing class?" he said.

You, shirtless, on a stallion?

"Um . . . what do you mean?"

"To eat?" He frowned. It made his nose wrinkle upward,

like it was tethered to his forehead. I was so flustered about him knowing my name that I'd forgotten where we were—in line, at his job. He was being nice because he worked service. For god's sake, he flirted with the elderly. Even more blood rushed into my cheeks. If you poked them with a pin they'd probably burst everywhere. Like that scene in *The Shining* all over the Apple Prairie Mall food court.

"Oh, duh. Sorry, my blood sugar must be really low," I said. That's always Monique's excuse when she gets ditzy or snippy. "I was thinking, um, french fries?"

"Small?"

"No, large," I said quickly. I was starving. He grinned a little, which reminded me that the girls Kyle Bonham hung out with did *not* eat large fries. They'd probably cumulatively eaten half an order of fries in the last ten years, which was why they looked like miniature supermodels and I looked like the funny friend. "I like how the large container makes my hands look extra tiny and stunted. It helps me get perspective on life," I added.

Oh dear god, someone take this shovel away from me so I can stop digging my own fricking grave.

He laughed though, shaking his head slightly. "You're funny. Okay. One large fry is gonna be four thirty-six."

I dug in my purse for the money. He counted out my change and went to grab the fries. I could feel my heart rate slowing back to "not having a coronary" speeds.

"There you go," he said. "I *think* this is the right size for your hands," he added, grabbing one of my tiny fingers and playfully lifting the whole arm up in the air.

His touch was like an electric shock tingling up my entire arm. I almost snatched it back; guys don't usually go around grabbing my hands. Only guys like Kyle—guys who win state sports titles and homecoming king crowns—have the balls to do stuff like that in the first place. I hoped I hadn't nervous-sweated enough to pit out my shirt.

But somehow I managed to keep it together long enough for him to squint back and forth between my hand and the fry box, measuring the two against each other before finally nodding as though I'd passed muster.

"Yup, looks like a fit," he said.

He dropped my hand. I tried to breathe again.

"HA." I forced a laugh. Poorly. "I should go. I have to meet up with my mom." Awesome, Rachel, add to your intrigue by reminding him you hang out with your mother.

"Enjoy the fries, Rachel from writing," he said, grinning. "See you tomorrow."

"Sure." I gulped, nodding too many times, too fast. "See you around."

I walked away as slowly as I could force myself to, which was just this side of a sprint.

Breathing hard, I plopped onto a bench near the fountain. That had been disastrous.

But at least I'd gotten my picture. That had been the point, right? To flit something goofy to Monique? I finished typing her handle, then—because of course I'm oh-so-witty the *minute* actual guys have disappeared—I typed in a hashtag.

Send.

Immediately, I felt a little twinge. What if he saw it? He'd know it was me.

But that wouldn't happen. Kyle didn't follow me—maybe ten people did. I flitted all the pictures in the game to Monique, I'd been doing it for months; no one had ever noticed them before. I think the most attention any of the pictures ever got was a single non-Mo luv, and that squirrel vest had been AWESOME. Why would anyone suddenly care about this one?

My phone pinged with the sound that meant I had a reflit.

I opened my feed to see what Mo had said.

@attackoftherach_face tonight's brain food.

The picture I'd flitted was below. That sweet, goofy half grin lingering around his lips was too adorable. So much so that it had made me feel sassy enough to flit:

@Mo_than_you_know I'm digging what they're serving up at Burger Barn today.
#idlikefrieswithTHAT

God, I am *such* an idiot.

## chapter two

KYLE

TUESDAY, 5:00 P.M.

The girls who stepped up to the register looked about thirteen. Middle school age, probably. And they were all giggling.

Jeez, what was with the giggling today? I knew I looked like a tool in this hat, but it had never been noteworthy before. Middle schoolers: utter mysteries.

The ringleader: slick, straight, dirty-blond hair and what had to be fake fingernails. Finally she spoke up, hushing her crew with a wave of one hand.

"Okay, so, um, we'll take three chocolate quake-shakes, please, and a burger for Lau-*rie*." She said it with an exaggerated eye roll. Laurie must be the one in the back with the hunched shoulders, staring at her feet. Girls were so crappy to each other. "And a Diet Coke, please."

I typed it into the register.

"Anything else?"

"Oh, um, yes, actually," she said, biting her lip and looking back over her shoulder at her little posse. The group simultaneously giggled and squealed, sort of like a bagpipe laughing. I could see the bands on Ringleader's braces. She'd chosen bright pink. "I'd like fries with THAT."

Ringleader burst out laughing and buried her head in the nearest minion's shoulder. The whole group was giggling louder than ever, whispering "I can't believe you did it," and raising their eyebrows at one another dramatically.

Jeez. These middle schoolers: extra annoying.

"That's gonna be twenty-three eighteen," I said, trying to make my voice as flat as possible. The less you give middle school girls to work with, the better. I'd learned that pretty thoroughly coaching lacrosse camp last summer. "Soda machine is to the right," I added, pushing a cup with a plastic lid stuffed inside it across the counter.

After several seconds of dramatic breath-catching and hand fluttering, the girls paid and ran off, staring at me over their shoulders with googly eyes. Oof.

A middle-aged guy with a gut spilling out of the bottom of his polo shirt ordered a "Lite and Tasty." Then another group of girls squealed their way up to the register. These ones looked older. They were maybe freshmen. But they were all still giggling. Like, a lot. Usually even girls couldn't find anything funny about the Burger Barn. And I couldn't remember the last time our clientele had been so female.

Could there be some sort of event at the mall? A pop star or something? One of the girls was pointing at me and taking out her phone, like she was gonna take a picture. Which was weird and kinda creepy. I felt like telling her I wasn't whoever she thought I was, but that would have made things worse. She might have started talking to me.

This shift could not end fast enough.

#

I had never seen so many girls order fries in my life. I would have snuck back to my locker to google what was going on, but I was the only person on the register on Tuesdays; usually it was dead my whole shift.

By five forty-five we'd run out of fries. We'd never run out of anything before. By six fifteen, Jim, the manager, decided to close for the night, even though it was two hours early. We were running out of too many things. The only thing left was chicken tenders, minus the sauce.

At that point, the line went past the China House and around the corner by the Gap. It was mostly groups of girls, with a couple annoyed adults stuck between them, and it had to be fifty people long.

Which didn't make sense at all. I eat this stuff, like, every day. There's no good reason to wait around for it.

I headed to my locker, rolling my shoulders the way I did after a tough practice. All the girls had been laughing. Most had been taking pictures. The whole thing had been . . . terrifying. It had been kinda terrifying, all of them staring at me, placing the same exact order, even using the same exact words. It was like I was stuck in a french-fries-themed *Body Snatchers* sequel.

At first it seemed harmless. Like maybe some girls JV team was doing, like, extra-dumb hazing. But after the third or fourth giggle-giggle-FRIES-WITH-THAT-giggle-giggle, I wondered if someone was trying to mess with me. Like, me specifically. It could have been Dave Rouquiaux, from lacrosse. He was always doing stuff to try to get a rise out of us after games, or in the locker room. One time he put about half a bottle of laxatives into Eric Winger's Gatorade because he thought Eric had been hitting on the girl he liked. Another time he stole the entire starting line's shoelaces before practice, just 'cause. He even took his own, to throw everyone off the scent. Dave might do something like this out of boredom. Dave: just that dude.

But how would he have convinced about a zillion girls to mess with me at the Burger Barn? Did Dave even *know* that many girls? Not likely.

Sighing, I opened the locker and chucked my hat inside. I checked the pile of T-shirts on the shelf. Only one clean shirt left. I'd have to take the rest home and do laundry tonight. Weak.

I jogged back to the register to grab a plastic bag to put them in.

CLICK, CLICK, CLICK, CLICK.

Two girls had been lying in wait. By the time I yelled "What is going *on*?" they were already halfway across the food court, dodging and weaving around customers holding trays. If they had any stick skills they might have been good at lacrosse. One was making this wheezing sound of excitement, like she might faint. Or pop. This day: definitely getting weird.

I walked as fast as I could back to my locker, stopping to check my reflection in the mirror alongside Jim's office for pulsing zits, or, like, a full-on snot mustache. Something worth lying in wait to photograph. Maybe something mangled and evil had started growing out of my neck. What were those things called? Parasitic twins?

But there was nothing out of the ordinary. I looked exactly the same as always, except I was still in my grease-splattered Burger Barn shirt. I headed to the locker and started stuffing dirty shirts into the bag. I needed to get out of here. Like now.

After I'd changed and checked the schedule to see when I was on next, I grabbed my phone from the back of the locker shelf. We weren't allowed to have them when we worked the register.

I pressed the on button.

10 notifications . . .

The little refresh wheel at the top kept spinning.

36 notifications . . .

And spinning.

492 notifications . . .

Dang.

Then it just totally died. Turned itself off. Blip.

Seriously, what the heck was going on?

I turned the phone back on and set it on the shelf. It convulsed with notifications. Finally it chimed loudly, buzzed one last time, and came to a stop. Cautiously, I picked it up.

13,178 notifications

It buzzed again.

14,256 notifications

My eyes went out of focus for a second. This made no sense. I clicked my texts.

It looked like I'd gotten one from everyone in my phone book, plus a few numbers I didn't recognize. The top one was from Ollie, my best friend on the team. I liked Ollie. He was quieter than the other guys, and he never tried to prank people or anything, but he wasn't all judgmental when other people did. He just didn't seem to care. It drove Dave nuts how unconcerned Ollie could be. *That* was flipping hilarious.

(**From Ollie**): Dude, you're a trend topic

What was he talking about? I scrolled back through his messages.

> **(From Ollie):** Did you see this picture of you? Some junior chick has a crush

> **(From Ollie):** Everyone is sharing it, you need to check this out

> **(From Ollie):** You're blowing up Flit

I opened my Flit app.

@jenDintheHEE and 15,822 other users reflitted a flit you were mentioned in.

I looked. It was from Erin Rothstein, this girl on dance team that sometimes hung out with my girlfriend, Emma. Actually, Emma: technically my ex. Anyway, it was just someone else's flit that Erin had added "OMG that's @YourBoyKyle_B" to.

I opened the original.

62,414 reflits

My legs kinda went out from under me then, until I was sitting on the peeling linoleum floor in front of the lockers.

It was a photo of me behind the register, looking like a

dork in my uniform. The hashtag said #idlikefrieswithTHAT.

It looked like it was taken today. And it already had how many reflits? I frowned, trying to make this make sense. That was what all the middle schoolers were saying all afternoon. "I'd like fries with *that.*" So clearly they'd all seen the picture . . . since my shift started. At four.

I took a deep breath, closing my eyes as I exhaled. Coach Laughton said it helped you focus, but it just made me feel dizzier.

First things first: who had taken the picture? The original flit seemed to have come from "attackoftherach_face." That could have been anyone. The name on the account was "oh RHEally" so that didn't help. I peered at the tiny thumbnail picture. It was mostly an explosion of curly, dark-brown hair.

I squinted.

It was totally that Rachel girl, the strange, quiet one from writing class. We'd talked at the start of my shift. I smiled a little. *She* had a crush on me? She seemed like the type that would be dating a twenty-year-old who smoked cigarettes end-to-end and wore skinny jeans and played bass in, like, some punk band.

Huh. Rachel: unexpected.

Without thinking, I clicked to follow her. It brought her count to twenty-nine. She only followed fourteen accounts herself, and one of them was Alec Baldwin, who had to be older than my parents. Who *was* this girl?

Oh, wait a second.

I clicked back to my notifications.

11K new followers.

K. As in thousand.

This morning I had 289, as in 289. I had checked.

I could feel my heart beating too fast, thumping against my rib cage. What was happening? Why would anyone even want to share a picture of me? I'd always figured I was decent looking. I never could have landed Emma otherwise. But I wasn't anything special. My brother, Carter, was the handsome one. Or Ollie, he had that brooding movie star thing going on. I could see this happening to Ollie. But me? Seriously?

I stuffed the bag of dirty T-shirts into my backpack and jogged to the back of the store. The door there opened onto an employee parking lot near the food court dumpsters. It was deserted. I'd never been so happy to park next to trash.

I got into my car and gripped the steering wheel until my hands stopped shaking. Thank god the middle schoolers hadn't figured out where I was parked. I didn't know how they would have, but I couldn't work out how they'd found the right Burger Barn so fast, either.

My phone lit up again. I grabbed it, ready to turn the stupid thing off. This was too intense. I needed time to process what was going on.

Emma's picture popped up, the one she'd put into my contacts a year ago, right after we first got together. She had on bright-red lipstick and was making an exaggerated, ducky pout. She thought it was a better picture of her than I did.

I decided to answer.

"Hey, Em."

"Ohmygod, KYLE. I have been trying to call you ALL. DAY. Didn't you get my messages?" She was talking fast, even for her. She sounded breathless.

"No, sorry. I was at work."

"You saw Flit, though."

"Yeah. Yeah, I saw it." I squeezed my eyes shut, frowning. I still couldn't wrap my head around what had happened. It kinda hurt to try. I rolled down the car window; the air inside, still heated from the sunny day, suddenly felt claustrophobic. Even with the smells of rancid fryer grease and a thousand kinds of rotting vegetables, the outside air was better.

"Who is that girl anyway? I can't believe she took that picture. Totally pathetic."

I didn't like Emma calling Rachel pathetic, but I didn't know what to say. I guess it had been sorta weird. "She's just some junior."

"Isn't that cute."

Emma's voice was low and monotone. I shouldn't say any more about Rachel. Emma had always been kinda jealous.

"I guess."

"Anyway, what are you doing right now?"

"I was gonna go home. We closed early. Ran out of food."

"Really? I thought you guys had, like, five freezers full of stuff in back."

"We do. Usually. A lot of middle school girls came by to

get fries. I guess because of the picture?"

"Whoa." Emma whistled. "They tracked you down? That's insane. Are you okay? That almost sounds scary."

"Yeah, kinda." I exhaled. Emma had always been really good at hearing what I wasn't saying. It was one of the things I liked best about her. Maybe it was 'cause we were both used to people not paying much attention to us. Emma's dad was too busy marrying and divorcing new women every couple years to be around much. Her mom and stepdad seemed cool, but she always said they loved their kid, Nathan, more than they loved her.

My stuff was less drama. My brother, Carter, was the golden child with the grades and the ambition and the looks. I was like the knockoff version. The crappier mini-Carter that my parents had stopped paying attention to ages ago. At least I was taller.

"I'm just glad they don't know what I drive. For a second I thought there might be a few camped out in the backseat." I leaned over to make sure I wasn't right, but it was empty.

"If you closed early you don't have to go home right away, do you?"

"I dunno. Why?"

"Maybe you can come over. I was supposed to have dinner with my dad but he bailed at the last minute. Again. I guess Lindsay had some event, I don't know." Emma trailed off. She never said much about her dad's current girlfriend. "Anyway my mom and Martin are out somewhere, and Nathan is over at a friend's, so I don't even have him to play video games with. Pretty pathetic, huh?"

I squeezed my eyes shut tight and leaned my forehead on the steering wheel.

Was she inviting me over because she wanted to get back together? Or was she just lonely, and curious about the flit, and she figured I'd answer? If I came, would it smooth things over, or would she think I was whipped? Emma wasn't the kind of girl who would get back together with someone she thought she had on *too* short a leash.

Girls: I definitely need a translator.

"It'd be pretty hard for you to be pathetic," I said. It was the least puppy-dog thing I could come up with that was still true.

"You're sweet."

"Just honest."

"So are you coming over? I've got the whole place to myself, I think all night. Plus, if you go home there will probably be middle schoolers camped out at your house. And you just said you don't have any more fries."

I laughed.

"That's an excellent point." I tried not to think about how it might *actually* be an excellent point.

I couldn't say yes until I knew what she wanted. If she was trying to push me into the friend zone, I should go home. It would be easier in the long run.

"Does this mean . . . I thought we were broken up?" It had only been a week since Emma had told me she "needed to just be alone for a while." That put her two weeks ahead of schedule for "missing me so much," if our last two breakups were any guide.

I know it's pathetic that I didn't just ditch her already, but there was something about Emma. She was really hot, obviously, but she was also good at reading people, at reading *me*. Like if I was down, or if I wanted to leave wherever we were, Emma always knew, sometimes even before I did. It was like she noticed me more than other people. And when no one was around, I'd catch glimpses of this side of her that was so . . . fragile. For most people she was on all the time, but when we were alone she was different. Smaller somehow, and sadder. It made me want to make her happier. And she had this way of looking at me sometimes that made me feel . . . I dunno, like something legit amazing. Emma made you want to be cool enough to hang out with Emma.

"Well we *were*," she said slowly. "Do you still want to be broken up?"

"I never wanted to be at all," I said truthfully.

"I never wanted to be broken up, I just needed me-time, you know? It'd be nice to see you. It's lonely over here." She sighed. The sound made my heart squeeze tight.

"Okay," I said, "I'll be over in a little."

Maybe this picture blowing up wasn't such a bad thing after all.

chapter three

RACHEL

TUESDAY, 5:15 P.M.

It honestly didn't occur to me that anyone would see the picture.

Sure, Monique had reflitted it, but so what? I was annoyed at first—she had to know I wouldn't want people to know how drooly I got over Kyle Bonham—but it's not like it was some big secret that he's good-looking. People might not even know I'd flitted it. Ever since middle school I'd been working to ensure I was one of Apple Prairie High's least-known students; better to be nobody than have a target on your back. Besides, Monique barely has more followers than me, and half of them are her cousins.

When I checked my phone as my mom pulled into the

driveway, though, it had jumped to ten reflits.

I only recognized one of the profiles, which meant that eight strangers had shared the picture. That was weird. Not bad, but definitely not great.

"Rachel, for goodness' sake, get out of the car." Mom looked at me through the driver's-side door. "Honestly I sometimes think we should never have let you have that thing," she muttered.

I fumbled at my seat belt with my left hand, refreshing the app with my thumb.

39 reflits

Crap-muffins. Someone from school was going to see this soon, and it wouldn't be hard for them to put it together, if they hadn't already. If Kyle found out, I wouldn't be the strange girl from writing anymore, I'd be pathetic.

A notification lit up my screen.

@DanceQueenErin reflitted your flit:
OMG that's @YourBoyKyle_B @attackoftherach_
face I'm digging what they're serving up at
Burger Barn today **#idlikefrieswithTHAT**

Dammit, dammit, DAMMIT.

Then it really exploded.

It seemed like the entire school was reflitting the picture.

First the girls on dance team with Erin, then a handful of ath-letes, then the names stopped even being familiar (I kind of tried *not* to know the meatheads). They were multiplying too fast for me to work out who most of them were.

One name I recognized, though.

@jessieflozo mentioned you in a flit: OMG I should've known @attackoftherach_face was up to something weird I totally saw this happen **#idlikefrieswithTHAT**

@jessieflozo replied to a flit you were mentioned in: Sorry for not saving u from the stalker, @YourBoyKyle_B, I didn't even know u were working

@jessieflozo replied to a flit you were mentioned in: Don't feel bad, though, @attackoftherach_face always liked fries with that **#idlikefrieswithTHAT <img: r-e-burger .jpg>**

I would've assumed Jessie burned any pictures of us together back in middle school, to destroy all evidence of hav-ing been friends with a weirdo. Since then, she'd clawed her way to the top social tier. Making the Wolfettes dance team sophomore year helped.

The picture she chose was from the worst of my awkward phase—I'd put on my puberty weight before having a growth spurt, I had one big caterpillar eyebrow I hadn't learned to pluck yet, and I was still in braces.

. . . and I was biting through a massive cheeseburger, the poster girl for childhood obesity. I swallowed hard. After this, if Kyle didn't find me actively repellant, he'd probably just pity me, which was possibly even worse.

I couldn't believe she'd flitted it. She'd laugh along in middle school when her "cool" friends ragged on my hair, or the plays Monique and I wrote (I used to just write stories, but Monique wanted something she could perform), but she'd never *started* things.

I should turn off my phone. The smart thing would be to turn off the phone for the next half hour until this went away.

But Mo was the smart one. I compromised and slid it into my shirt pocket.

I ran upstairs to my bedroom, flopped onto my back on the puffy black-and-white zigzag comforter, and tried to focus on something else. Anything else. Think up a new scene for *Twice Removed*; Mo would be pumped the play was coming along. Just whatever you do, don't look at your phone again.

What if Jessie posted more pictures? Who else had them? There had to be a dozen just from that awful sleepover at Lorelei Patton's in the fifth grade, when Mom had called Lorelei's parents and forced her to invite me.

I ran to the oak bookcase in the corner and started pulling out yearbooks.

"Rachel!" Mom's voice ricocheted up the stairs. "Dinner!"

I flipped through manically. Here I was with a full-on fro, touching my tongue to my nose. Here I was around the height of my weight gain in a too-short shirt that showed my doughy belly. Jesus, they had me as an "orphan" in the seventh-grade production of *Oliver!*, tooth blacked out and dirt on my face. And these were just sitting in yearbooks, waiting for anyone to find . . . and flit. I'd always figured hiding in the corner with my handful of arty friends would mean this kind of thing couldn't happen again. But Jessie's followers were already piling onto the picture. Being invisible at school was my line of defense. And they were rolling over it like a tidal wave, disintegrating the only protection I had . . .

"Rachel, I mean it! Get a move on!"

I swallowed hard and dropped the yearbook. I thought about leaving the phone upstairs, but I couldn't make myself do it. I'd just see how many notifications were coming through.

I slid into my usual seat at our tiny kitchen table, wedged into the corner next to the door to the backyard we left permanently deadbolted. Jonathan sat across from me, fanning Pokémon cards across his place mat and squinting at them through his wire-rimmed glasses.

He frowned, rearranging his card fiefdom, then grinned, nodded, and swept them together to stuff them into the kangaroo pocket of his sweatshirt. His Pikachu sweatshirt.

God, the kid was hopeless, but I loved him for it. I wouldn't have known how to handle a little brother who cared about seeming cool. People like that confused me—Jessie confused me.

Maybe I should have spent more time trying to decode her.

My phone buzzed right as Mom set the salad bowl on the table. I pulled it out to look at the screen.

592 notifications

My stomach pirouetted. Even Jessie didn't have that many followers. Who else was talking about me?

"Rachel, phone away," Mom said automatically, turning to the counter to load plates with lasagna. "Dinner is a technology-free zone."

I slipped it into my pocket, tapping my toe against the ground as Dad sat down at my left. They were probably mostly luvs. That wasn't so bad, right?

I hadn't even made it through a bite of lasagna before the phone buzzed again. I breathed in deep, stuffed my fork into my mouth, and swallowed as fast as I could. The still-molten cheese burned the roof of my mouth, making me tear up a little.

"Jonathan, tell me one way you expressed yourself today." Mom stabbed her salad precisely until she'd speared one of every element.

Jonathan squinted thoughtfully.

"I finished my vocabulary test early, so I drew pictures of the words around the edges."

"I'm glad you added more beauty to the world."

This was how they talked to us at dinner. I'd only realized in middle school that most people's parents weren't total hippies, but I didn't mind that mine were. They'd always made us feel like what we were doing mattered. It was nice—and dorky—but today it made me want to spit acid.

My phone buzzed again as Mom asked him about Odyssey of the Mind. She was focused on Jonathan; I could sneak a peek.

1,385 notifications

I almost choked on my cherry tomato. That was more people than all of Apple Prairie High. Without thinking I clicked the screen; I had to know what they were saying.

"Rachel." Dad tilted his head down to peer at me over the top of his glasses. They were identical to Jonathan's—he was Dad's doppelgänger, wiry and myopic and narrow-faced, while I looked like a darker version of Mom, with her frizzy hair, single dimple, and permanent extra ten pounds. "Active listening shows respect."

"Okay." I dropped the phone into my lap. I could feel its heat radiating into me like a burning brand. L, maybe, for loser. Or TP, for total pariah. "Monique's been texting about homework," I added. She had been a few hours back, so it wasn't totally untrue.

Dad frowned in a way he thought was menacing. He couldn't pull off menacing.

"Well, tell me something new you learned today, Rachel."

"How to apply a majolica glaze," I squeezed out. I stuffed as big a bite of lasagna into my mouth as I thought could fit. Swallowing was becoming harder and harder—my stomach felt like a knotted garden hose, tangled and twisted and unwilling to take anything in—but I had to make a dent in the food or they'd never let me leave the table. "It was harder than I thought." I'd also learned how to commit social seppuku, but opted not to mention that.

"Jonathan," Dad said, "what's a difficult problem you overcame today?"

Jonathan sat, thinking hard. He was still young enough to enjoy my parents' earnest . . . well, probing. The phone buzzed again. Mom and Dad were both turned toward Jonathan. Surreptitiously I dropped my hand under the table, clicking it to life.

1,529 notifications

The most recent ones showed up below:

@RickiTicki_TAVI mentioned you in a flit:
@attackoftherach_face goes to APHS? where'd

she come from? i've nvr seen her before
#idlikefrieswithTHAT

I exhaled. That wasn't so bad. But there were more:

@GabiBaby mentioned you in a flit: Ugh, cld
@attackoftherach_face be any more pathetic?
She was always weird but this is just sad.

It was Gabi Ruiz, from ceramics club. I'd assumed my weird-kid activities were safe. She was low on the social totem pole, but clearly angling for more.

@BethaneEeeEEE mentioned you in a flit: Found
another middle school gem of
@attackoftherach_face. Awkward phase much?
#idlikefrieswithTHAT

@chzfries mentioned you in a flit:
@BethaneEeeEEE @attackoftherach_face
she looks like one of those loner serial killer
types. @YourBoyKyle_B shld slepe w/1 eye
open haha

Kyle wasn't tagged in many, but enough that there was no way to avoid embarrassment. The whole school knew about my stupid crush, and now they were digging up proof of my long-standing patheticness. I was barely past seeing myself that way. Now Jessie was ensuring everyone would. Wouldn't be able to *not*.

I might actually implode from humiliation, like one of those stars Ms. Feldman talked about last year in Planetary Sciences, the ones that are too small and unimportant to explode when they die, so they collapse into themselves until there's nothing left.

"Rachel. Our family is here in the real world, waiting to engage with you." Dad put his hand out.

"No, please—" I breathed in too fast, in a choky kind of way. "Can I be excused? There's a . . . thing I have to deal with . . ."

"Rachel, what's going on?" Mom's voice was soft. She laid her hand on my arm. "This isn't like you."

I knew I should have left the phone upstairs. Now I had to figure out the best way to lie about this.

When I was little I told my parents everything, like Jonathan—ideas I had for plays, crushes, even when I got my first pubes (I know, totally mortifying). Besides Monique, they were basically my best friends.

So when Lorelei Patton started calling me "oo-bee" in the fifth grade (short for "unibrow"—Mom hadn't taken me to get waxed yet), I told Mom. I told her about Lorelei leaving a bottle of Nair on my desk with a drawing of my "monster brows." I told her about everyone but me getting invited to Lorelei's slumber party.

Then she turned around and called Lorelei's mother, and the teacher, and the fricking principal, and said they needed to deal with "this horrific bullying."

"If bullies aren't confronted they find new targets," she'd said, with this maddening, patronizing smile. "Kids will respect you for standing up to her."

The whole class knew I was the reason we had that stupid presentation in the gym, with middle-aged actors taunting the "shy kid" on a "bus" that was nothing more than chairs lined up in rows and a detached steering wheel for the actor at the front.

Mom didn't realize that this *was* like me. The me who spent the night of Lorelei's sleepover pretending to be asleep so the girls wouldn't know I could hear every mean thing they were saying. The me who lied the next day and said it was fun.

We'd had intensely awkward conversations about how she and Dad wouldn't punish me for "exploring my sexuality" or "experimenting with substances," so birth control or calling home drunk for a ride was neutral ground.

But when I told her something—a big something—she'd ratted me out to the entire fricking school. Not *everything* was neutral ground.

So not everything was up for discussion anymore.

I looked down at the smear of brown and creamy red I'd smashed out of the lasagna. I had to say enough that they'd buy me being stressed, but not so much that they'd look into it.

"It's dumb," I started. "It's this . . . flit. I flitted a picture, and some people at school have seen it, and I'm mildly freaking out." I could feel my ears getting hot. Who gets hot ears? Was that one of those body signs that you're lying?

"What kind of picture?" Mom said slowly, leaning forward to look at me more closely. Her eyes were buggy, and her mouth was pulled tight.

Oh god.

"NOT that kind of picture. Wow. No. Nothing like that." She nodded, obviously relieved no one had seen digital versions of my naughty parts. "It was of this random boy who's out of my league. Mo reflitted it, and now people at school have seen it . . ." I had to tread lightly here. Mom barely went on social media; she wouldn't look unless I gave her a reason to. "It's just embarrassing."

"So you're worried because people know you think this boy is cute?"

I grimaced. Even though I was deliberately feeding her a sanitized version, it did make the whole thing sound silly.

"I mean . . . yeah, I guess."

"Attraction is a natural thing, and nothing to be ashamed of." Dad looked at me meaningfully.

Mom glared at him, eyebrows raised, and squeezed my arm.

"What your dad means is this is going to blow over before you know it. By tomorrow morning, everyone will have forgotten about it. They probably already have."

I tried to force a smile, but it felt like my cheeks were stuck in the off position. At least I hadn't succumbed to stress tears. If I'd been on my period (when my balloon-skin of normal is barely able to cover the ever-expanding explosion of emotional wreck and snotty cries), this game would have been over.

"Trust me, sweetie. This is barely a speck on people's radar." I nodded, mute. I couldn't tell her otherwise, and besides, I *really* wanted to believe her.

"I'm sorry I was looking at my phone. But can I be excused? I'm not hungry."

"We want you kids to live your lives *off*line." Dad shook his head. Mom gave him a *Jesus, Dan, give it a rest* face. "But I suppose it's all right this once."

I practically ran to the sink, slopping the gory mess of pasta sauce and drowned leaves into the disposal. I'd just thought of one way to keep this from going any further; I could deactivate my account. If Kyle hadn't seen things yet (possible—he was still at work) he might not realize it was me. The mean pictures weren't addressed to him; he might miss those entirely.

"Rachel," Dad said as I was rushing out the door. I turned, fingers tapping my impatience out against my leg. "There's no such thing as a boy that's out of your league. If he doesn't realize that, he's not good enough for you in the first place."

God, dads were so perpetually blind to reality. Still, *your* dad should believe that. Even if he's wrong.

"Thanks, Dad."

I checked my phone on the stairs. A new batch of mentions filed down to the bottom, but sitting above them, separated out, was a different notification.

@YourBoyKyle_B followed you

So much for that idea—he definitely knew. I dug my fingernails into the butt of my hand.

Was he messing with me? Getting in on the joke? I thought back to the afternoon. He'd seemed so genuine. So nice.

Maybe we could actually get to know each other?

Not likely, but it's not like I could somehow be more humiliated by this whole debacle. Before I could think better of it, I followed him back, then tapped out a quick private flit.

Sorry about the pic. I had no idea it would blow
up. Also, you're welcome for the massive ego
boost.

I immediately refreshed my account to see if he'd responded. Instead I just got another notification.

@Lolobear1899 mentioned you in a flit: eww
@attackoftherach_face is so fat and disgusting.
just kill yourself girl ur gonna die a virgin anyway
haha

I dropped the phone on my bedroom floor so fast it might as well have stung me. Why would someone say that? My stomach roiled, and I could feel my cheeks getting hot. Before this whole thing had been embarrassing, but now I felt . . . ashamed. Like someone had just pantsed me in the middle of the commons. Was there something wrong with me? I'd never thought about it before; Mo was still a virgin too.

Cautiously, I picked up the phone, and pecked at the girl's profile picture to see who she was.

She wasn't familiar. Maybe because she lived in California.

She didn't even know me—she couldn't, she lived a million miles away—and she was telling me to kill myself.

My mouth started watering painfully. If some random chick from California was saying that, how far would this go? What else would people say?

Bile started crawling the sides of my throat.

I turned the phone off.

## chapter four

KYLE

TUESDAY, 7:00 P.M.

My phone rattled on the coffee table, the screen lighting up.
I bent over to check it. Which was stupid, I was getting notifications about every second, but it was habit. Like muscle
memory.

@attackoftherach_face followed you

@attackoftherach_face has sent you a private
flit

A PF after all this? I opened her message. It was kinda . . .
like, funny. If it were me, I'd have tried to pretend nothing had

happened, but she just owned it. And she didn't seem angry, even though some dance team girls were turning catty. Not like that was my fault, but holding it against me seemed like something a girl might do.

"Okay, I get that it's fun being Apple Prairie High's flavor of the week or whatever." Emma waved her hand in front of my phone screen until I looked at her. "But you have to leave that alone." She grabbed the phone and put it on the far corner of the coffee table. "I asked you over because I actually wanted us to hang out. If I only wanted a warm body in the room, I'd have bought a cat. Or called Dave." She smirked.

We were sitting in Emma's wood-paneled basement, on a couch her mom had gotten sick of for the upstairs. The room was always a little too cold and smelled a little musty, like some corner had gotten wet and never quite dried out, but it was the best place in the house. Even if her mom and stepdad had been home, they'd never come down here. Emma's basement: total bonus.

"All right, what do you want to do?" I said.

"We could download a new game? As long as it's something I can play with Nathan. PG stuff." Emma always pretended she only got video games for her nine-year-old half brother so she wouldn't have to admit to liking them.

"Are you paying? I barely have enough hours this week to cover gas money."

"My dad is." Emma turned on the TV and her console. "In fact, we should get a dozen. He won't say anything about it. If he even notices."

"He's okay with that?" My parents would ream me if I did something like that. They'd made Carter and me get jobs as soon as we could drive. Apparently it taught us about money and "built character." They loved character.

"He'd have to talk to me to not be okay with it," Emma murmured. She flipped past the war games rapidly. "Anyway, he should have spent the money on me tonight at dinner." She turned, grinning hard. I must have been frowning, because her smile immediately curdled. Whoops.

"We don't have to." She tossed the controller on the couch. "I just thought you'd like it." Emma burrowed backward, pulling her knees to her chin and looking away from me.

Jeez. Ten minutes: longer than I can go without doing something completely idiotic.

"Do you want me to go, or . . ."

"No, please stay," she said, so quiet I almost couldn't hear. We sat in silence for a minute. Suddenly, she lunged toward my phone. "I know, let's see how many freshmen are into you." She smiled, eyes wide and mischievous. "You'll be, like, the new picture in their lockers tomorrow, right? I better not have to fight one for you."

"Not likely. But sure, okay." I made myself smile back. Something about the idea made me uncomfortable, but at least Emma wasn't legit mad. Plus, it *was* kind of awesome. I should call Carter to tell him about this. He'd never believe it.

Emma leaned into me, handing me the phone to enter the

pass code. She was wearing a plain long-sleeved T-shirt and plaid pajama bottoms. I could feel the heat of her skin through the thin fabric. I held my breath, focusing on the warmth of her body. And on not letting it make me forget my own pass code.

Emma grabbed the phone back and buried her head in my neck. Her curls tickled my cheek, but I didn't reach over to scratch it. It was nice having her there. Trying as hard I could not to move her, I freed my arm from between us and draped it across her shoulders.

"Holy wow, Kyle." I opened my eyes. I'd been busy inhaling the faint cherry scent of her hair.

"What?"

"Let's just say this has *definitely* moved beyond the freshman class."

I took the phone. At first I couldn't figure out what Emma had seen.

Oh. The number under my name had jumped a *lot*.

Followers: 152K

I blinked. I hadn't wrapped my head around a *K* showing up in my followers count. Now, an hour later, it was in the hundreds of thousands? My heart beat faster.

I started scrolling through the notifications, really paying attention for the first time. People hadn't just followed me, they'd flitted about how hot I was, how they wanted to hang out, how if I followed back they would . . . whoa, that was *not* rated PG.

Emma squeezed my arm a little. "Have you already found my replacement?"

"Just one sec." I squinted. Should I respond to these girls? I should flit something, right? I still wasn't sure why they were following me. I wasn't the one who took the picture. What did they expect me to say? It made it impossible to say *anything*.

I tapped my thumb against the screen, thinking. What do you say to a million girls telling you they're "totally in love"? Carter would know. Carter: *actually* the cool guy, not just someone understudying his older brother.

"Kyle? Hello?" Emma waved a hand in front of my eyes. When I didn't respond, she started tracing a finger along my arm. It tickled. "Do you need help coming up with a flit? I bet we can think of something funny."

I scrolled down farther. A girl with the handle DarkAngelina403 had sent a photo of her in a bikini. A really tiny bikini. And it was kinda see-through.

Emma squirmed over me until she was sitting on my lap, facing me. She smiled hard, running a finger along my jaw.

"Kyle . . ."

"Just let me finish this." Some of these girls were ridiculously hot.

Emma leaned in to kiss me on the cheek, her curls making it impossible to see my phone screen. I leaned to the side, trying to focus, or just get a sight line.

"I thought you came over to hang out with *me*." Emma ducked under my arms for a kiss. Instinctively I pulled back. "Can't you leave that alone? You don't even know those girls."

"But I have to say something, right?"

"*I'm* here. They're not."

She leaned in again to press her lips against mine. Her tongue slid into my mouth.

It felt so good I couldn't focus on anything else. I dropped the phone and wrapped my hands around her hips, pulling her toward me. Emma moaned softly.

Then she started biting my lip. The bites: not sexy, just hard.

"Whoa, settle," I said, pulling back. "That hurt."

"All right, I'll be gentle." She leaned in to nibble on my ear. "Even though that's no *fun*."

"Slow down." This was starting to feel weird. Hot, obviously, but still: she was never this aggressive when we were both sober. Also: still technically not a couple. "There's nothing wrong with going slower, right?"

"But Kyle, I want to be with you," she murmured. "Don't you want to be with me?"

It sounded like something out of a movie. An X-rated one.

I jerked my head back. Suddenly it didn't feel hot anymore.

It felt forced, like she was playacting. Which made me feel dirty, like I should brush my teeth or watch a Disney movie or something.

"Emma, what's going on?"

"What do you mean?" She looked past me. "Did I do something wrong?"

"No, you're just acting . . . I dunno, weird. I mean, we're sitting here, doing nothing, and out of the blue you're, like, more into me now than the entire year we dated?"

She grimaced. I could have punched myself in the face.

Why was I saying this? She's all over me, and I'm pushing her away? Jeez, the Flit stuff must have temporarily fried my brain. Or hers. Was that it? The reason she was acting this way? I didn't want to believe it, but it made sense.

"I've always been into you." She shrank back, wrapping an arm around herself protectively. "I don't know why you'd say that."

"But why are you acting like this?" She hadn't told me I was crazy. In fact she was clearly avoiding the question. Oof. "Where did this come from, Em?"

"Seriously?" She still wouldn't meet my eye. "What's so bad about wanting to make out? You said on the phone you wished we were back together, now you're going to be all—" Emma rolled off my lap onto the couch. She scooted away, putting a solid six inches of cushion between us. It might as well have been a wall.

"It's not bad, but it's like . . ." I exhaled and looked at my lap. I wouldn't have the courage to say it if I could see her reaction. "Are you only into me right now because of what's happening with the picture?"

"What? It's not even that good of a picture of you."

Answer: not a "no." It might as well have been "obviously." The idea made me so angry my temples throbbed.

"Awesome. So when I'm just me, you're over it. Don't call, don't need me."

"Who ever said . . ."

"You. You said *exactly* that. That you were actually *trying* 'not to need anyone.' I know because it was less than a week ago." I could feel my hands balling into fists. "But now that my picture is everywhere, you invite me over and throw yourself at me."

"Kyle, it wasn't like that at *all*," she said softly.

It felt like my stomach was collapsing it was sinking so fast. I forced out a laugh.

"I'm right, aren't I? You're ready to do anything because I'm suddenly, like, pretend famous. For a second. On *Flit*. Jeez, Emma, do you know how gross that is?"

"You know what? Leave."

"Am I hitting too close to home?"

"No, you're being a massive jerk, and I want you to leave," she spat, her voice stronger. She was looking at me now, eyes narrowed to angry, dark slits. "You know why I asked you

over? Because my dad ditched me again, and I wanted someone around who didn't think of me as just some obligation
that they don't *even* have to fulfill. Someone who actually
wanted to see me." She blinked rapidly. "But apparently I was
wrong, and you think I'm half a step from an actual prostitute,
so just . . . go."

It felt like she'd popped some balloon that had been puff-
ing up in my chest.

"Emma, don't be like that. I'm not accusing you of anything, but I had to ask—"

"In case I'm some fame whore." She folded her arms across
her chest.

"I didn't call you that."

"Right. Just implied it."

"Emma, don't be—"

"I asked you to leave. I don't need you, remember? So leave.
Go find someone who cares about you for real. Maybe that
Rachel girl. I'm sure she's deeply available." Emma sniffed, lips
curling in disgust.

I grabbed my phone and backpack. At the bottom of the
stairs I turned, but Emma wasn't in sight. I could hear the
blare of the TV turning up. Sighing, I headed upstairs. I'd
managed to screw that up pretty fast.

On the way to the car I opened Flit, just to see what had
happened. There were too many notifications to sort through,
thousands and thousands of mentions, and follows, and reflits.

I clicked to Rachel's page. She hadn't flitted since the picture. The last thing before that had been a couple days ago. It was a picture of a cat in space with a cat sweater on. She'd captioned it "meta-sweata."

Man, she was so weird. But funny. Like, in a way I didn't quite get.

I luvved the picture and stuffed the phone in my pocket.

chapter five

RACHEL

WEDNESDAY, 7:19 A.M.

"Really, Mom, I don't feel well. I should stay home in case I'm contagious."

"Rachel, enough." Mom plopped a slice of whole-grain toast in front of me, staring until I nibbled a corner. "I understand you're worried about Flit, but skipping school isn't going to make it go away. Going will be good for you. You can see firsthand how much of a molehill this really is."

I knew Mom wouldn't let me stay home—she never did. But I had only myself to blame. She always said monitoring my social media feeds would be "like reading my diary," so there was no reason for her to know how ugly things had gotten.

I'd woken up to 23,208 more notifications (besides the luvs and reflits), mostly vicious. I was fat, I was ugly, I was pathetic and deluded. Not like I'd never thought those things, but seeing other people say them almost made me vomit. It made them feel true.

And even without those, almost a million people had reflitted the picture. That's the population of a major city—or minor country—looking at my stupid picture of Kyle.

But if I told her that, there was no telling what she might do. How much worse she might make things.

"Fine," I mumbled. I forced another bite of toast in. It felt too dry to even chew, a square of burny sawdust, so I gulped some coffee to help choke it down. "Bye then."

I grabbed my backpack and coffee tumbler and headed for the front door.

"Rachel, what kind of reaction was that? RACH-el," Mom called after me.

Usually I would have dashed back to give her a quick hug good-bye.

I slammed the door behind me and ran to the car before she could follow.

Staying home wasn't worth having every one of my profiles shut down, and a dozen parents called, and whatever else Mom decided was the "appropriate" response to this. It was easier not to explain it at all.

So I was really, completely on my own.

# # #

I sat in my beat-up blue Toyota Corolla, hands gripping the plastic steering wheel, molded to look like stitched leather. I'd parked toward the far end of the junior lot, up against the spindly pine "woods" where kids went to smoke pot between classes. The spot had a good vantage point.

Though it's not really hard to see a couple of news vans parked outside the main entrance to your high school.

If there had been a legitimate problem, like the time Sophie Laurentis's brother had called in a bomb threat to get out of the PSAT, kids would have been flooding out of the parking lots like some retreating human tide before the teachers had gotten organized enough to stop them.

It had to be about football. We always played homecoming against Sunny Valley, and both towns acted like it really mattered which group of high schoolers had the longest streak of beating other high schoolers at a head-injury buffet.

Still, I couldn't get too near. With my luck, they'd want to interview me about the team—which I had only seen play from under a marching band hat—and the internet would have one more thing to make fun of.

I'd have to go through the middle school.

Unlike East Apple Prairie, West Apple Prairie Middle School wasn't freestanding; it huddled up along the short wall of the high school. One narrow hallway connected the two schools, lined with lockers that always got assigned to freshmen. Chances were good it would be less of a crapstravaganza than the main entrance.

I breathed in and out a few times, closing my eyes and trying to focus on something calming, like a smooth lake. That was supposed to help, right?

Probably someone on the internet was telling me to drown in one just like it.

Smiling bitterly, I got out of the car and headed for the door.

I slid inside and turned left down the mostly empty hallway, walking as quickly as I could without drawing attention, head down. The tube lights overhead buzzed; it sounded like I was being watched by a million insects.

"You're her, aren't you?" I heard from my right.

I stopped midstride, without really meaning to.

"Oh my god, you totally are. You're Attack of the Rach Face." Her voice was getting higher and faster, like someone had pressed fast-forward on her. "You must be *mortified*."

I glanced at the girl, standing at one of the lockers that lined the hallway.

She was a couple of inches taller than me and weed-thin, with long, dark-brown hair with just a hint of waviness. She had to be a freshman, and she was arrestingly pretty. "Date seniors already" pretty. She had a hand over her mouth like she'd said too much, but her eyes were smiling wickedly.

I started walking again.

"Weren't you worried people would think he was too hot for you?" she called after me, banging her locker closed. She sounded interested, but I'd seen the mean-girl trick in action before: sweet voice, eviscerating statement.

I sped up.

"If it makes you feel better, you're a lot less fat than I expected."

I tried to ignore her quiet laughter and the thickening in my throat. I didn't care about baby mean girls, right? But no, apparently I did. The thought made me clench my fists in frustration.

I didn't look up again until I made it to my locker.

Stuck on the front were dozens of copies of the picture, the largest cut into a heart and smacked dead center. Around the edge pictures of middle school me formed a border of ugly. Some were from sleepovers with Jessie, pictures no one would have but her. It was like joining the popular crowd made her want to out-mean them all. Across the whole array, scrawled in red Sharpie, someone had written "#loser." Then other people—the handwriting was different—had added on. Smaller scribbles proclaimed "#notgonnahappen," "#lose-someweight," "#freak," "#pathetic," and a bunch more things.

I couldn't read the others because I was tearing the pictures off one by one, slowly, so the people watching—cell phones out to capture the moment—wouldn't think I was losing it, eyes squeezed extra tight to try to keep from crying.

## chapter six

WEDNESDAY, 7:54 A.M.

I was gonna be late for first-period Physics. And if you handed in homework more than five minutes after the bell, Ms. Casey docked you an entire letter grade.

I whipped into the first parking space I could find, grabbed my backpack off the front seat, pulled my phone out of my pocket, and typed out a quick flit.

> Feels weird to be going back to school after everything that happened yesterday. Wish me luck!

It was kinda dumb, but apparently that didn't matter. Last

night, after spending maybe an hour in my room debating what to say, I'd finally just flitted:

Wow. Um, hi everybody (?)

It got 3,297 reflits in the first five minutes. Seriously. Already I could feel my phone rattling against my hip bone. I grinned. It was hard to wrap my head around the idea that people cared what I had to say. Maybe I was more interesting than I thought.

It was only when I was closing in on the main entrance that I registered the cars taking up all the visitor spaces. They were all news vans.

It was probably about homecoming. Local news ran that story every year. I could see the principal, Dr. Rheim (we just called her Ream), standing near the doors. She was craning her long, narrow neck back and forth like she was taking a head count. Maybe waiting for someone to throw on the mascot costume?

I walked up the lawn so I wouldn't have to weave through the cameramen bunched on the sidewalk. There were at least two, plus a couple other people hovering around whose jobs I couldn't figure out.

Ream sprang into action first.

"Kyle, come here, please." She gestured me over with one of her claw hands. Her back was even stiffer than usual. Was I blocking her shot or something? I started toward her, but it was already too late.

"Kyle," a woman in a navy dress with some sort of twisty thing happening at the waist yelled. She was smiling triumphantly, like she'd just found the prize in the cereal. "Kyle, the Now News Five team would like to speak to you!"

She started jogging toward me. Her narrow skirt and high heels made her steps jerky and straight-legged, like a Barbie. She didn't get far before more people started yelling and pressing forward. Out of the corner of my eye, I saw Ream marching toward me, mouth pinched tight.

Then it clicked. The reporter knew my name. She'd picked me out by sight.

I *was* the news. They were here about me. Dude.

"I'm not entirely clear on why these reporters are here to see you, Mr. Bonham. They mentioned Flit?" Ream said in an insistent undertone.

I nodded, my throat tightening.

"You don't have to speak to them. This is clearly outside the bounds of the school-use image release your parents signed. Until we reach them, the school can act in loco parentis and—"

"They won't know what you're talking about." I hadn't told my parents about the flit. What was there to tell? *Hey, Mom, a lot of internet randos like a picture of me.* She'd just nod, tell me to be careful about what colleges might see, then go back to whatever she was reading on her iPad. Dad would be locked up in his office, on some call, like he was most nights he was in town.

"They're really here to talk to me?" She nodded. I tried not to grin. Ream was taking this so seriously.

It felt like nerves were weaving through my chest, expanding it until it was too big for breaths to fill. Talking to reporters would be like public speaking times a thousand. But on the other hand, it was flipping *cool*. Even Carter had never been his own news story before. And both years he was captain, lacrosse won state. I tried to imagine Mom and Dad seeing me on television. They'd be so surprised.

"*Can* I talk to them?"

Ream raised a drawn-on eyebrow at me.

"As I said, I haven't been able to reach either of your parents, so legally I'm not—"

"I'm eighteen. And they'll leave faster if I give them what they want, right?"

Ream's mouth, pinched so tight it looked like the sucker of the tapeworms we dissected in tenth-grade Bio, softened into a smile. She tried to act tough, but she was kind of a pushover.

"Oh, fine. Just keep it brief. And I'll be informing your parents that I told you to wait, so figure out your story, buster." She took a step away and nodded toward the reporters. Game on.

I smiled, but it didn't feel like it was working right. At least I wasn't frowning. I gave a two-fingered wave to the cameras. A super-blond reporter in black had squeezed up next to the first one. Both thrust their mikes in my face.

"Kyle, why do you think your picture struck such a—" Navy started.

"—taken by someone you know?" Blond finished.

I couldn't tell where I was supposed to look, or which question to answer. The sun was still hidden behind the building, and I could feel goose bumps prickling my forearms. Repressing a shiver, I fake-smiled harder and looked between them.

"I'm as surprised by this as anyone," I squeaked out. "Like my girl—" Foul. "My, um, friend told me last night, it's not even that good a picture of me."

"Hundreds of thousands of Flit users would disagree, Kyle," Blond Reporter said. "What do you have to say to them?"

"I guess that they're lucky no one's invented scratch-and-sniff flits? After a shift, I'm best appreciated from a distance. Like, ten feet or greater."

The reporters chuckled. I wasn't doing so badly. Still, I felt like I had that time Ollie and I went cliff-jumping at his cabin. Stomach: lodged in my throat. I should get out before I said something seriously stupid.

"Anyway, I have to get going. A flit is *not* a good enough excuse for being late to Ms. Casey's class." I grinned. It felt less rubbery. "Though feel free to try and help me out. Maybe if the picture gets a million reflits she'll let me off the hook."

I waved, turned, winked at Ream, and jogged around the cluster into the school.

I made it to Ms. Casey's room six minutes after the bell. One minute too late.

"Here's my homework," I said, panting. Out of the corner of my eye, I saw a couple girls pulling out phones to snap a picture while Ms. Casey was distracted. Me yesterday: just another kid they went to school with. They probably didn't even think about me. Me today: worth posting pictures of to their feeds. I tried not to grin.

"You know the rule. Late is late."

"I know, but I swear it wasn't my fault."

"Really." Ms. Casey tilted her head to the side to make sure I got a better look at her smirk. Casey: champion smirker. Usually it meant she was about to be funny, which was impressive since she taught one of the most boring subjects ever. Today it clearly meant "I'm calling you on your crap, Kyle."

"There were news vans waiting for me at the door." She raised an eyebrow. "Seriously, ask Rea—, uh, Dr. Rheim. I got by as fast as I could, but I didn't build time for that into my commute, you know?"

A couple kids snickered.

"What did you do that's so newsworthy, Mr. Bonham?"

"Nothing. Someone took a picture of me and it sort of, like . . . I dunno, it blew up."

She raised an eyebrow.

"He's telling the truth, Ms. Casey," Erin Rothstein said in her squeaky-high voice, raising a belated arm over her tight blond curls. "He's totally famous now."

"I saw the vans on my way in," Caleb DeLeon offered to no one in particular.

A couple kids nodded. Ms. Casey frowned, then rolled her eyes and reached for my homework.

"Fine, for now you get a bye," she said, shooing me toward my seat. "But if I don't hear your name on the evening news, regular rules apply."

"All right," I said, grinning. "You will, though."

chapter seven

RACHEL

WEDNESDAY, 11:20 A.M.

I should have been angry to see Monique beckoning me toward our usual lunch table near the fro-yo bar, like nothing had even happened, but I was mostly relieved. Jessie must have been in the crowd around my locker; she'd posted a video of me pulling off the pictures on Flit with the caption "Saving them for her scrapbook?"

It already had over three hundred luvs. Seeing anyone who didn't look like they were half a second from laughing, or ready to drip patronizing pity on me, was a relief.

"Hey, Rach," she said carefully as I walked up. I nodded at Mark Majors and Britta Goldberg, leaning over a manga together at the end of the table. Mark nodded back, his floppy brown hair falling over his eyes. Britta raised a few fingers before turning back to the comic, absorbed. Neither laughed and pointed, like I was a circus animal that had just done something hilarious with its own poop.

So now I had a solid three people in my corner, which sadly felt like an improvement.

"Hey, Mo." I slid into a seat across from her.

"Did you see I called last night?" She pushed her vegetable medley around with her fork, glancing at me quickly.

"Not until this morning. I turned off my phone." I shrugged and took a bite of the apple I'd grabbed in line. It was flavorless and mealy, but I forced myself to swallow. With everyone watching, I'd felt too weird taking any more than the apple, a yogurt, and a vegetable side. I knew I wasn't a bikini model, but I'd never thought of myself as fat. The fact that all the snippy comments were getting to me almost stung worse than being *called* fat in the first place.

. . . but I wasn't going up for seconds.

"Listen, I know you're probably livid, which I get," Monique said, holding up one long brown hand and talking fast. "But let me say—"

"I'm not livid, Mo." I sighed. "I mean, I'm annoyed. But I'm not angry."

"I never intended— Wait, really?" Monique jerked back a little. She blinked her amber eyes a few times, frowning slightly.

"Really. I know you didn't think anything would happen any more than I did."

"Yes. Exactly, I had no idea." She nodded rapidly, neck held erect so only her chin moved, more up than down. Sometimes her dancer tics looked out of place in normal life. "I honestly didn't even know what had happened until after dinner; I'd put my phone on silent so I could study. Which wasn't enough; I totally bombed the test."

I chose to ignore her fishing.

"Even if I were mad, you're pretty much the only person left in this school, possibly the entire state, who I can still trust—mostly." Mo blushed slightly. "So I suppose I have to keep you on my good side."

"So . . ." Monique looked away toward the far end of the table, scanning the cafeteria slowly. "What are you going to do?"

"Besides invest in radical, identity-disguising plastic surgery?"

"I'm serious, Rachel." Monique tilted her chin down, looking at me from under her eyebrows. I rolled my eyes.

"I mean, I guess I'll be more careful about what I flit. Other than that, wait it out? That's all I really can do."

"You're not going to try to . . . you know, take advantage of it?"

She couldn't be serious.

"Oh my god, Rach, stop looking at me like that."

"I'm sorry, just . . . take advantage of *what*? Everyone thinking I'm pathetic? Here, do you wanna see what they're saying?" I pulled out my phone, clicking Flit open. I could feel my heart beating faster in my chest. The idea of even Mo seeing all of it in one place was terrifying. Would she see me differently? Pity me? I'd see it in her eyes.

Mo held up a hand, shaking her head rapidly. I exhaled, more relieved than I wanted to admit.

"You're being too sensitive, Rachel."

Through massive force of will, I managed not to spit hot lava at her. Is there *ever* a time it's okay to tell someone that? She didn't seem to notice all my muscles clenching, though, because she plowed ahead.

"They're just jealous. Think about it. They're still nobodies, but they all know who *you* are. If you played it right, they wouldn't be the only ones."

Did she mean Kyle? She couldn't possibly think there was a chance there . . .

"You could use this to get us into the workshop."

Mo and I had been planning to apply to the Budding Playwrights summer program together. It was incredibly competitive—you got to live in New York City and work with real actors and directors, and they hand-selected attendees based on tons of "creative response" questions plus a full one-act play. We were planning to enter *Twice Removed* as a team. The website said they had "limited" spots for playwriting duos, but we figured fewer people would apply for them;

all the theater kids we knew were all about their "personal vision." Plus, if we applied separately and one of us got in and the other didn't—especially if Mo was the "didn't"—things could have turned ugly.

"How?"

She shrugged. "My cousin's doing drama at Yale, and she said everyone knows famous kids get preferential treatment." Mo pushed her tray across the sticky wood veneer of the table. I forced myself not to pick the scraps off it. "Apparently there's a kid from a boy band there who didn't even take the SAT. And another whose dad is some big L.A. producer who gets all the parts, even though he's barely literate."

"Being famous because everyone hates you is different. No one wants that." Monique frowned, opening her mouth like she was about to say something to contradict me. I hurried on. "Anyway, I don't see how it would get us in."

"Programs want publicity. If you're an internet sensation with a million followers, they'll want you talking about them. Period."

"Yeah, but I'm not."

"You could be." I rolled my eyes. Mo ignored me. "There are two ways to think about this. You can let everyone be evil and jealous and do nothing—and really, who knows how long that could go on." Monique twisted a tight curl around her fingertip. She'd been wearing her hair natural since school started, and she couldn't seem to stop touching it. "Or you can try to take advantage of it before everyone moves on."

"I don't think I'm up for that, Mo. I just want this to go away."

She sniffed, pointing at the TV hanging about twenty feet away. In the morning the cafeteria TVs were turned to announcements, like the ones in all the classrooms, but after eleven, they got real channels. Well, network. Usually everyone ignored them, but today it seemed like a lot of faces were locked on the screen.

"I don't think you'll be able to swing that," she said.

There was Kyle, smiling easily and waving to the camera before he loped into school. He looked like he'd been doing this his whole life. The screen cut to a blue background and the Flit logo. "893,271 reflits and counting" scrolled across the top. I turned back to Mo, my stomach plunging to my kneecaps.

My parents didn't watch local news much, but if someone from Apple Prairie was on it? Would someone mention it to Mom at the flower shop? She was always chatty with customers.

And once she knew, what would she do? Strap me to my bed until she thought my mental health was "stable" again? Would she even let me apply to the playwriting workshop?

Maybe I *would* be able to survive on a diet of almost nothing. The world kept making it impossible to keep food down.

## chapter eight

KYLE

WEDNESDAY, 12:54 P.M.

In morning classes, girls tried to sneak pictures. Even ones like Erin Rothstein, who probably had pictures of me already from summer parties I went to with Emma.

After the newscast aired I could barely get through the halls.

A crowd of freshmen I'd never seen formed around me in the commons after lunch. One asked me to autograph her shoe. Was she walking around barefoot, or had she brought an extra? It was already in her hand when she asked, and I couldn't see Shoe Girl's feet through the crowd.

But I signed it. Signing a shoe: totally rock star. Not quite signing a bra, but close.

I felt a heavy slap on the back.

"Man, who would have thought a tool like you could get this much ass?"

I turned to Dave. He was staring at a skinny brunette a foot shorter than him with this dazed half smile. With his buzzed head and beefy build, it vibed creepy. The whole team knew Dave was all talk. Dave in the locker room: endless stories about what he'd "tapped." Dave with actual girls: too nervous to string a sentence together. The girl's eyes widened, she sorta cough-giggled, and she squeezed through the people behind her. The other girls melted away after her. Dave's his own buffer zone.

But we'd both played lacrosse so long we were half friends by default.

"What's up?" I said finally. Dave was not a conversationalist.

"Nothing really." He yawned. The yawn: obviously fake. "I'd been wondering, since you're gonna be up to your balls in willing underclassmen for the next few months, is Emma, like, up for grabs?"

I bit back my automatic no. After last night, wasn't she?

"You'd have to ask her," I said flatly. "Things have been weird with us."

"So you wouldn't mind if I tried to hit that." He stuck his tongue between his lips. It looked like a slug crawling out of his mouth.

"I mean, yeah, dude. I'd mind."

I wanted to add that only a massive tool would even ask, but Dave burst out with a laugh like a motor backfiring.

"Calm down." He raised two ham-steak hands in mock defense. "I'm messing with you, bro." He punched my shoulder. I forced myself not to flinch. "You think I'd break code that way?"

"No." My mouth felt too full of spit. I had to swallow just to not drool. I laughed weakly. "I guess I get, like, weird about Emma."

"Who wouldn't? Emma is . . ." He made a boinging sound, flipping his hand up in front of his waistband. I forced a laugh, even though I could feel my stomach muscles tightening like my body was trying to make me lean in and shove him.

He cocked his head to the right. "This is me. I'll catch you later." He hulked toward the classroom. "Try not to get any freshmen pregnant between now and the bell."

"No promises," I muttered. Dave snorted loudly and disappeared into the room. It made me realize it was probably a crappy thing to say.

I made it the rest of the way to Creative Writing without getting mobbed. Which was good, since I felt like punching something.

The minute I walked through the door, whoops filled the air. I glared at Mr. Jenkins, sitting at his metal desk in the back corner of the room. He smirked, shrugged, and turned back to the magazine he was reading with a look of concentration. The bell hadn't rung, so he was opting to ignore it. I looked for Ollie at the back of the room, but too many people were up on their desks.

"Is it true? Have we really been graced by the famous Kyle Bonham?" Cam Eaton mock-bowed at me.

Cam: class-clown junior, usually kinda annoying. But right this second, the distraction was nice. People were laughing at Cam, bowing over and over, lower every time, to me, the kid who was suddenly famous. My jaw still felt painfully tight, but I threw on my biggest smile, playing into it. I wasn't gonna stay worried about Emma. She wouldn't be mad forever.

"At your service." I nodded toward him like some king.

Cam threw himself to the floor of my row. More people were watching now. It almost made me nervous. Like I was performing. Which was dumb. I walked slowly down the row, chin up, until I got near Cam. Then, without looking at him, I extended my hand. He grabbed it and faked a fit of ecstasy, rolling around gibbering, "FRIES! Oh, my lord's hand even SMELLS of fries!"

I looked to the back of the room. I could see Ollie now: sitting low in his chair, rolling his eyes like I was the annoying kid brother.

It made me want to milk the moment harder.

"Someone should take a picture of Cam." I grinned, looking around. Ollie was staring intently, like he was trying to get some point across. I couldn't figure out what. "Who knows, it could make him. Look at me. It's not like talent factors in."

People laughed, especially guys. I could feel myself

warming up to this. Having everyone's eyes on just me: exciting in a way lacrosse games had never been. Off in the far corner I noticed Rachel's explosion of curls. Her back was to me, like she was looking out the window. Why wasn't she getting in on this?

"But if we want Cam's picture to go anywhere, we need it to have the right . . . *how do you say* . . ." I did my most Cam-worthy French accent. "*Panache*. There's only one choice, of course." I walked back down the aisle. I could see movement from Ollie out of the corner of my eye, but I ignored it. I made it over to Rachel's desk, but she wouldn't look at me. "It needs the almost supernatural photographic skills of Ms. Rachel Ettinger."

She looked up then. Her lips were pinched together so hard they were almost white, and her eyes were huge and shiny with tears. She looked like I'd just stabbed her in the stomach, her face a mix of pain, and anger, and something else . . . contempt, maybe.

She stood, pushed past me as well as she could (she was a little unsteady, and stumbled into the edge of the desk), and rushed out of the room, not even turning back for her bag. Dimly, I heard a few girls' high, thin laughs.

What the heck? I glanced back at Jenkins, but he was still buried in his magazine. He always read through passing time. I looked at Ollie. Ollie: shaking his head, obviously disgusted.

"The artist's temperament, that one," Cam said. People laughed. I smiled weakly and wove back to my seat.

"Dude," I said, turning to Ollie. He was staring straight

ahead, jaw rigid. "What just happened?"

"Have you looked at her mentions on Flit?" he murmured, not looking at me.

"No. I can't even dig through my own. Why? What's wrong?" A heavy, sinking feeling settled in my chest, like someone had tied weights to my ribs. "Seriously, Ollie, what did I do?"

He turned to me, his face loosening slightly. He sighed.

"I know you didn't mean it, Kyle, but that was a messed-up move you just pulled."

"Really?" Ollie cocked an eyebrow. It looked exactly like "I like you, but you're a mega-idiot." "I thought everyone was having fun. I was the one acting like an idiot."

"Kyle. C'mon."

My phone started buzzing in my back pocket. I pulled it out. It was my mom.

"Sorry, dude, I think I have to answer this." I turned to Jenkins, who was standing and stretching, and mouthed "My mom?" with the phone up in the air. He nodded briefly, pointing at the clock. Passing time was almost over. "You know it was just for fun, right?"

The phone rang again, insistent. Ollie nodded and gave me an exasperated half smile. "Yeah, *I* know that. Just . . . pay more attention, Kyle."

I frowned, but I didn't have time to talk about it. Heading down the row past Ollie to avoid Cam's sprawled legs, I jogged out the door.

"Hey, Mom," I said, craning my neck to see up and down the hallway. There was no sign of Rachel. "What's up?"

"Kyle, why do I have news reporters calling me? And your principal? Why did I have to pretend I knew why my paralegal saw you on television during her lunch break?" My mom's voice was high with strain. "What in Pete's name is going on?"

"Do you have a minute?" I sighed, leaning back against the wall. "It's kind of hard to explain."

chapter nine

RACHEL

WEDNESDAY, 1:15 P.M.

I was halfway across the junior lot before I realized I'd left my bag in Mr. Jenkins's room.

It was devastating enough that I actually stomped up and down in the middle of the rows of cars like a rampaging toddler, screwing up my face against tears just a pinprick beneath the surface.

How was I gonna get in my car and drive as far and fast and recklessly as I could if I didn't have my fricking keys?

I moved to the curb and plopped down, hanging my head between my knees.

This day would end—it had to eventually—and people

would move on. How could they not? It was Flit for Christ's sake.

Besides, who cares about people so devastatingly shallow that they spend their free time trolling strangers over the internet? Or pulling mean-girl stunts so cliché I wouldn't even put them in a play? I'd never cared what people thought of me before, why start now?

I was not making very convincing arguments.

"Are you okay?"

I looked up, startled. Not like the junior parking lot is some sacred space, but I didn't think I'd run into anyone.

"Yeah, I'm fine," I lied. I blinked; the sun reflecting off the cars was so much brighter than the space I'd created between my knees. The girl in front of me wasn't very tall—maybe half a head taller than me. Her short, dark, shiny curls were like a rebuke—curly hair doesn't have to look like a metaphor for chaos theory.

I didn't know much about Emma Stashausen, beyond the fact that she was on the Wolfettes. They were like the ur-cheerleaders at Apple Prairie—if you weren't on top of the social ladder when you made the team, you were from then on. It made Jessie even more confounding—what else did she have to prove?

And of course I knew Emma and Kyle were a thing.

"You're her, aren't you?" She squatted down to my level. "You're that girl who took Kyle's picture."

I sighed, looking down at the blacktop. "Sorry," I squeaked.

"I really didn't mean anything by it."

Emma squinted for a second, tilting her head to one side to take me in.

"I know," she said finally, rocking back on her heels to stand again. "You didn't know what would happen."

Something around my lungs loosened for the first time all day. I drew in a deep breath, a little ragged around the edges, and squeezed my eyes shut hard. Tears started sneaking out the corners.

Emma patted me softly on the top of the head. It was the kind of thing you'd do for a child, or a dog, but still, it felt good.

"It'll be okay." She sounded calm, like she had practice at this. It made me feel better and sadder at the same time.

"Sorry, I'm totally embarrassing right now." Deep breaths, Rachel. Focus on deep breaths. "What are you even doing out here?" I asked, once I thought I could speak without ripping through the spiderweb-thin net currently holding my insides together.

"Sinning." Emma smirked mischievously, and brought two long fingers up to her lips to puff an air cigarette. "I don't usually, but it's been a stressful day."

"Uh, yeah."

Emma laughed lightly.

"I should go, I'm super late. Just remember, people are awful, but it's not about you," Emma said with a half smile. "It's almost always about them."

"Thanks," I called after her already-retreating form.

Then I was alone again.

Now what?

I had to get my backpack. Even if I skipped Chem too, I'd need my keys.

I'd just wait until class let out, then duck in for my bag after everyone left. If I was lucky, I wouldn't have to talk to anyone, except maybe Mr. Jenkins. He was cool though. If I told him I was having emotional issues today, he'd probably hand me a copy of *The Bell Jar* and tell me to tap into the pain for my art.

Ha. Right.

I pulled my phone out to see how long I had until I had to head back in.

296 notifications

That was encouraging. It was only since the beginning of lunch, but maybe it meant things were dying down.

I clicked to Kyle's page.

Jesus, he had over two hundred thousand followers.

I felt the tiny bubble of hope that had been floating up through my chest pop and dissipate. Of course it wouldn't be that easy. Sighing, I wove my free hand into my tangle of hair and started scrolling through his feed.

So far all he'd flitted since the picture were a couple

inoffensive sentences—"hi everyone," "wish me luck!" It was kind of adorable, how straightforward they were. If I had that many followers I'd try to mess with them—post something weird to see how people would react, if they'd pretend to like it or something.

But that's why I still had fewer than a hundred, even with rubberneckers and hate-followers. Act that sweet and oblivious and even flits as "I ate a sandwich" as what he'd written so far racked up thousands of luvs.

I almost felt like writing him a PF:

> You should see how much power you have—
> say you like girls w/shaved eyebrows and see if
> it starts a trend.

But then I thought about class. Kyle making a big joke of it all—of me—for a cheap laugh from Cam Eaton, as though it's worth anything to impress someone who tries that hard. He'd probably only followed me back to see who the freak was who had taken the picture. We weren't friends. We never had been.

I closed Flit and played phone games until it was time to go back inside.

I was at the end of the hallway when the bell rang and people started pouring out of classrooms. I stared at my feet so I wouldn't have to make eye contact with anyone, a skill I'd been perfecting since sixth grade. I was just about to duck into the safety of the empty classroom when I felt a hand on my arm.

"Hey, do you have a sec?"

I turned to see Kyle, the pained look in his big green eyes making them softer and wider. It almost seemed like he'd been waiting for me; no one else was around.

The idea made me feel unsteady, like my body had suddenly become too light and I might start floating upward any second.

What was wrong with me? He'd just humiliated me in class, and that stupid picture was the reason I'd probably get egged every day until graduation. Besides, he was a year older, this confident, normal athlete, miles away from interested in me. I frowned. Why couldn't I have a crush on pretty much anyone else?

"K," I said. He dropped my arm. I could feel all the sparkles he'd shaken up floating back down to the bottom of my insides, making it easier to see straight, but less worth looking at anything.

"About earlier, I wasn't trying to . . ." He scrunched his face small, searching for the words. "I should have, like, left you alone."

"Oh, um, okay. Thanks."

"I just wanted you to know I will from now on."

"Great," I said flatly. He frowned for a second, as though he couldn't figure out whether the conversation was over, then shrugged and grinned, his face lighting up like he'd flipped a switch on himself.

"Okay, that's all I wanted to say. See you tomorrow?"

"Sure." I rolled my eyes to the side. "I'll be here."

I pushed through the door. I couldn't stand seeing how he looked at me any longer, like I was some kid sister whose skinned knee he'd cleaned up. At least when he hadn't been aware of me I could pretend there was some chance we'd get together.

"Did you know, Rachel, you're actually scheduled for my *fifth*-period class."

Mr. Jenkins was staring at me from behind his desk; he hadn't stood up. His mouth was set in a straight-across line, but his eyes looked smiley.

"I'm sorry, I couldn't handle it after . . ." I couldn't think how to frame it. Jesus, this whole thing wasn't just killing my social life, it was leaving me dumber too.

"I know. And I get it," Mr. Jenkins said. I could have hugged him. Mr. Jenkins, savior of awkward moments. "Believe it or not, I'm capable of seeing what's trending on Flit. And I probably should have stopped things sooner; I wasn't paying attention—I usually try to block out Mr. Eaton's antics between classes."

I could feel my cheeks getting hot. I walked over to grab my bag.

"So you get a pass, since it's my fault. In exchange, can you make the effort to attend from here on out? Or at least not make it painfully obvious to everyone else that you're ditching? I need my best student to lend me some credibility."

I smiled. It felt weird; I don't think I'd done it all day.

"Yeah, I think I can handle that."

"Good, thank you. Can't let those animals think I'm soft." He smirked. Sometimes Mr. Jenkins almost made me believe teachers got it.

I walked over to my bag, still sitting underneath my desk.

"Rachel," he said as I was heading out.

"Yes?"

"I know it's hard to believe right now, but this *will* blow over."

"Thanks, Mr. Jenkins," I said, trying to sound upbeat.

When he was making such an effort to be nice, it didn't feel fair to mention that it might blow me over with it.

## chapter ten

WEDNESDAY, 2:08 P.M.

That: hadn't gone like I'd expected.

What *had* I expected? It hadn't been bad. Just kinda awkward. It's hard to talk to someone who won't look at you. That must be why I still felt like it was . . . I dunno, unfinished?

Or maybe I was still riled from Cam. He'd spent the entire class finding ways to keep making me a thing.

When Mr. Jenkins asked for help handing out a photocopy, Cam volunteered, and then kneeled to give me mine. During free-writing, he just kept staring at me with this dreamy look on his face. Eventually the whole class noticed, giggling and elbowing each other until Jenkins shut them up.

Then when Jenkins asked people to read their pieces,

Cam jumped up and started talking about "eyes like brightest jade" and "hair tendrilling out from 'neath a peak-ed paper cap" and "teeth like really great teeth," stealing furtive looks at me the entire time. Even Jenkins laughed. He tried to hide it with a hand over his mouth and a threat of "detention if you don't cut the bull, Cameron," but you could tell. I just froze my smile and pretended I thought it was as funny as everyone else seemed to. Me: not amused.

I was ready for this day to be over. It was starting to feel . . . sour.

I headed across the commons toward the stairs to the language hallway. It was the fastest way; my feet autopiloted me that direction.

Bad idea.

The commons was always crowded, but usually you could weave through the knots of people pretty fast. Sometimes I'd even pretend I was on the field and roll dodge around people, fake stick in hand.

That didn't work so well when random sophomores kept pulling you in for selfies.

"I've really got to get to class," I said to the third girl to scooch close and pout her lips for the phone over her head.

Sophomore #3,972: didn't hear or didn't care. She took another shot. "Thanks, Kyle," she said. Like we were friends or something.

I fake smiled and pulled away, edging around a group of band geeks huddled against the windows.

"Ky-LE. What's up, bro?" A heavy hand clapped me on the back. It was attached to Lamont Davis, all six foot five of him. He was grinning chummily from the middle of a pack of football guys in letter jackets. Lamont's crew: all waiting for Lamont's cue on when to laugh.

"Hey, Lamont." Lamont didn't suck, but we'd never been friends, and I had nothing to say to him. After the last hour, and that conversation with Rachel, I didn't have much to say to anyone.

"We were just talking about the kegger at Anderson's Friday," he said, nodding toward one of the guys. "His parents are at some medical conference. You in, bro?"

I'd gone to a few football parties. Emma's friends on the Wolfettes always went, and the parties always got huge. But I'd never been invited directly before.

"Yeah, for sure. Sounds fun." I smiled at Lamont and tried to push past him. He stopped me with a hand on my shoulder.

"Bring your new friends, huh?" Lamont tilted his head at a couple sophomores surreptitiously snapping photos. One was Erin Rothstein's little sister, with her same tight blond curls and exaggerated curves. The rumor, mostly spread by guys like Dave and Lamont: "Baby Rothstein puts out." I tried not to look disgusted.

"Flit that you're coming," Anderson chimed in, eyeing Lamont eagerly. "And that you'll be waiting to meet them in my bedroom." A couple dudes laughed.

I could imagine it: dozens of underclass girls sloppy on

free beer. When I turned them down, what would happen? Looking at Anderson's sneer, I had a pretty good idea.

"Dude, don't make it like that."

"Like what?"

I couldn't exactly tell Anderson I thought he was a massive skeeze.

"I don't want to be, like, bait for freshmen."

Lamont snorted exaggeratedly. He'd positioned himself so I couldn't get past him without pushing by. "It's not like we're desperate for you to be there, bro."

"No, I didn't mean that." Lamont: suddenly bigger. He wasn't just six-five, he was a *thick* six-five.

"You're lucky I even *asked* you." Lamont shoved me with the hand he'd left on my shoulder. It wasn't hard, but I hadn't been expecting it, and I stumbled backward. I could feel his cronies watching.

"You're right." I nodded, a little frantic. Lamont leaned in, his already-small eyes narrowed to tiny slits. I could feel the muscles in my arms and stomach tensing, ready to strike out at a moment's notice. Or take a punch. He leaned back, sneering.

"You know what? Screw that. Don't come. I don't want you there."

"Lamont, I didn't mean anyth—"

"I'm serious, you better not show up. You might think you're hot all of a sudden, but I'm not impressed." He folded his arms across his chest. It made him even wider.

"All right," I said, voice flat. Why the heck couldn't I keep my mouth shut? What did I care if Lamont's friends were creeps? But at least he didn't want a fight. Lamont had fifty pounds on me, easy.

He wouldn't move, so I had to squeeze between his elbow and the guy next to him, a kid I barely knew named Judd, or maybe Josh. Judd-Josh snickered as I forced my way through.

"And Kyle," Lamont yelled at my back, loud enough so everyone around us could hear. "Watch yourself. Not everyone is as nice to idiots as I am."

I kept walking, head down, trying not to look at anyone.

He was right about one thing.

I felt like a massive idiot.

chapter eleven

RACHEL

WEDNESDAY, 3:15 P.M.

I walked into Chemistry tense, my whole body coiled tight like it was ready to spring at something—at someone—all nails and spit and screeching.

But nothing happened. I caught one eyebrow-raise from Jemma Aitkinson as I shuffled past her to my seat, but Jemma had always sucked. I wasn't going into freak-out mode over *Jemma*.

No one talked to me in class. No one even looked at me. By the time the bell rang, I was starting to hope Mr. Jenkins had actually known what he was talking about.

He hadn't.

It probably only took fifteen seconds to brush all the

fries piled on the hood of my car to the ground. There were hundreds—krinkly ones from the cafeteria, skinny ones like at the McDonald's near the hockey arena, even some waffle-cuts I didn't recognize. They left different-shaped grease streaks across the hood, little ghosts of themselves that I'd have to find a car wash to get rid of if I didn't want Mom to ask questions.

But with Jessie Florenzano's braying laugh drawing a crowd that stayed just far enough away to not look like they'd done it, it felt like hours.

chapter twelve

WEDNESDAY, 3:25 P.M.

"Kyle, wait up." I was halfway across the parking lot when I heard Emma's voice behind me.

I'd made up some confusion about the subjunctive tense so I could talk to Señora long enough for the halls to clear out. Apparently I hadn't waited long enough.

I still felt . . . not bad, or angry, more like *tense* about the run-in with Lamont. Uncomfortable, like it was something stuck between my teeth.

I stopped to let Emma catch up, trying not to focus on the tension knots forming in my shoulders. After last night's blow-up, I couldn't help dreading what she had to say. We hadn't seen each other since second-hour Econ, and she hadn't looked at me that entire class. Message received. She jogged the last few steps, shiny brown curls bouncing against her pale cheeks.

"Hey, Emma," I said cautiously.

But she didn't look pissed now. She looked . . . like Emma. Eyes sparkling with some secret joke, the girl you'd see across a room and want to meet. I tried to ignore the part of me that just wanted to grab her and throw her on the hood of my car. Dude, focus. You and Emma: not even together anymore.

"I was hoping I'd catch you. I wasn't sure if you were staying after, or if you'd left early for work . . ." Emma smiled slightly, almost like she was shy of me.

Jeez, did she know how hot that was? I couldn't figure Emma out on good days. Emma today: might as well have been in Japanese. Was she trying to get something out of me too? Or did she just feel as awkward as I did, like we'd never met, never dated, never . . . dude, focus.

"Yeah, no," I choked out, barely keeping my voice from breaking like some pimply thirteen-year-old. My cheeks went hot. Like Emma could see what I'd been thinking about? Get it together, Bonham. "I'm not scheduled for the rest of the week." Actually, Jim's text had implied I might not be scheduled for the rest of ever if this didn't blow over.

"That's cool." Emma looked at the ground. She was pushing her feet up and down in some kind of ballet move. "I'm glad I didn't miss you."

"Why?"

Emma smirked.

"I wanted to talk to you, obviously. About last night."

"Oh. About that . . ." I searched for the right words. How could I explain how surreal things had felt in that moment, like the volume had been turned up too loud and my whole body was made of nerves? Would that sound like I was making excuses, or—

"I wanted to say I'm sorry."

"What? Why?"

Emma rolled her eyes and bent a little farther over her feet.

"I wasn't really mad at *you*, and I wasn't very understanding, I guess. Of how weird this must be, I mean."

"No, I didn't mean it that way. I meant, why are *you* sorry? I was the one acting like a jerk."

Emma looked up at me, eyes grateful.

"We can both be sorry, then. Or we can both be jerks."

"Okay." I wondered what had changed her mind since lunch. I almost asked, but it felt too lucky that this was even happening; I didn't want to mess it up.

"Anyway, if you're not doing anything tonight, it's just me and Nathan holding down the fort. Surprise, surprise." Emma rolled her eyes.

"I would, but I think my mom wants me home. She called during Creati— um, during fifth hour." References to Rachel: possibly still land-mined. Besides, I didn't want to tell Emma about our encounter after class. It felt unfinished. "She was kinda freaking out. Which makes sense. I'm still kinda freaking out."

Emma laughed.

"That's cool. Maybe call me later, then."

"Yeah, for sure."

I wasn't sure what to do next, wasn't sure where this left us, but Emma put her hands on my shoulders, stretched up on tiptoe, and kissed me softly at the side of the mouth. Just as I was leaning into it she pulled away, smiled, and dashed off toward her car.

I would never understand girls.

chapter thirteen

RACHEL

WEDNESDAY, 4:15 P.M.

"I think you're making the wrong decision."

Monique leaned over from where she was sitting—at the rickety, scuffed antique desk Mom bought me in the fourth grade—to reach the box of cupcakes she'd put on my equally rickety, spindly-legged nightstand. They were her way of saying sorry for being so pushy at lunch. Monique wasn't big on apologies—in fact, I don't think I'd ever heard a "sorry" from her that didn't have a "but" right behind—but she was good at knowing when to do something like show up unexpected, bearing cupcakes.

Her long, slim fingers circled slowly over the box for a few seconds, conjuring mysteries from the depths of the glossy white cardboard. Then, with a darting movement, like a snake attacking prey, she plucked out a red velvet with a half-baseball-sized mountain of cream cheese frosting.

"Fine. Give me one of your pro/cons for why I shouldn't delete my Flit account," I said. I was sprawled out on the bed, head facing the bottom, so I wouldn't be able to reach the cupcakes easily. I really, really wanted one. Maybe three—they were from Sweet Tooth, the chichi bakery tucked into a half-sized storefront in Apple Prairie's "downtown" area. But I still couldn't get all the "fat" comments out of my head.

"Okay, pros are for keeping the account, cons are for deleting it," Monique said, setting the cupcake on the desk so she could tick off her arguments on her fingers. "Pro number one: the Budding Playwrights application. I still think you could leverage this to get us in, which is what we both want more than anything."

"Con: I've only got maybe a hundred followers right now, so I'd have to do something pretty crazy for this to do us any good."

"All you'd have to do is write an article about it. Maybe even about how mean people were right away? Feminist websites would love that." I glared until she rolled her eyes, sighing loudly. "Fine, pro: you'll be able to see what's happening with the picture, and Kyle, and what develops."

"Con: the only things that have developed are more people swooning over him and piling onto me. And my locker. And my car."

Monique pursed her lips. I took that as a sign I'd made a decent rebuttal.

"Okay, yes, that sucked, but people at school are not what we're pro/conning. For better or worse, they already know you exist." I rolled my eyes, but Mo ignored me. "All right, pro: you have a serious crush, and Kyle actually followed you back and responded to your PF. Flit is the best link you have to him."

"Con: I never actually had a chance, and now he thinks of me as some pathetic kid with a crush. At *best*."

Monique twisted her mouth off to the side, thinking.

"Pro: if you delete your social media accounts, you may as well not exist."

"No way, that's totally con: if I delete it, people might finally be able to forget I exist."

"But why let them do that to you?" Monique leaned forward, forehead crumpling in concern. "Listen, Rachel. I know it *sucked* seeing all that stuff. Having Jessie and people get mean about your pictures. People are terrible. That's a given, right?"

"Yeah."

"But it's already petering out."

She had a point, at least about the online stuff. In the last few hours only a couple of dozen notifications had come in. Most were just late-to-the-party luvs and reflits.

"Yeah, but Mo, they were *vicious*. I didn't even tell you some of the worst ones, you have no idea how nasty it got."

"I have no idea?" Monique sat back, raising an accusatory

eyebrow. "I know it's easy to forget in Apple Prairie, since I'm one of maybe five in the entire school, but I'm actually a black girl?" She lifted her forehead in feigned surprise. "'Mixed' doesn't change anything for trolls. Trust me, I know *exactly* how awful people get."

I jerked my head back involuntarily. She was right, it was easy to forget. It never really occurred to me that Monique had to deal with that—no one I knew treated her any differently. Did I actually know that, though?

"I'm sorry, Mo, I didn't mean . . ."

"I know you didn't. But . . ." She shook her head, squeezing her eyes tight. "Look, you can't let it get to you. That's all. People can be terrible, but letting that affect how you live your life? That's just . . ." She tilted her head back until she was talking to the ceiling. "Don't let them win, Rachel, okay?"

"Okay," I murmured.

I spun around on the bed so I could see into the cupcake box. There were three double-fudges. If I had still been a little mad at Monique when she'd texted that she was outside my door, I definitely wasn't anymore. I grabbed the nearest one and took a big bite, then rolled back onto my stomach, continuing to fortify myself with chocolate and gooey-thick frosting.

"Okay," I said again, "so I won't totally delete my accounts and attempt to melt into the earth and cut out a big red letter *P* to wear on my chest every time I leave the house."

"It was an *A*," Monique said automatically. Trust Monique to correct me on school stuff at the moment she's trying to repair our friendship with cupcakes and moral support.

"I know, but I'm not an adulteress, I'm pathetic."

"Rachel, how many times have I—"

"No, no, I get it." I raised my cupcake-free hand to stop her. "I'm just saying if I had a shame badge, that would be the one. Let's say it stands for photographer, will that make you feel better? Pathetic, puppy dog, pitiful photographer. Either way, I'm not planning on actually wearing it."

Monique smirked, but she kept her mouth shut.

"But just because I'm not going to pull a total disappearing act doesn't mean I'm ready to become everybody's favorite hate-follow. That's too much."

"Okay," Monique said tightly, dipping her pointer into her cream cheese icing and circling it around until it looked like her finger was wearing an old-lady wig. She sucked on it thoughtfully, staring at me. "I still think we could figure out something that gets you attention that *isn't* a hate-follow. But fine. What's your plan?"

"No more picture game, for one. Especially since I'm apparently so good at it that the world can't help but get on board."

Monique reddened slightly, nodding once.

"In fact, I'm going radio silent until this fully blows over."

Monique pulled her finger out of her mouth with a small, wet pop. "It'll happen sooner than you think. Today was as much blowback as you're gonna get, I bet."

"Great, then you can expect amazing GIFs of squirrels

acting out romance novel covers as soon as next week."

"You're so weird, Rachel."

She rolled her eyes at me. It made me feel a tiny bit better. Like things were inching back toward normal.

We ate our cupcakes in silence for a few seconds. Eventually, Monique couldn't help herself anymore.

"But you're gonna keep an eye on it, right?"

"On what?" I knew what.

"On his profile, Rachel."

"Why would I?"

"Oh come *on*. You've been swooning over this guy for how long now? How can you not?" Monique smirked knowingly.

"Yeah, but why would I want to be reminded of the fact that I will never, *ever* have a chance with him? I mean, I didn't have a chance with him when he was the pretty-cool senior at Apple Prairie. Now that he has what, three hundred thousand followers?"

"Five, last I checked."

"Okay, five hundred thousand. That just makes my point more valid. Now he's all the things he was before, plus famous . . . ish. For being hot. *You* come on."

"Yeah, but you're curious."

I didn't respond. It had been a few hours since I'd looked at Kyle's page, but only through sheer force of will. Maybe that's why I had none left over to resist cupcakes.

"Besides, have you seen his flits? The boy isn't Shakespeare." Monique snorted. "Maybe seeing all the *brilliant* musings of Kyle Bonham's brain will be the cure you need."

"They are pretty ridiculous, aren't they?"

"My *aunt* flits more interesting stuff than that," Monique said. "'It's great to feel great, isn't it, guys? Today's awesome! Go sports!'"

I giggled in spite of myself.

I grabbed my phone and pretended I was clicking through to his page so Monique wouldn't know it was already up. It was the last one I'd looked at.

"So?"

I scrolled down to see what he'd been doing.

"Mostly it's a lot of 'Thanks, so-and-so.' People must be telling him how gorgeous he is or whatever."

"Nothing good, then?"

"Yeah it's all . . . wait. He just flitted, but . . . Jesus, that can't be for real." I refreshed the page. Maybe it was a mistake. Or was he flitting his how-this-pans-out wish list? My mouth felt like someone had shop-vac'd out every little bit of moisture. I tried to swallow.

"What?"

"Look for yourself."

Monique walked over to stand at my shoulder, leaning down until she could see the phone in my hand.

Suddenly, she sat down on the bed, like a puppet whose strings had been cut.

"I think we might have to revise our estimate of when this is going to blow over," Monique said.

## chapter fourteen

WEDNESDAY, 3:55 P.M.

When I walked through the door, Mom was waiting at the kitchen table, legs crossed in one of her pantsuits. The floaty feeling I'd had the entire ride home hit the ground fast. Her jaw was set so tight I could see muscles quivering. Mom: total buzzkill.

"Where have you been? I called Jim, I know you don't work today."

"Settle." I threw my backpack on the chair nearest the back door. "I stayed after to talk to Señora, but it was only for, like, ten minutes."

"You could have called."

I raised an eyebrow.

"Why are you home, anyway? Don't you have to be at the office?" Mom had always worked late, but since Carter left for school, she never walked through the door before takeout o'clock.

"I was worried about you."

"It's no big deal, Mom, honestly."

"Nice try. I looked online—this is a *very* big deal. There are already stories about your flit on all the local stations' sites, *and* on a gossip blog out of New York."

"It wasn't my flit," I mumbled.

"Don't be tedious." She waved a hand in the air exasperatedly. "The point remains: you should have told your father and me."

"I'm sorry. I just figured it would blow over by this morning. I mean, you saw it. It's not even a very good picture of me."

"Oh, I don't know about that. I thought you looked very handsome." Mom eased back into the spindly wooden chair she was sitting in. She'd actually been waiting for me on the edge of her seat. Mom caring that much about *anything* I do: definitely new.

"Not a-million-reflits-overnight handsome."

"Okay, explain that for me." She scrunched up her eyes, putting her fingertips to the side of her forehead. "Because I can't understand why everyone cares so much about this picture. Why news teams care about it."

"I think they only care that it's popular." I tried to say it with authority, like Carter would. She nodded thoughtfully, as though I'd said something smart.

"Well, let's make a plan."

Classic Mom: she would spreadsheet a party if she could. It's probably why she was such a good lawyer; she was equal parts interrogation and list making.

"What sort of plan? I don't really have a say over this."

"Of course you do. You certainly have a say in how you react. For example, you didn't have to agree to be interviewed by those reporters this morning."

"I guess not." I could feel my back tensing up.

"I think you were quite poised." Mom gave a rare smile. I exhaled. "I was proud of how you handled yourself. The goal now is to make sure you get more of those opportunities and use them to your advantage."

"Look at you, Stage Mom."

"No, I'm just trying to be smart," Mom said pointedly. "If you play this right, it could put Princeton back on the table. An essay about this—with Rosie's help, obviously"—Rosie was the SAT tutor Mom had hired a year ago who had transitioned recently into a college apps guru—"well, it would definitely stand out. And colleges have always liked applicants that are visible, doing something different; the ones that have that 'something special.' This could be what makes you special, Kyle. It could be everything we've wanted for you."

I swallowed. I'd thought my parents were mostly resigned to the idea that I wasn't going to follow Carter to the Ivies. I didn't have the grades, I wasn't half as good at lacrosse; it just wasn't going to happen. It had actually been a relief when my most recent SAT scores came in; even they could see I was nowhere near Princeton's averages.

The first thing I manage to do that's different than Carter, better even, and they want to use it to put me back on track to being his Mini-Me.

The house line rang from the little paneled nook at the back of the kitchen. Mom stood up automatically. Usually it was either a telemarketer or one of her clients.

"I'm gonna do some homework," I said, starting across the kitchen.

"We're on the same page, though?" Mom walked to the phone but didn't pick it up, watching me with raised eyebrows. "We're going to optimize your . . ."

"Media appearances?"

She rolled her eyes. "Yes, I guess that's what they are. You'll discuss any 'appearances' with your dad or me first, okay?"

"Yeah, okay. Sure."

She nodded once and grabbed the phone off the cradle, putting a hand over the receiver and mouthing "shoes off" before putting it to her ear. I kicked them off and started upstairs. I figured I had at least an hour of video games before I had to start on homework. After all, I'd expected more shifts this week.

I'd barely turned on the Xbox when Mom's voice ricocheted up behind me.

"Kyle, come down here, please?"

I clicked the game open, so it could at least be loaded when I got back, and padded back downstairs.

"Yeah?"

Mom's eyes were extra wide and the blood had drained out of her face. She was still holding the phone at shoulder level, but I could hear the tinny flatline of the dial tone from the doorway.

"What happened? Is everything okay?" My heart started beating faster, pulsing hard through the veins in my neck. "Mom, what's wrong?" Had something happened to Dad? A car accident? "MOM."

"Nothing, everything is fine." Her voice was robot-flat, and she was staring past me, frowning slightly. "I'm just a little shocked. That was a producer from the *Laura Show*."

The cage of barbed wire that had clamped around my stomach loosened slightly. People we loved: not dead or dying. Mom just *looked* like she'd gotten gut-punched.

Then her words registered.

"Wait, like the talk show?"

She nodded slowly.

"Why?"

A dazed smile started to pull up the corners of her mouth.

"They want you on the show. Friday's show, but they'd tape tomorrow. They said they'd fly you out on a red-eye. Tonight."

The *Laura Show*? Wanted *me*? I'd only seen it once or twice when I was home sick. It was on in the middle of the afternoon, and it seemed to be aimed toward goofy moms.

Still, even I knew it was big. "Real celebrities selling their latest movies" big.

It was exactly what Mom wanted. She always seemed to be able to make what she wanted happen. My whole body started to feel too light, like even my arms were dizzy. It wasn't particularly pleasant.

"What do you think?" I finally said. I couldn't have answered the question if she'd been the one asking.

"Oh, Kyle, it's fantastic!"

She leaned forward and hugged me hard around the shoulders. I wasn't sure if I agreed or not, so I just focused on trying to keep my balance.

chapter fifteen

RACHEL

WEDNESDAY, 4:35 P.M.

"It has to be a joke, right?"

Monique had collapsed onto the bed beside me, but I was still staring at the phone, transfixed.

@YourBoyKyle_B: Just got a call from the awesome people at the Laura Show. Who wants to see me on TV? ;)

"I don't think it's a joke," Monique said to the ceiling.

"But Laura? She has on TV stars. She got the president to do karaoke with her that one time. She can't seriously be interested in Kyle Bonham from Apple Prairie High."

"Why not? She had Melodramatic Husky on a few months ago."

"What, do you DVR her or something?"

"My aunt sent me a YouTube clip."

"Oh."

My heart fluttered away from its usual spot, bounced off my stomach and the sides of my throat.

"You don't think . . . I mean, people had started to let up on me, but if he's on *Laura*, will they . . . will I be . . ." I couldn't get out the tail end of the thought; it was like it had spikes that had sunk too deeply into my tongue for me to spit it out. It was a thought wearing cleats.

"Honestly, I don't think so." Mo rolled over on her elbow, facing me. "And I'm not just saying that to make you feel better. I think it would be worse, psychologically, to feel like this had blown over and have it flare up again than it would be to deal with the idea that it would continue to be crappy for a while longer."

Only Monique would turn me into a case study at a time like this. It was oddly reassuring.

"So many more people are going to be aware of it, though."

"Yup. But since you don't *want* to make yourself part of the story, he's all they'll be aware of."

"Mo." It was what I wanted to hear, but she sounded so annoyed.

"Think about it. Have you gotten any calls from the *Laura Show*?"

"Obviously I haven't."

"Well, if *they* don't think you're the interesting part of this, why would anyone watching?"

That was good news. Right? It was what I wanted—for people to leave me alone, stop trying to give me cliché complexes about the size of my butt, and let me go back to being anonymous. The girl you didn't really notice at the back of the class, unless her ridiculous brillo-pad hair was obscuring your view.

Still, it felt sort of . . . sad. Like I was losing something, something I'd never even had. Kyle would be fully famous and I'd be fully irrelevant. A footnote at best. He wouldn't think of me as the weird, quiet, stalkery girl anymore, because he wouldn't think about me at all.

But I couldn't say that out loud. I'd been the one insisting that I wanted *less* attention from all this.

"I've gotta go," Mo said finally, rocking herself up to a sitting position. "I have a problem set for Chem I have to finish before dance."

"Okay, thanks for coming over," I said, voice flat.

"You should be happy." Mo swung her messenger bag onto her narrow shoulders. "People are going to be over you by tomorrow. By Monday, they'll have forgotten you were even involved."

I nodded. That was exactly what I was starting to worry about.

chapter sixteen

WEDNESDAY, 8:55 P.M.

"I'm gonna get a Starbucks. Do you want anything?"

I shook my head. Mom was acting even more nervous than I felt, and we still had half an hour until boarding. Ten minutes of her drumming her fingers somewhere else: necessary. Though I would have to deal with her being hypercaffeinated.

She strode off rapidly, a woman with a plan. Always.

I looked around for something to distract me. We were at the farthest end of the terminal, at a gate that didn't even have places to plug in near your seat. The airport felt worn out. Everyone walking by looked like they needed a nap, and half the shops had metal grilles pulled down over the entrances. Even the carpet looked tired, all the neon geometric designs in it dingy from the feet that had rushed over them.

I needed to talk to someone about the show. Besides the people responding to my selfie with the sign above the gate, proving we were going to L.A. They'd all been positive, but they all sounded the same.

My thumb tapped it out automatically before I even realized what I was doing.

"Hey, Kyle," Emma said. I could hear her sleepy smile through the phone, and somewhere in the background, twinkly *boing* sounds. Apparently she'd found the right game for Nathan.

"So do you want me to pick you up anything from L.A.? I hear they have great . . . smoothies?"

Emma laughed. My arm twitched, like it wanted to reach out and bury her head against my chest from miles away.

"If you could get your name on one of those stars, that'd be great."

"Just that?"

"Yup. I'm easy to please."

I laughed. The muscles in my neck and shoulders released a little. I must have been tensing them.

"Have you practiced what you're going to say?"

"What is there to say? 'I guess people like how I look covered in grease'?"

Emma snorted.

"No. I'm just saying if it were me, I'd be practicing

one-liners in the mirror until the second I had to go onstage."

I *had* practiced a couple things before we left the house. My name, where I worked, where I went to school: things I knew I'd have to say. But I didn't need to tell Emma that. Worrying about messing up your own name: kinda embarrassing.

"I don't know. Not really. I'll say what happened, I guess. Rachel took a picture of me, and it blew up."

The name came out before I had a chance to think. I held my breath, waiting for Emma to . . . I dunno. Get pissed, most likely.

"You should try to keep the focus off Rachel," Emma said quietly. Almost . . . sweetly.

That voice: completely unexpected.

"Any reason?"

"I don't know." I could almost hear her look up at the ceiling, like she did when she was trying to explain something complicated. "People can just be . . . mean to girls. Online. And generally, I suppose."

"People?"

"Not me, if that's what you're implying."

"I didn't mean that."

She sniffed but kept talking. "I just feel bad for her. It would be one thing if people were asking her on *Laura* too, but they're not, you know?"

"I thought you didn't like her. For taking the picture." Jeez, sometimes it's like there's no filter between my thoughts and my mouth, especially with Emma. No wonder she keeps dumping me.

"Yeah, I was annoyed at first," she said slowly, considering. "I guess I got over it."

Wow.

Luckily even *I* wasn't stupid enough to say that out loud.

"Okay, yeah, I'll do my best. I honestly have no idea what they'll ask, though."

"I still can't believe you're going to be on *Laura*," Emma said. I exhaled, relieved. The conversation was starting to feel less land-mined.

I could see Mom slicing through the crowd, chin up, Starbucks cup raised like a weapon.

"Hey, I gotta go," I said. "My mom's back. Call you tomorrow?"

"I'll be waiting by the phone," she said. Her voice was smiling again.

"Cool. Later."

"I'll be thinking of you, Kyle."

Mom slid into the seat across from me. She sorta hovered forward on it, like she might have to make a run for it.

Looking at her made me more nervous. I turned to my phone instead.

I had a few hundred notifications. I swiped to clear them off my screen and opened Flit, clicking the search icon.

My phone autofilled the handle before I'd even typed

three letters. Jeez, I hadn't looked at her page that many times, had I?

@attackoftherach_face

She still hadn't flitted anything new. And she still had fewer than a hundred followers.

I wondered what she was thinking about all this. I clicked open a PF window, ready to type something stupid, just like, "hey what's up," but I stopped myself. What would be the point?

After all, Emma was right. I'd seen those flits from Jessie, and Erin, and a couple other girls at school. It didn't seem that embarrassing to me. So Rachel had an awkward phase: Who didn't? But you could tell they were trying to humiliate her. Even if Rachel didn't blame me for that, she probably didn't want to hear from me.

I clicked my phone dark. I wasn't going to write the message, and there wasn't time to worry about this right now. They'd started boarding the plane to L.A.

chapter seventeen

RACHEL

THURSDAY, 7:45 A.M.

The last twenty-four hours, the only thing I could think was how much I wished people would forget about me, let me fall through some hole in the stage and stay there.

But it was kind of surreal to realize how quickly they had.

I walked into school Thursday morning bracing my brain for the very real possibility that a picture of me from the heyday of middle school awkward would be lining every single hallway. My insides felt like someone had tied rubber bands around all the important parts, restricting all the flow. I even started mentally reciting one of Mom's mantras, "I choose joy, I choose joy," which immediately made me feel snarky about how ridiculous her mantras were, which didn't seem like the point.

But there was nothing there. My locker was covered in its usual seafoam green paint, no spectators in sight. The halls were plastered with exhortations to sign up for debate, many of them covered with Sharpie pictures of penises. It was any day at Apple Prairie High.

Maybe people got over it quicker because of Kyle's whirlwind trip to L.A. It was the only thing anyone seemed interested in talking about.

"I heard he might get a part in a movie or something."
—A COUPLE OF SOPHOMORES IN THE COMMONS
AFTER SECOND HOUR

"Did you know he already has more followers than what's her name from last season's TRAINWRECK'D? *And she has, like, a shoe line."*
—JENNA ARROYO, SENIOR COLOR GUARD MEMBER
WHO PERSONALLY KEEPS THE WORLD'S HAIR
BLEACH MANUFACTURERS IN BUSINESS

"All I'm saying is that show made *Melodramatic Husky. I read the owners pull down something like a million a year from endorsements and appearances now."*
—CALEB DELEON TO CAM EATON, WHO LOOKED A
LOT SOURER THAN YOU'D EXPECT FROM A GUY WHO
HAD LITERALLY KISSED KYLE'S FEET YESTERDAY

Kyle was doing even newer, more exciting things than he had been yesterday, and yesterday had already been hard to wrap my mind around.

I guess that was why I wasn't at the front of anyone's mind anymore.

People hadn't let up entirely, of course. A couple of sophomores gunning for the Wolfettes tripped me in the math hall between first and second hours, then acted concerned while their friends laughed uproariously. At lunch, someone had pasted a sign, "Rachel Ettinger approved!" with the cheeseburger picture, on the front of the fry warming tray. And of course people snickered, and stared, and gave me pitying looks.

But there were no buckets of blood on my head. It all felt kind of anticlimactic. I'd thought I was starring in some intense drama, but it turned out I was just a B plot.

This was what I wanted. I had to remember that. It probably only felt strange and anxious and unfinished because I was subconsciously waiting for the other shoe to plop down in a big pile of catty and splatter it all over me again.

# # #

The message came in about an hour after I got home from school.

I was sprawled on the beige Berber carpeting in the basement, staring at a muddle of $x + y$ over fractions to the nth power equations. Algebra II might as well have been in cuneiform for how much sense it made. Geometry had been so much better. Shapes you could *see*. This was just . . . alphabet soup.

My phone pinged from the coffee table. It hadn't been going off much all day. A few notifications before lunch, but since then, radio silence. Maybe Monique was texting. I *did* still have a couple of real-life friends willing to talk to me.

I levered up—the carpet painfully peeling away from my elbows, where it left a series of red ridges and bumps—and scooted over to the low coffee table on my knees.

@YourBoyKyle_B has sent you a private flit

Wait, what?

A thousand centipedes started scuttling around the inside of my stomach, trying to escape up my throat.

Wasn't it enough that my total social annihilation had bought him overnight fame—couldn't he just leave the deluded idiot alone now, like he'd promised? But of course a huge part of me was whole-body-electrified-excited that he hadn't forgotten me yet. Totally pathetic—it was like some deep, buried part of my brain was okay with him treating me like the dorky sidekick as long as he talked to me. Stupid fricking subconscious. Get with the program.

Weakly, I touched the screen.

Q: were you gonna watch the show tmw?

I blinked for a minute. Kyle had to be sending this from L.A. Oh god, that had to mean something about me had come up on the show. The thought made me want to vomit. I typed before I could lose my nerve entirely:

Probably. You've finished filming, right? Should
I be worried about mobs with pitchforks?

Kyle's response came in before my screen even went fully dark.

Yeah, wrapped about an hour ago. And no,
nothing like that. But you should def watch.

Am I going to like what I see?

Oh my god, was I seriously trying to flirt right now? Also, was that maybe the worst attempt at flirting that had ever happened in the history of ever?

Hope so. But I don't want to ruin the surprise.

For Christ's sake. Is there anything more maddening than people telling you you'll be surprised by something that won't happen for ages? It's like dangling a piece of salami over a dog's head, exactly two inches higher than the poor thing can jump.

Obviously I wasn't going to tell Kyle that.

All right, you have me intrigued. I'll be watching.

Good. BTW, what's your #? Txts wld be easier.

Statement retracted. Kyle could dangle all the "surprise!" salamis he wanted if he was going to throw requests like that in there. Pathetic, I know, but I was too anxious to care. Thumbs shaking, I typed the number into the message window. About a minute later, a text arrived from a number I didn't recognize.

> **(From 763 . . .):** Hey, it's Kyle. Now we can talk easier! Gotta go. Make sure to watch and txt me after it's over. Later!

Hands fully seizuring now, I carefully clicked to save the number. Kyle Bonham, also saved to SIM.

I collapsed onto the carpet, my cheek pressing hard into the rough beige divots. I'd probably wind up with a topographical map there too, part of a matching set with my elbows.

I closed my eyes and breathed in as deeply as I could, trying to calm the fluttery feeling taking over my stomach and lungs.

How was I ever going to get through the next twenty-four hours knowing there was something on the show Kyle wanted me, in particular, to see?

And what could it possibly be?

## chapter eighteen

KYLE

THURSDAY, 11:45 A.M.

The dressing rooms at the *Laura Show* had no windows. Had: huge overstuffed couches, bright-white walls, fresh flowers, and baskets filled with, like, every kind of junk food ever, plus some hippie ones I'd never even heard of. Didn't have: windows.

It made it even harder to sit still. The room felt claustrophobic, like a well-decorated prison cell. But with an attached bathroom instead of a can in the corner.

We'd been waiting for three hours, but no one had come by since the thin, prim woman manning reception when we showed up dropped us here. She'd offered to show us around first, which seemed cool. But she'd locked her smile in place right away, walking down the long, narrow hallway with all the dressing rooms (currently next door: the band Five-Step Boogie), and she was smiling just as hard for the camera storage room.

It made me wonder if she ever *didn't* smile.

I walked the length of the room again. The light: too bright, like an operating room. I thought all the time between when we were supposed to arrive and when we started taping would help me calm down, but I was getting crazy nervous. I shook my hands out and bounced up and down on my toes like I did before lacrosse games, trying to release the energy.

Someone knocked softly at the door. Mom's head whipped around so fast I thought she might do damage. I froze midway through a bounce, heels not touching the ground.

The door opened, and a man's head appeared around the crack.

"Knock, knock!" he said cheerily. He had dark-brown hair, slicked back in a perfect pompadour, and the barest hint of black stubble on his narrow chin. He was smiling just as hard as the tour lady, but it didn't seem fake.

Neither Mom nor I said anything. For the split second before the man's head appeared I had this weird hope that one of the Five-Step Boogie guys had come by to say hey. Which was pretty embarrassing; all but two of them were younger than me and their fan base was entirely tweeny-boppers.

Still, they were, like, *massively* famous.

"Can I come in?" He arched an eyebrow.

"Sure, yeah," I sputtered. "Please." I leaned back on my heels and spread my arm in the universal "enter" gesture.

"Great." He stepped inside. He was wearing a multicolored tank top with armholes that went all the way down to the waistband of his jeans, which were tucked into snakeskin boots. He looked cool. In an L.A. way.

"I'm José. I'm gonna be helping you with your hair and makeup."

"Oh. Okay."

"Don't worry, it's just so the stage lights won't wash you out. Though you could *definitely* pull off that five-year-old beauty queen thing."

I frowned. The corner of José's mouth twitched. Jeez, and that was an *obvious* joke. Me: way too tense right now.

I forced out a laugh.

"How'd you know my going-out look?"

José smiled and pointed me to sit at the counter running along one wall, in front of a light-bulb-studded mirror. He pushed the snacks aside to make room for a massive black box filled with dozens of bottles and brushes and tubes of makeup.

"Should I change first?" I asked as he started pulling out colors and holding them to the light.

"That would be good. Pulling on a T-shirt might mess up your hair."

"Right." My first time on TV: wearing my fricking Burger Barn uniform. At least I'd be comfortable.

I put on the burnt-orange shirt, and José got to work.

Having him there, smearing at my face and asking me boring, everyday questions about where I went to school and whether I'd been to L.A. before calmed me down a little. By the time he was done, I wasn't even tapping my toe against the tiled floor anymore.

"All right, my job here is done," he said, snapping his case closed. "You look adorable, by the way. They're going to love you."

"Oh, uh, thanks," I said.

"Someone will be by to get you in about fifteen minutes. Break a leg, okay?"

José whisked out the door, taking all the calm with him.

It felt like seconds later when Tour Lady walked in.

"They're ready for you, Kyle. Would you like to follow me backstage?"

I nodded. If I tried to talk I might puke on her.

We walked fast down the dressing room hall, wound through a couple quick turns, and reached a door marked "Backstage."

If my stomach hadn't been so churny I would have made a joke about how glamorous it was. Tour Lady probably would have just kept the same perma-smile in place. I swallowed. I felt exactly like I did before every lacrosse match: like puking.

She put her hand on the door.

"Once we go through, I'm going to ask you to be quiet, since we're filming. I'll take you up to the stage entrance, and you'll hear Laura introduce you. Once you hear your full name, walk out onto the set and sit in the chair opposite Laura. Got it?"

"Yup," I squeaked. Jeez, what if I sound like a Muppet through the whole interview? "Simple."

"Great." She turned and eased the door open silently. They must keep the hinges super-greased. She gestured at me to follow, not looking back. She clearly didn't care how I was doing as long as I followed orders. It was a relief. Her acknowledging my nerves would have made it worse. Like, I'd be hyperaware of them or something.

We walked into a dim, cavelike room. Waist-high metal cabinets, like the ones my grandpa used to hold his tools, were pushed against the black walls. Random crap piled everywhere: a spool of wire, a rusty film tin, a plastic alarm clock, weird canned foods with foreign labels, and a dusty picture of Frank Sinatra, to name a few. A couple tan director's chairs were pushed into a corner, the canvas edges fraying.

The chaos and the darkness calmed me down a little. That dressing room had been so bright and polished. It was too perfect; it made me feel like I was going to mess up. But this space felt more down to earth, like real people worked here. Already I was . . .

"Welcome internet sensation—seriously, people, this kid is HUGE—all the way from Apple Prairie, Minnesota, it's Kyle! BONHAM!"

In case I hadn't been planning to step onstage, the sharp poke of a pen in my back from Tour Lady told me it was time.

I walked out, grinning as hard as I could, unsure where to look. I think people were cheering, but blood was pounding through my ears so hard I wasn't sure. A couple steps past the false wall that had been hiding me, I saw the huge white leather chair with Laura in it. She was smaller than I realized, shorter than Emma even, wearing a tailored pantsuit with a T-shirt underneath, like this was all just casual.

If I were cooler I would have done something with my walk across the stage. People do that on TV, right? Like, dance or, I dunno, mime making burgers?

But I'm not that cool, so I walked straight over to the open chair and sat, turning to smile at the crowd. Jeez, there had to be at least two hundred people, maybe more. They were screaming and jumping around, but I couldn't make out faces. One bonus of stage lights: they turn the audience into people-shaped blobs.

"Kyle, we're so glad you could make it out to the show!" Laura smiled. Her teeth were bright white, but they weren't totally straight, and even stage makeup didn't cover the slight crookedness of her nose and the little wrinkles around her eyes. She looked like a more-polished version of your favorite aunt. Already I liked her. No wonder she was so popular with moms.

"Thanks for having me," I said automatically, looking out at the audience and waving a little.

"Did you have any trouble finding someone to cover your shift at the Burger Barn?" she leaned in, feigning concern.

(((**129**

"Not really. They don't want me on too many shifts right now."

"Why's that? You must be a huge draw for them."

"Yeah, that's why we ran out of food last time."

The audience laughed so loud I could almost feel it pouring over me, like a wave. I smiled wider. They *wanted* to like me. I'd never felt so charged with adrenaline in my life, not even during lacrosse playoffs. I was nervous, but my senses felt sharper. Like I was performing at a higher level. Like I was the best version of myself I'd ever been: Kyle 2.0.

"So walk me through what happened. You're just working at the Burger Barn like usual, right? Then someone took your picture."

"Right. I didn't even know it had happened."

"And when did you realize something weird was going on?"

"I can't have my phone with me when I'm working. Because of the grease," I said, turning toward the audience and smiling ruefully. They giggled. Point. "But a lot of girls started showing up about halfway through my shift. And they were all saying, 'I'd like fries with *that*.' Which of course just sounded strange to me. Like they didn't know which word in a sentence to *emphasize*." The audience roared.

"And that was the hashtag on the photo."

"Right."

"So your shift ends . . ." Laura raised her eyebrows, urging me to go on. It was so easy to talk to her. Like we were team-mates passing back and forth.

"Because we'd run out of food." Laughter. "So I check my phone, and I see that I have, like, over ten thousand new fol-lowers."

"How many did you have before your shift?"

"Two hundred eighty-nine."

Giggles.

"Wow. That must have been really strange for you."

"It definitely still is."

"You have a few more followers now, I take it."

"Uh, yeah. Like, a few hundred thousand? And I still don't have anything interesting to say." The audience laughed again.

"That is just fascinating, Kyle. But there's another side to this story, right?"

I tried to keep my smile on, but I was confused. I couldn't see the play she was trying to make.

"Because the girl who took the photo wasn't a stranger, was she?"

"No, not a stranger. I mean, we don't know each other well."

"But she goes to your high school?"

"Yeah. We're in Creative Writing together. She's really good. Her stories are always way more interesting than what other people come up with." Would Emma think that was too much? Or would she be jealous? But Rachel *was* good. She couldn't be upset about me telling the world she was good, could she? I started to feel less sure of myself. Like I'd forgotten my lines in a play.

"She sounds like a fascinating young woman. We're going to take a break now, but when we come back, we'll have more with Kyle Bonham, the young man who's taking over the internet one triple-stacker with cheese at a time."

The audience clapped loudly, and the stage lights dimmed. A producer I hadn't seen before ran up to hand Laura a water bottle. Laura accepted it with a slightly tired smile. The producer was older than the one who had shown me around, and less put together. Her look: oversized oxford only half tucked into her pants, mousy-brown hair mostly falling out of the off-center, sloppy bun on the crown of her head, hand tapping nervously against her thigh. She looked like someone who ran things.

"Kyle, I wanted to talk to you before we start taping the next segment," the producer said, smiling widely at me. "I was chatting with your mom backstage and she came up with a great idea. I'm very excited about it. It could be a really fantastic way for you to keep your story fresh."

"Okay," I said tentatively.

"You were planning on going to your school's homecoming dance, right?"

Laura looked at me expectantly. Without the cameras on, she was a different person. More attentive. Her stare was actually kinda intense.

"Sure. Yes."

"Have you asked anyone yet?"

Emma insisted I ask her officially to every dance, even if we hadn't broken up recently. Which we had. Were we still? Lately she'd been hot and cold, then warmish but noncommittal.

"No, not officially."

The woman smiled with half her mouth. Her dark-brown eyes glittered with excitement.

"Perfect. Let me tell you what we came up with—and I have to say, I think this could be a *huge* hit with our fans—then you can tell me if you're on board, okay?"

For some reason, even though the producer and Laura were both smiling, my heart started racing. What did they want? If Mom came up with it, that meant I should say yes, right? She kept saying I had to make more opportunities out of this, turn this into an application Princeton couldn't turn down.

Somehow that made me even more nervous.

"Okay," I said, trying to return the producer's smile. "What were you thinking?"

chapter nineteen

RACHEL

FRIDAY, 7:08 A.M.

A car horn honked from the driveway. Even from the upstairs bathroom it sounded annoyed. *Beep! Be-be-be-beeeeep!*

"Jesus Christ, Mo, I'm coming," I muttered to my reflection. It was taking me longer than expected to get my eyeliner right, maybe because I almost never wore eyeliner. Still, over the last couple of days it had somehow started to feel more necessary, like another line of defense. Yesterday hadn't been so hard. Maybe I was just too tired after this week to manage even the most basic of motor skills on a Friday morning.

Finally, I sighed, smeared my finger through the black—it was morning-after chic, right?—and ran down the stairs.

"Bye, Mom," I yelled on my way out the door. I didn't wait

for a response. I hadn't really wanted to talk to her lately; I was mildly afraid that if I got too near her for too long, she'd somehow smell it on me, the truth of what had happened with the picture. My parents hadn't said anything about it since Tuesday's dinner, and it's not like they'd suddenly joined Flit. Still, sometimes my mom was creepy good at knowing when something was going on.

I was almost out the front door when I heard her running through the hallway.

"Rachel, can I talk to you for a second?"

So close.

"Yeah, what's up?" I kept a hand on the open door.

"What's your plan after school?" she said. She seemed stiff. Like when she had been angry with me earlier and wasn't quite over it yet. But we hadn't fought.

"I was gonna come home with Mo and watch some TV. Ashlee is having a slumber party tonight, so Mo didn't want to be home. Why? Is it okay if she's over?"

"No, no, I just wanted to make sure you'd be here. I have my flower arranging class at the adult education center, so I'm gonna need you to help your father with dinner. You know how hopeless he is."

Mom was looking at some point just to the left of my head, trying—and failing miserably—to be casual and unconcerned. Jesus, she must have been terrible at lying to her parents.

"All right, so I'll be here. I'm gonna go," I said, taking a step through the door.

"Isn't a boy from your school going to be on the *Laura Show* today?"

Crapberries. I thought my parents didn't watch local news.

"Yeah. Kyle Bonham."

"And that's the boy whose picture—"

"Yeah, Mom." I stared at the toes of my Chuck Taylors. No wonder she'd been acting so weird. She knew.

"Will you and Monique watch it?"

I looked up, ready to tell her to stop judging and leave me the hell alone, YOU DON'T UNDERSTAND ME, like some teen in an eighties movie, but she was . . . smiling. She was trying to hide it, but Mom was *definitely* smiling. She couldn't have known everything; she was too calm. This had to be her "I'm a mom who's involved and knows what's happening!" bit.

I tried to seem just standoffish enough that it would cover my relief. I didn't want her getting suspicious, after all.

"Yeah, probably. Why?"

"No reason."

"Okaaaay." I frowned at her, but she just kept that idiotic half grin on her face. "I'm going now."

"All right, have a good day at school, sweetie." She looked like she was trying not to burst out laughing. Jesus, she needed something of her own so she wouldn't have to get so much vicarious satisfaction out of my crushes—my pointless crushes. "And remember, straight home after so you can help with dinner."

"K," I said, shaking my head as I ran out the door.

I slid into the front seat of Monique's SUV. She whipped out of the driveway almost before I'd managed to get the door closed.

"You're early," I said. We were leaving at least fifteen minutes before I would have, and I always made it to school way before the warning bell.

"What do you mean? This is when you have a chance to talk to teachers."

Oh, Mo. As though anyone else *wanted* to talk to teachers.

I kept my mouth shut. It was nice of her to drive—it was the easiest way to ensure we were both in the same room the second the show started; I needed her there with me, otherwise I might totally freak out and turn the stupid thing off. Plus, it allowed her to bypass the bevy of catty thirteen-year-olds that Ashlee hung out with, and her mother's inevitable requests for help keeping them happy. And I wouldn't have to face school alone today. Win-win-win.

Full disclosure—a tiny little part of me wished he *would* mention me on the show. I'd already seen the most vile things trolls could possibly say about me; it couldn't get any worse than it already had, right? And it would mean his messages had meant something other than pity for the loser.

. . . which would mean I could still pretend, in my most pathetically ridiculous fantasies, that he might still fall for me someday.

But I definitely couldn't say that out loud.

Especially since I hadn't told Mo about Kyle's messages. I should have, probably, but I hadn't wanted her to confirm what I already knew—that he was just being polite, or worse, treating me like another fan to cultivate. The original. Fan 0.

Keeping them secret let me hold on to the fantasy of them a little longer. Mo was too practical to understand why I'd want to do that. Plus, as soon as she knew about them, she'd be all over me to try to milk the Kyle connection for the application, even if it didn't really exist.

Mo swung into a space near the front of the mostly empty parking lot. Already I had to face this day. Dammit.

"All right." Mo turned to me, chin pointed toward her chest, the better to stare me down. She must be nervous about something; usually she reserved her "pay attention to what I'm going to say" face for times when she was leading a group project, or assistant teaching one of her kindergarten dance classes. "I'll see you at lunch. But in case something happens and I don't, the plan is to be here, at the car, immediately after classes end, right?"

"Right."

"And you don't foresee any reason you'll be late, do you?"

"No." I raised an eyebrow. This was a little plan-happy even for Mo.

"And you'll keep your phone out in case we get separated and need to find each other then, right?"

"*Yes*, Mo."

She exhaled dramatically.

"I'm sorry, I just want to make sure we have a plan. It will be tight getting home in time for the show."

We had nearly an hour to make it the fifteen minutes from school to my house. And I was the one with skin in the game—except I probably wasn't, since I almost certainly wouldn't come up. Still, this was how Mo showed you she cared. Via micromanaging.

I nodded, forcing my lips into a strained smile.

"I'll be here. Don't worry."

Mo looked me up and down, evaluating for god-knows-what, then nodded and whipped the door open.

"Good," she called from outside. "I have to get going. I want to talk to Mr. Sandvaal about last night's Chem problem set before French."

She slammed the door and strode off toward the school ahead of me, too fast on her long legs for me to catch up. Sighing, but smiling to myself, I got out of the car and headed in after her.

And then the day became *endless*.

No one was paying any attention to me, finally, which was good. But that left nothing to worry about besides class. Everything I was supposed to be doing was simultaneously boring and somehow too hard to focus on, which made time feel like a lead weight I couldn't manage to drag forward.

I spent most of French in some sort of fugue state, not even deciphering the sounds coming out of Monsieur's mouth as words in any language. In Art we were supposed to practice figure drawing, but I couldn't hold the little wooden doll's shape in my mind long enough to get the proportions right. I just pretended to play in band. The notes were too swimmy.

Finally, after several years of painful imprisonment, the last bell rolled around. I pushed past all the kids in class and half ran out to the junior lot.

Mo was already waiting by the car.

"You'd think you were the one about to be embarrassed on national television," I called to her.

"You don't know that," she snipped. Monique pinched her eyes closed and shook her head slightly, as though clearing the Etch A Sketch. "All I mean is I don't think he'd say anything to embarrass you. He's a good guy."

Jesus, everyone was being *extremely* weird today.

Mo sped back to my house, barely slowing down at stop signs. She always drove impatiently, but today was noteworthy. We practically flew into the driveway at 3:19.

"I'm gonna grab snacks," I said as we walked into the house. I headed for the kitchen. Mom had already assembled a casserole and left it on the counter with a note: "in oven at 5:15, 350 degrees, 1 hour." Seriously, Mom? Even Dad couldn't screw that up.

"Good. You do that." Mo had pulled out her phone and started texting furiously.

"Anything important?"

She whipped her head up and squinted at me in . . . wait, was she pissed?

"No, just mom stuff." Mo blinked rapidly. "I'll be down in a sec."

"Okaaay." I headed to the basement alone, turning on the TV and checking the guide to make sure the channel I knew was right was still, in fact, the right channel. Eventually Mo appeared. She was obviously still keyed up, but she didn't seem to want to talk about it, and I was too nervous to dig.

Finally the *Laura Show* theme came on, all blaring trumpets and cheery, regular beats. The camera focused on the stage, then quickly flipped around to catch Laura dancing down the aisles into the studio, grabbing people from the ends of the rows to pull them out with her.

She hopped onstage and made a big show of catching her breath.

"Happy Friday, everyone! Welcome to the *LAURA SHOW*!"

The crowd roared.

"Have we got a great show for you today. You know who's here? You know, don't you?" The cameras cut to shots of the crowd, leaning forward eagerly, manic grins plastered on every face. I'd never realized how cultish these audiences were. "Five-Step Boogie is here, and they're going to play us a song!"

You wouldn't think so many middle-aged women would

care about a tween boy band, but judging from their frenetic shrieking, you'd be wrong.

"But that's not all. Halloween is right around the corner, and I'm sending one of the show's producers, Tim, to all the best haunted houses in California!" Cheers. As though anyone actually cared who Tim was.

"And we'll also have a chance to meet the internet's biggest sensation. I swear, you will never be able to look at an order of french fries the same way again. Put your hands together for Kyle Bonham!"

They flashed the picture on the screen. I dug my nails into my palms. My heart felt like it was squeezing tighter and tighter, so tight I thought it might pop, exploding through my chest in a splatter of gore, like some grisly water balloon.

I leaned forward, mesmerized. Any minute now, Kyle would walk out there and fully transform from a regular (if exceptionally adorable) kid at my school into something else, something big and dense with its own impenetrable orbit.

The minute he set foot on that stage, he'd be legitimately famous.

And I'd be left behind forever.

## chapter twenty

FRIDAY, 4:24 P.M.

The van shuddered to a stop along the curb. I couldn't tell exactly where we were. It didn't have any windows in back. This van model: choice of kidnappers everywhere. When I stuck my head between the front seats and looked out the passenger door, I could just see a black SUV parked in the driveway of an unremarkable house.

"Don't wrinkle your tux," a voice behind me said. It was the producer I'd met at the show, whose name, I'd learned, was Mary. She was even more disheveled after the flight and the hassle of getting all the equipment into the huge white van we'd rented.

I should have felt nervous, but all I felt was vaguely guilty.

This was not a good idea. For lots of reasons. And I was the only one who seemed to get that. But Mom was clearly convinced this was what would get me into Princeton with Carter. The school I wasn't actually good enough for. Mom: very persuasive when she's set on something.

We'd dropped Mom back at the house after we landed, so it was just Mary; me; the massive, cue-ball-bald, mostly silent cameraman, Eddie; and Charles, an assistant on the show. He hardly looked older than me. It seemed like he was there mainly to do the things no one else wanted to, like taking food orders and driving.

"Is it time yet?" I asked. Mary was bent over a tablet, watching intently.

"Not yet," she mumbled. "Eddie, get out and set up; we're about ten minutes away from launching this puppy."

Eddie unpacked himself from the front seat and went around to the back of the van, cracking open a black plastic case and hoisting a huge camera onto his shoulder. He started fiddling with knobs.

I felt like I might be about to puke. Partly because the whole van smelled like old fast food, but more from everything else.

Would Emma be watching? What would she think about this, the sequel?

chapter twenty-one

RACHEL

FRIDAY, 4:36 P.M.

"I can't believe they're bringing him back after the commercials," I said, twisting around to look at Mo. "Laura must have loved him."

"Mm-hmm," she said tightly, staring at her phone. I could hear movement overhead. It sounded like Mom's step—deliberate and heavier than you'd expect—but she wasn't home. Jonathan must have tripped over himself trying to walk and organize his Pokémon collection at the same time.

I bit the inside of my lip. Mo had been this way the entire show, hardly paying attention, focused on texts, apparently annoyed about something. What the heck?

The theme song started playing again, and Laura appeared onstage with Kyle.

"Hey, folks. We're back with Kyle Bonham, the overnight internet french fry sensation—give me credit if you paint that on your bus, Kyle." The audience laughed indulgently. "And over the break, I got to thinking. Now that the world is swooning over Kyle, he needs a new look, don't you think?"

Kyle smiled broadly into the camera as the audience cheered their approval.

"He needs to up his game!"

"I definitely do," Kyle said, grinning harder.

They cheered louder.

"That's what I thought you'd say. That's why we're going to take Kyle backstage, spruce him up, and send him on a very important mission. We'll show you what happens on Monday's show! Kyle, *good luck*," she said, leaning toward him, feigning fear.

He stood. "I know it'll be a tough job, but I'm ready." He opened his eyes wide and mouthed, "Help me!" Then he laughed, waved to the crowd one last time, and jogged off.

God, he was so good at this. It was almost exasperating. How could someone be so comfortable putting himself out there in front of thousands of people?

"Next up, we're going to get you in the holiday spirit . . ." Laura said. Apparently they were done with Kyle for now.

"What do you think they'll do Monday?"

"Don't know," Monique said vaguely.

"Probably he'll go serve fries at some red carpet event or something. They love stuff like that."

"Totally," Mo mumbled.

"It wasn't so bad, what he said about me, was it?" It must have been why he'd told me to watch, to make sure I knew *he* thought I was good at writing. It was sweet, if a little anticlimactic. It made me even happier I hadn't told Mo about the texts. I'd already built the whole thing up too much in my own mind, imagining ridiculous scenarios where Laura enlisted me to take her "perfect selfie," or Kyle declared his love for me on air. It would have been so much worse to see the inevitable pity in Mo's eyes when nothing happened.

"Mm-hmm."

"I mean, it was embarrassing, but at least he was being nice, right?"

"Right."

The doorbell rang. Mo's head whipped back so fast I thought she might break her neck. She looked like she was trying to x-ray the ceiling, which was a little intense even for Mo. Finally, for the first time since the show started, she looked straight at me.

"Are you going to get that?" Her jaw looked tight.

"Jonathan can. Or my dad, if it breaks through his office door to his brain."

"You should."

"Why?" I frowned at her. "Kyle might be on again." Yes, I was that pathetic.

"Your dad's working, right? You should get the door."

"Who cares? It's probably evangelists trying to un-Jew my family or something."

"RACH-el." Monique fixed me with her green eyes. "Get the door. Trust me."

"All right."

Jesus, what in the actual hell was going on?

I could hear Monique trailing behind me as I padded up the basement stairs, but I didn't turn to look at her. She might hiss, and besides, now I was nervous. If I tried to look backward while walking upward, I'd probably get vertigo and fall and bleed out slowly while Monique tried to drag my body to answer the door.

"I don't know why you're coming, Mo," I called back. "Whoever it is doesn't need your input, I promise."

She didn't say anything.

Glancing at Mo, who'd stopped near the door to the basement, I walked the last few steps to the front door and pulled it open, ready to tell the visitor that my parents weren't home, and no, I didn't have any allowance to give to their cause.

But it wasn't a solicitor or a church or a secret murderer dressed as a utility-company employee.

It was Kyle, in a tuxedo, holding what looked like a massive bouquet of old french fries.

And there was a cameraman over his shoulder.

chapter twenty-two

KYLE

FRIDAY, 4:40 P.M.

Rachel stared at me for a second, then frowned.

Then she slammed the door in my face.

Ouch. I turned to Eddie. He leaned his head out from behind the camera, then shrugged, grinning slightly.

Thanks, dude. Big help.

I could hear muffled conversation behind the door, then nothing. Had she gone away?

I was about to knock when Rachel opened the door again, but only partway, like she wanted the option to retreat. This was not what was supposed to happen. We'd practiced and practiced, but not for this. Fry grease tickled my nose. It felt like someone was squeezing my lungs. It was hard to get a deep breath.

"Hi," I said in my most upbeat voice. It came out squeaky. Awesome. Monday on national TV: Kyle Bonham, reliving puberty. My heart thumped harder. Jeez, this was going to be a disaster.

"Hi," she said cautiously. Her face looked extra pale. "You're . . . here."

"I am."

"Why are you here?"

"Well, uh, I had been thinking about—"

"Aren't you supposed to be in California?"

"Oh. I flew back this morning. Early. They tape that stuff a day in advance."

"Oh. Duh." Rachel rolled her eyes. "Sorry, sometimes I can't help being a massive idiot." She looked at the camera again and gulped.

I laughed. Somehow, the fact that Rachel seemed totally unprepared for this made it easier to talk to her. I could be the smooth one. Or slightly smoother. Emma would have been playing to the camera the second she realized it was there. Though she would have probably been pissed that I hadn't given her a chance to fix her makeup.

Things to *not* think about: Emma.

"No, it's cool. I'm the one carrying a bouquet of fries."

"Is that what that is? Bet that makes all the ladies swoon."

"It's Romance 101. Box of chocolate-covered sliders and a

bouquet of cold fries melts any girl's heart."

"Or her arteries."

"Those too."

I heard a cough behind me. I turned; Mary was leaning out from behind Eddie, eyebrows raised expectantly.

Right. I was actually supposed to do something while I was here. I'd kind of forgotten.

I cleared my throat.

"Anyway, you probably guessed I didn't just show up to get our Creative Writing assignment."

Rachel's eyes widened so far I could see the whites all the way around. I'd never really noticed, but the brown of her eyes was shot through with little glints of gold, like some kind of buried treasure. And her eyelashes were so long, longer than I'd expected; I wondered if they tickled her face when she blinked. Like giving herself butterfly kisses.

She nodded slowly.

"I came because . . ." This was where I could get back on track. I'd run through it with Mary maybe a hundred times on the van ride over. Still, it stuck in my mouth a little. Be the golden boy for once, Kyle. "Because you saw something in me, and, uh, I wanted you to know that I see something in you too."

Rachel leaned a little farther out the door.

"What do you mean?"

I squinted, trying to remember what we'd practiced. This wasn't like lacrosse, where I could just go on muscle memory.

It was much, much harder . . . but also more exciting. Oh! I was supposed to bend down on one knee, according to Mary's plan.

But we hadn't had the fry bouquet before.

I started to squat down, but it was surprisingly awkward trying to balance a weird arrangement of fry cartons and get all the way down at the same time. Why hadn't we practiced with me holding something? I could almost *feel* the camera lens drilling into my back. You're messing it up, dude. Finally I just lunged forward, like when I was warming up for a game, until I got most of the way to the ground. Then I kinda fell, banging my kneecap hard against the concrete slab in front of Rachel's door. Smoother one: yeah, right.

"I mean." I swallowed. My hands were sweating against the cellophane enclosing the fries. This part we couldn't plan for. I didn't even know Rachel, not really. She might hate me. Girls like her weren't into athletes. And even if she hadn't hated me before, she might now. She hadn't gotten asked on any TV shows because of the picture. She'd just had catty girls call her names.

She might say no. She probably *would* say no.

How had this not even occurred to me before? Would they show that on TV? Me getting rejected, kneeling on the cement with wilted fries in my arms? It would be like flubbing the shot that could win the championship. Suddenly Mary's brilliant idea seemed full of holes.

It was too late now. Only way out: keep going.

"I'm saying, I was hoping you would . . . um . . . man, sorry, it's hard to get this right with an audience." I smiled, tilting my head to acknowledge the camera. Somehow, in the last three minutes, I'd transformed into the king of awkward. "Do you want to go to homecoming with me?" I finally spat out, all in one breath.

Rachel stared at me for a second. Oh jeez, here it comes.

Then the corner of her mouth started twitching into . . . a smile. One that she was pinching back like she was trying not to laugh. I started smiling too. It was pretty ridiculous, after all: the tux, the "bouquet," Mary behind me watching so hard it was making her lean forward, like this was life-or-death stuff.

I laughed.

Then she laughed.

"Of course, I mean . . ." She caught sight of the camera again and choked a little. "What girl can turn down . . . a fry bouquet?" By the end her voice was kinda shaky, but Mary burst out laughing behind me. Rachel smiled wanly.

"Awesome. That's awesome." I struggled to stand up. Rachel extended a hand. I grabbed it and let her help me to my feet. She looked up at me, smirking hard, face paler than ever. She was breathing too fast. She looked exactly like I'd felt the minute before I walked onstage at the show. Before I could think about it I pulled her into a hug. She let out a little "oh." The fries crushed in between us and started to spill out onto the ground.

She hugged back.

"Don't worry, you did great. Sorry for surprising you."

"No, it's okay," she murmured. I could feel her voice resonating in my chest. "It's a nice surprise."

She squeezed a little harder. I could smell her hair: sweet and soft, like some kind of flower. Kind of like her, actually. Her body loosened, like the tension was finally draining out. It made me realize how nervous she'd really been. It was hard to believe. Rachel was the best writer in our class, the one whose scenes Jenkins always chose to read out. I'd assumed she'd be more prepared for this than I was.

My heart started beating faster again. Or maybe that was her heart. With her body pressed up against me, it was hard to tell. It was weird, but feeling her that close to me, our entire bodies touching, part of me almost wanted to—

"Okay, cut. Good job, guys. Really, that was great. Super relatable."

Rachel let go of me and pulled away swiftly. She was looking at the ground next to her sneakers, like she didn't want to look at me. Rachel: clearly not thinking what I had been. Thank goodness I hadn't gone through with that one. I tried to will my body not to do something stupid like blush. Or worse.

"Cool," she mumbled. She started twisting the bottom of her shirt between her fingers. "So . . . now what happens?"

"That's the best part," Mary said, voice bright and shiny. Mary's exterior: thrift sale leftovers. Mary's interior: polished chrome. "We have some really exciting things planned for the two of you. Do you want to talk inside?"

"My mom's not home. And my dad is busy, I'm not sure . . ."

"Oh, don't worry, hun, we spoke to your mother when we were setting this up. And I believe she should be . . . ah, yes." Rachel turned as a woman who looked remarkably like her, but older, and in more hippie-ish clothes, walked up behind her. Rachel frowned and her mom reddened slightly. Before Rachel could open her mouth, her mom reached over her head to open the door wider.

"Come on in."

Mary plowed through, beaming so hard you didn't even notice the sloppy work shirt and rips in her jeans. She was already chattering at full speed. Eddie followed, camera hanging at his side now. I was just about to walk in after them when Rachel's mom came up beside me.

"You must be Kyle," she said. Her hair was even curlier than Rachel's, poofing out from her head in a kind of wiry triangle. Her smile was warm, but she barely looked at me. "You are even more adorable than in that picture." She walked into the house, calling out, "What can I get everyone to drink? We have milk, and pop, and wine if you want that."

Everyone seemed to have forgotten about me. It felt strange after the last few days. Unsure what to do, I awkwardly placed the bundle of fries on the ground and walked into the house, closing the door behind me.

chapter twenty-three

RACHEL

FRIDAY, 5:25 P.M.

"Well, that's everything," Mary said, standing up and smiling perfunctorily at me. Mom squeezed my shoulder. I shrugged out from under her.

"We'll just look these over as a family and get back to you. Is that all right?" Mom's voice turned worried. "I know you folks have tight deadlines, but these are big decisions."

"Of course that's all right. We won't be moving forward before midweek. If you could have them signed and back to us by . . ." Mary scrunched up her nose and looked at the ceiling, like she was fishing for an answer. It seemed contrived. Her whole "look at me, I'm so disheveled because I'm doing creative stuff all the time" vibe felt contrived, actually. She was nice enough, but I didn't really trust her. Or Mom. Or Mo. I glared at her, sitting on the edge of our brick hearth, just outside the circle discussing my fate. Mo knew better than to make eye contact with me, though.

"... Sunday evening?" she finished. "Pacific time, of course. That should give us enough time to come up with material for the next segment. And, of course, if you decide not to move forward, we'd like to know as soon as possible so Laura can plan an alternate segment for Monday's show."

"Sure, that shouldn't be a problem," Dad said. He was nodding slowly, like he was still taking this all in. I wondered what all Mom had told him. Probably not much; Dad was terrible at keeping secrets. "We'll talk it over tonight as a family."

"Shoot, depending on when your flight leaves, we might have an answer to you before you even land in L.A.!" Mom laughed nervously. Mary smiled but didn't join in.

"Great, then Eddie and I will just get out of your hair," she said, standing and brushing off the front of her pants. Eddie rose from the love seat he'd been dominating—it was kind of amazing how easily you forgot he was there, since he was approximately the size of an eighteen-wheeler—and they started getting their things together.

"Kyle," she said, not looking at him. "Do you need us to drop you home?"

He looked around awkwardly from his position against the wall beside the front door. I'd been sneaking glances at him throughout the conversation, but he'd just seemed really ill-at-ease, his arms folded, his head down. It confirmed the nasty, slimy feeling I'd been trying to ignore while Mary talked and Dad furrowed and Mom nodded, wide-eyed: that I was nothing but a setup to him. A chance to be a little more famous a little longer. It was stupid that it hurt. What had I thought, that he planned this whole thing on his own? Of course it had been a producer's idea.

He couldn't even look at me.

"That's okay, I can call my mom or . . . somebody. But do you need the tux?" Suddenly he looked so nervous, like a little kid who wasn't sure if he'd broken the rules, that I couldn't help but smile. Kyle definitely wasn't into me, but he *was* adorable. No wonder he was so much better on camera than I was.

He glanced my way. Seeing my grin, he frowned for a second, then smiled back, looking down at the floor like he was trying not to laugh.

And a sense of humor. Jesus, I'd be lucky if I didn't declare my undying love for him the first time they put us in a room together. There was no way this could happen. What they'd already shot was mortifying enough. Too bad there wasn't a way to say no to the show but convince him not to back out of homecoming.

"That's yours for now," Mary said. "It was tailored to you, after all. Just take it to the dry cleaners and send the receipt to the show. We'll reimburse you. It's possible we'll have you wear it to the dance."

Kyle nodded, eyes still down, cheeks still smiley.

"I'll drive him," Mo said. It was the first thing she'd said since we all sat down. "You guys probably have somewhere to be, anyway."

"Great. Thanks, Jo," Mary said, smiling perfunctorily. I could see Mo's jaw tense. Good. She deserved it. "We'll get going. Can't wait to get started on this!"

Mary shook Mom's hand, smiled in a big circle at the rest of us, and whisked out the door, Eddie in tow.

"Text me later, okay?" Mo stopped by the door to look back at me, eyes pleading.

"Don't worry, I *definitely* will." If only to ream her out.

"So was you asking Rachel something the show had planned from the beginning, or . . ." I heard her saying to Kyle as they headed out. Then the door slammed shut.

"Well." Mom leaned back into the couch cushions, looking dazed. After a few seconds of grinning at nothing, she turned to me. "What do you think about *that*?"

I stared at her.

"I can't believe you set this up. You knew they were going to come over, and make me look like a total fricking idiot—"

"Rachel, *tone*."

"And then they'd air it on national TV. You *knew*."

Mom's forehead accordioned into a pained expression. Dad was frowning at me unconvincingly. I had a sneaking suspicion Dad was thinking the same things.

"All I knew was they were helping Kyle ask you to homecoming. He was the boy you had a crush on, and Mo said this would help your plays somehow." Mom shook her head, waving the air in front of her as if it were full of flies. "I thought you'd be excited."

"To be the laughingstock again? For everyone to remind me that I'm too fat for him, too ugly, too worthless to—" I shook my head. Even now it felt risky to tell my mom about the really awful stuff. If she knew that, there was no limit to how far she might go: wrap me up in a thousand layers of bubble wrap, remove all the too-sharp internets and people from my vicinity, and pack me away in my room for the rest of high school, probably.

"Rachel, you didn't say anything about—"

"Of course I didn't." I could feel spit flying out of my mouth. I couldn't stop, I only seemed capable of talking louder, faster. "Remember Lorelei Patton? I told you about her, and you decided to turn it into a personal crusade. Everything you did made things a thousand times worse. Why would I be *stupid* enough to tell you something like that again?"

"Oh." Mom's face slid down, like it had suddenly turned to wax on a too-hot day.

It took all the air out of me. I shouldn't have said any of that. It was years ago, and everyone had moved on. I thought I'd moved on. Apparently not. It was horrible to see Mom look so hurt and sad and know I was the reason.

"Don't worry," I said, forcing my voice back toward calm. "People are crappy is all. I just feel . . . blindsided."

"Well, even without that . . . new information, I don't

think we should go any further with this," Dad said, looking at Mom meaningfully. She nodded slowly, face scrunched up like she had a headache. "It's your choice, Rachel—you know we want you and Jonathan to be your own people—but what that Mary described sounds . . . well, shallow. I want you to be recognized for your talent, not for liking some boy."

"Well of course. We both do." Mom shook her head, looking at her lap. "I just thought this—just the dance, you getting asked to the dance—would be fun for you. But that was stupid of me. I should have asked. I should have *known* you'd feel this way about being thrust into the spotlight. When have you been an attention seeker? Of course you feel this way. Here—"

Mom leaned over to the coffee table, sifting through the stacks of forms Mary had left behind until she found the right one.

"That's it." She slid a business card from beneath its paper-clip prison and leaned back from it. I smirked, though she probably couldn't see it. She absolutely refused to get reading glasses because they'd "make her look old," but she was willing to squint and keep adjusting her arm back and forth to find the right distance for five straight minutes, as though that was somehow better.

"I'll grab my phone, and you can tell me the number," she finally said, passing it to me. "And we'll tell her right now we're not interested. If we reach her quickly, they can even stop the invite from airing—they said that, right?" Mom's face was imploring.

"Don't do that." The idea of turning my back on it so definitively—turning my back on Kyle—actually made my stomach hurt. He might still take me to the dance, right? Then again, this was all a game for him. It had to be. Wouldn't I be setting myself up to be hurt more by agreeing to be his pity date? "I should at least talk to Kyle first."

"Okay, honey. What do you want me to do? Tell her no to the rest, or . . . ?"

How was I supposed to know that?

"Just . . . don't do anything yet, okay? I'd like at least as much time to think this over as you and Mo had," I added. It sounded sulky even to me.

Mom didn't even flinch, though.

"Okay," she said, staring at me like my eyes were some kind of life raft. "Take your time and make whatever decision feels right. And I mean that, honey. Whatever decision you make, your dad and I will support you, won't we, Dan?" He nodded solemnly. "I swear to you, I would have never said yes to even this much if I'd thought . . ." She exhaled heavily, eyes pinched closed.

"I know, Mom. I just need time to think."

"Of course. Yes, right. Take your time."

I nodded.

But really there was nothing to think about. Just one brutally painful thing to do.

chapter twenty-four

FRIDAY, 5:45 P.M.

We were barely a block from my house. If I didn't ask now, I'd miss my chance.

"Do you think . . . is Rachel mad at me?" I looked out the window at the lawns flying by. I could feel Monique looking over, sizing me up.

"No, why would she be?"

"No reason." I tapped my toes against the floor mat. "She just seemed weird."

Monique whipped her car into my driveway, probably still going forty. Girl seriously drives like a maniac.

"I think she was caught off guard is all. It's a lot to take in. We all had time to process the idea."

"Yeah." It made sense, but it didn't make the heavy feeling at the bottom of my chest go away. I looked over at Monique, trying to see whether she was hiding something. Rachel when I asked: seemed happy. Rachel when we left: like a bomb about to go off. And she wouldn't even look at me.

But what did I know? We'd only talked, like, three times. "As long as she's not angry."

"She's not mad at you. Trust me, I've known her since forever." Monique tilted her chin down, staring straight at me, eyebrows raised. I think it was supposed to be reassuring, but it seemed kinda cocky. We'd hung out for maybe fifteen minutes and already I could tell she didn't take crap from *anyone*. I wondered how she and Rachel had become friends.

"Cool." I pulled open the door and got out. "Thanks for the ride."

"It'd probably help if you spent more time together, though," Monique said just before I closed the door. I leaned in. "I mean, she doesn't really know you. And I'm not sure if you noticed, since you had a few hundred thousand new fans, but people were beyond evil to her. It's probably hard for her to feel all warm and fuzzy toward you after that."

Oof. Punch: not pulled.

"Yeah, okay. Maybe we can get . . . dinner or something."

"Or you could just ask her to a party. It doesn't have to be a big formal thing."

"Right. I'm not sure when there's a—"

"Beau Anderson and the football team are having a party tonight, right?"

"Yeah, I think so. I don't think I'm welcome since—"

"You're welcome anywhere, Kyle. You're famous now. Ask Rachel to the party. I'll get her to go. The whole thing will work better if you guys seem like friends, anyway. So . . . be friendly."

"Okay."

"I have to go. Text me once you've asked her."

I nodded and closed the door, staring at the car as Monique sped down the driveway in reverse.

Someday that chick was going to run countries.

In the kitchen, Mom was sitting at the table, talking on the landline.

"You'll see it Monday, it was *adorable*. They got him a tuxedo, tailored it to him . . . I know, isn't it? Like something out of a movie. Then they flew us back on the overnight flight . . ."

She waved at me with a couple fingers, smiling hard. I was glad she was tied up; I needed time to settle my nerves.

What I had to do next was going to suck.

I dialed the number.

"Hey, Kyle!" Her voice was light and sweet. I could hear her happiness through the phone. "I didn't expect to hear from you tonight. Where are you?"

"Hey, Emma. Home, actually."

"Oh my god, that's AWESOME. We can pregame Beau's

party, and you can tell me everything." Apparently I was the only one who thought I shouldn't go to Anderson's kegger. Though Rachel might agree. Emma kept talking at hyperspeed. "Did Laura look older in person? She looks good on TV, but she has to be, like, forty."

"She looked . . . I dunno, good. Normal. Like a mom. But, you know, a mom who takes care of herself."

"That makes sense." I could almost hear her nodding, fast like a little bird. She always did it when she was excited.

"What was the best part? Did they send a limo to get you? Oh, what was backstage like? Was the greenroom super shmancy, or was it a dump?"

"We can talk about it later. I have to tell you something before tonight, though."

"Oh. Okay. Is it good?"

"Kinda." I closed my eyes, trying to focus. "They want me to do a whole series of segments for the show."

"Oh my GOD. KY-LE!" She was squealing. Jeez, this was even worse than I expected.

"Yeah, it's cool. There's just one thing." I breathed deep.

"Do you have to move to L.A. for a while? Oh my god, I can't *believe* this. Probably you're going to have a movie star girlfriend by next week and totally forget I exist."

Oof. Emma: not making this easier.

"No, that's not gonna happen. But the thing about the segments—"

"Do you think they'll let me, like, guest star? I can pretend

I don't know you if they want. Oh my god, this is *crazy*."

I was never going to get a word in if I waited for her to stop, so I just broke in over Emma's excitement.

"The segments are with Rachel. They had me ask her to homecoming, and the show is going to, like, follow us leading up to it. It wasn't my idea. The producers came up with it. They think it will play well 'for the *Laura Show* audience.'" I could feel myself getting off track. Why was I still talking? Like it was going to make Emma take it any better? "Anyway, I thought I should be the one to tell you."

I waited for Emma to say something. Tell me she understood it was all make-believe, or scream that she hated me, or even say something catty about Rachel.

But the other end of the line was dead silent.

Then she hung up.

chapter twenty-five

FRIDAY, 5:55 P.M.

There was no way around it: I couldn't do the show, so I couldn't go to the dance with Kyle.

Now I just had to tell everyone. Mo would be pissed. But then, I was pissed at Mo.

After the "family discussion," I ran up to my bedroom and threw myself onto my bed, staring at the ceiling. I was doing a lot of that lately.

I already knew I couldn't go through with this, but some part of me didn't want to admit it. The part that thought Kyle looked adorable in his tux, and noticed how he had laughed at the same ridiculous moments as I had, and smiled at me in a way that felt so real, even while the rest of me—my actual *brain*—was screaming at me not to be so fricking gullible.

Pros is doing the show, cons is saying no.

Pro: I get to go to homecoming with Kyle.

Con: It's fake, he only asked me because a producer made him, and I'll probably embarrass myself by forgetting that.

Pro: We'd be on TV.

Con: Being on TV is basically begging all the mean girls to comment on how ugly the dress I chose was, how much hotter Kyle is than me, how ridiculous my hair looks, and, and, and. They'd probably point out things that were wrong about me that I hadn't even thought of yet. Maybe my jokes suck. Or maybe I have a lisp. Or a mustache—a massive handlebar mustache that curls at the ends that somehow I've *never even known I have*. Whatever it is, they'll tell me.

Pro: Kyle clearly wants to stay in the spotlight longer. I could give him that.

Con: He probably wouldn't even realize I was the one doing it.

Pro: Mo might not be totally wrong about this helping our application.

Con: Even thinking about what I'd be like on TV made my stomach hurt. Remembering the moronic things I'd said in the two minutes at my front door, when I hadn't been expecting everyone to show up, made my whole face feel hot. If I knew I had to do it—mug for a camera—I'd almost certainly try too hard and be even more brutally awkward. There's a reason I *write* plays, not audition for them.

Con: The more I put myself in the spotlight, the lower the chances of this ever blowing over.

Con: Kyle doesn't like me that way, which sucks enough already, but the more I get to know him, to actually see him, the worse that's going to feel. Doing this would be like starting with a paper cut and trying to bandage it with a machete.

If I'd learned anything from the past week, it was that other people could be cruel—needlessly cruel—for no reason at all. They'd probably already forgotten what they said to me. Even Jessie seemed to be over it by now; all the internet trolls wouldn't know me if they tripped on me. But it would almost certainly start up again—and be way worse—if they *did* know who I was. I couldn't go through that again.

So it had to be no. Everyone might hate me for a while, but how was that any different from my life right now? Mo would come around eventually, hopefully around the same time I was ready to be on speaking terms again. And Kyle . . . well, Kyle never really liked me in the first place.

Out of the corner of my eye, I saw my phone light up, the harsh metallic glow of its screen reflecting off the folds of my comforter.

(From Kyle): Hey, what r u doing tonight?

I wasn't ready to hear from him yet. Knowing I was going to single-handedly end his star turn was way easier when he was an abstract concept instead of a real contact.

Could I text that the whole thing was off?

No, he'd never speak to me again. Plus, it just felt cowardly. Like breaking up over social media or something.

> **(To Kyle):** No plans yet. I know, hard to believe of a social butterfly like me.

(From Kyle): Come to Beau Anderson's party it's gonna be huge.

Beau Anderson? The senior football player? I had never in my life gone to a party like the ones he threw, with multiple kegs and random hookups happening in any room with a door that closed and kids vomiting into bushes or toilets or tubs "then rallying!" They sounded more like something out of a movie than Apple Prairie. Frankly, I'd never *wanted* to go.

> **(To Kyle):** Maybe. I doubt I'll know anyone there.

(From Kyle): You'll know me. And Monique.

Wait, what?

I typed Mo a text.

> **(To MO-MO):** Beau Anderson's? Really?

(From MO-MO): Don't automatically say no. It could be fun. Besides, if you and Kyle are going to homecoming you should hang out. Which is easier and more likely to lead to sloppy makeouts if you're drunk.

(To MO-MO): Nothing in your text is ever gonna happen.

(From MO-MO): Stop being a drama queen and let's do something fun for once.

Great, now Mo was doubling down on being evil.

(From Kyle): Say yes? Promise I'll shower so I don't smell like fries AGAIN

If I didn't go they—well, mostly Mo—would berate me all night. And every new text from Kyle would just make it harder to tell him what I had to.

Besides, if I wasn't going to take the coward's way out and text him the bad news, how *was* I going to tell him? The longer I waited, the harder it would be. I needed to do it before Mary sent today's footage to wherever footage goes before it embarrasses you in front of a national audience.

(To Kyle): Fine, you've convinced me. Make sure to use chzburger aftershave though otherwise I won't know for sure who you are.

(From Kyle): Obvs.

I'd go to the party and tell him there.

After that, I probably wouldn't have to worry about hearing from him much anymore.

## chapter twenty-six

KYLE

FRIDAY, 7:42 P.M.

I could have offered to pick Rachel up to go to the party, but after the conversation with Emma—the half a conversation she let me have—it seemed like a bad idea, at least if I ever wanted Emma to speak to me again. Rachel being there was enough. Getting to know each other better didn't have to mean being besties right away.

But I wasn't gonna show up alone. Everyone else might not care about it, but I hadn't forgotten that Lamont and his crew were *not* my fans. Being on TV today: probably not helping that any.

I threw myself onto one of the worn-out denim beanbags in the Xbox corner of my room and scrolled to Ollie's number.

He was always hit-or-miss with texts. If you didn't catch him at the right moment, he wouldn't respond. Which was fine usually, but I needed a wingman now, not tomorrow.

He picked up on the first ring.

"Hey, Kyle," he said. I could hear a sports announcer shouting in the background. Ollie always had ESPN on. Sometimes he even watched ESPN Classic. "How's L.A.?"

"Actually I'm back already."

"Really? That was fast." The background noise got softer. "I saw the show. I thought they were going to have you back. Are you flying out again?"

"No, they did the follow-up here. That's why we came back so fast."

"Yeah?"

"They staged a homecoming invite."

Ollie didn't say anything for a second.

"Who'd they have you ask?"

He sounded suspicious. I should have known Ollie would cut right to the awkward part. Ollie: always able to smell when you weren't telling him everything. It was part of why I liked him. Who wanted friends who never called you on your BS? You'd wind up . . . being Dave. Oof.

"Rachel."

Ollie exhaled thoughtfully.

"Are you sure that's a good idea?"

"Why wouldn't it be?"

"Well it's good for you, obviously, but what about Emma?

Or Rachel. She's already getting death threats now."

Death threats? Jeez, what had people been saying to her? Sending a death threat to someone over a meme: legit crazy. Besides, Rachel hadn't done anything wrong. And it took all of two seconds talking to her to realize how nice she was. My left hand clenched into a fist.

"Have you even *told* Emma?"

That brought me back to the moment. With a thud.

"Yeah." I sighed.

"And?"

"She hung up on me."

Ollie snorted.

"Dude."

"Sorry. I didn't mean to. It's just . . . what did you expect?"

"It wasn't my idea, it was the producer's. Anyway, I told her to come to Anderson's tonight. Rachel, I mean. I figured we should, like, get to know each other. Before we have to do more stuff for the show."

"You want someone to roll up with?"

This. This was why Ollie was the best ever, even now.

"That would be awesome, dude. Thanks."

"No worries. Leave your car here and we can walk. He only lives a half mile from me."

# # #

Ollie and I headed over to the party early, like eight thirty, but there were already a few dozen people milling around the kitchen, the keg jammed into a laundry bucket full of ice. I looked around for Rachel, but I didn't see her.

Good. I needed to talk to Emma in person before Rachel showed up.

"I thought I told you not to come to this," a low voice said from over my left shoulder. I looked at Ollie, hoping he could somehow save me from Lamont's wrath, but he just shrugged and mouthed, "Get it over with."

"Hey, Lamont." I turned to face him. Man, I always forgot how *big* he was. "Sorry for the other day, I was being a tool."

"You were born a tool, Kyle," Lamont said, raising an eyebrow. "But I never took you for stupid."

"I know." I could feel my palm sweating against the neck of the bottle I was gripping. "That's why I brought a peace offering. To make up for it."

I swung the bottle around so Lamont could see the more-than-half-full liter of rum I'd pulled out of the back of Carter's closet. No one hated having backup liquor around.

"I thought you might want it for later." Lamont was still staring at me like I was dog crap he hadn't scraped off his shoe yet. What would make him change his mind? Or at least not punch me? "Plus, chicks love doing shots, right?"

He leaned closer, so close I could smell his aftershave, minty and sharp beneath the musky cologne he was wearing. His fingers were twitching at his sides, like he was getting ready to do something he didn't want me to see coming.

Oh, jeez. Stomach muscles: clenched in preparation.

He swung his arm around suddenly. I forced myself not to

flinch. If he was gonna punch me, it was gonna hurt as bad as it was gonna hurt, whether or not I acted like a wimp.

But instead of concussing me, he reached for the rum. A wave of cold relief washed down my entire body, leaving my muscles shaky in its wake.

"Okay, we're cool," he said, a smile cracking his square, stubbly jaw. "I *did* tell you to bring chicks, though. Ollie's pretty close, but I don't think even I can drink that much." He laughed, showing bright-white teeth. Ollie shrugged and leaned against the counter behind me.

"I did, actually. Just a couple junior girls."

"Oh yeah? Where are they?"

"They're coming." What would plausibly explain why they hadn't come *with* me? "I wanted to talk to you first to make sure we were cool before I had them come."

"I hear that. Well, call your girls. If you parked on the street, move your car a couple blocks down so the cops don't come. Woods behind the house and the fire pit are on-limits, pool is closed for the night. Anderson says it's hell to clean puke out of the filters. Yo, Lu-SEEE," Lamont yelled, turning away from me to bear-hug a stick-thin brunette in six-inch heels who had just tottered in the side door.

"All right, I guess we're cool to stay," I said to Ollie. I could feel myself grinning stupidly. Not getting your ass kicked: feels pretty good.

"Well, maybe," he said, looking down the hallway toward the main entrance to the house.

My eyes followed his.

Emma was striding down the hall, flanked by three dance-team friends.

I could see her register me, her extra-fast blinking the only indication of the split-second of shock.

Then she turned and whispered something into Erin Rothstein's mass of shiny blond curls. Erin cracked up, then pulled Jessie Florenzano's arm so she could pass on Emma's secret. Jessie's dark-brown eyes widened. She turned over her shoulder to Willow Agners, who had been smiling with nervous eyes, waiting to see if she was the butt of the joke. All the while Emma watched them, serene, making sure I knew how in control she was.

Suddenly the night didn't seem to be going as well as I had thought.

chapter twenty-seven

RACHEL

FRIDAY, 8:50 P.M.

"Why are you stopping? We're at least three blocks from his house."

I thrust my phone at Mo, the line on the GPS app still defiantly long.

"He'll just make us move the car if we park closer. This is good. Plus, the woods that run behind his house let out over there, by the park." Mo pointed over to the left where a few straggling trees tottered up to the plastic fencing around the playground. "If the cops come, it's better not to have to walk down his street."

Trust Mo to have planned additional exit routes in case of emergency.

"We're not going to be here long enough for it to matter."

"Noted," Mo said tightly, clicking her key fob. The car chirped behind us. "It's literally the only thing you've said to me since I picked you up. It still doesn't hurt."

Whatever. She couldn't know how short our stay would *really* be. She was right; we hadn't spoken the entire ride over. I figured I didn't owe her any warning about turning Kyle down; she hadn't given me any. She'd prattled on about how to stay natural in front of a camera, and which stores had the best dresses for homecoming, and which of the apparently myriad smiles I had was my *"good* smile," trying to fill the dead space.

I just stared out the window. I needed a ride—there was no way I was delivering the bad news entirely sober—but that's all Mo was to me right now. Besides, even if I weren't pissed at her, why would I want to party with a bunch of strangers who were almost certainly responsible for "decorating" my locker on Wednesday? If I hadn't wanted to deliver the news in person, Mo wouldn't have even gotten a text back.

I'd never been to Beau's house, so I didn't know how secluded it was until we were almost there. It was big and blocky and white, with dark-green trim and a porch that wrapped all the way around the back of the second story. You could hear kids shouting and music blasting once you got right up to the front, but it was tucked way back into the woods, the last place on a dead end, and the next house was too far away for the neighbors to hear anything at all.

Everyone was right. It was the perfect place for a party.

I looked over at Monique. Her mouth was pinched closed and her eyes were wide—maybe she was regretting coming as much as I was. After hesitating on the flagstone sidewalk that wound up under the front portico, I shrugged and started walking across the lawn toward the back. The night was cool, and the damp grass tickling my ankles made me shiver. I heard Monique following, steps soft and squishy in the grass.

Out back, people thronged the deck overhead, but we'd either missed the stairs or there wasn't a way to get up to it from outside. At ground level, light spilled out from a pair of sliding glass doors leading into a big, open room with a few people clustered in corners. I turned to Monique. Her face looked pale in the glow from the basement. I felt my stomach flutter slightly. These were *not* my people.

Not that I really had people. There weren't that many artsy weirdos at Apple Prairie.

"Are you coming?" I snipped. She nodded mutely but didn't move. Neither of us really knew how to enter a party like this. Suddenly the doors flew open and a huge figure stepped toward us, backlit so it was hard to make out his face.

"Ladies! Come on inside," he boomed. It was Lamont Davis, the absolutely massive captain of the football team. He put an arm around my shoulder. His hand felt about the size of a baseball glove. "You know Anderson, right?" He tilted his head toward Beau, standing just inside the door and grinning at us. "It's his party, so you better be nice to him."

"Okay," Monique squeaked. She cleared her throat and pasted on a huge, stagey smile, ready-made for a dance recital, or an audition. "As long as he's nice to us."

Lamont roared with laughter and pushed me into the house, which was impossible to resist since his arms were approximately the size of tree trunks.

"Feisty, huh?" He followed us in and closed the doors. "I like that. I'm Lamont, by the way." He extended a hand. "Who do you know here?"

"I'm Monique," she said, smiling and thrusting her hand forward. "And this is Rachel. Kyle Bonham told us to come."

"Oh man, I thought he was making that up," Lamont said, chuckling.

"What do you mean?" I said.

"Nothing. Here, let's do a 'nice to meet you' shot," he said, pulling a bottle off a thin table running along the back of one of the two couches that dominated the right half of the basement. "Anderson, you got glasses?"

Beau crossed over to a dated, wood-paneled wet bar at the bottom of the stairs and returned with four glasses, each painted with the name of a different spring-break location. They had clearly been used recently. I could see the ghostly outline of a lip crescenting the top of "CANCUN!"

"We don't need a shot, we . . . pregamed at Mo's," I lied. I hated shots.

"Who cares. Now you're at the game!" Lamont poured rum into the glasses, filling the first so full it spilled over the top. Beau handed it to Monique. She smiled at him, ignoring my glare in her direction.

He passed the next glass to me. I took it. Even if shots sucked, I needed the liquid courage before I found Kyle.

Lamont filled the last two glasses and looked down at Monique with a wolfish grin.

"To new friends!" he said, clinking his glass against hers. She raised her glass toward the center and pounded back the rum. There was really no other option but to do the same. It burned going down but left a pleasantly warm feeling behind.

"All RIGHT," Lamont shouted, slamming his glass down through the air, throwing himself forward and a little off-balance. He giggled as he stumbled forward. "Now you guys are ready to party! Keg's in the kitchen, and there's booze up there and pop for mixers. Pool's off-limits, at least till Anderson STOPS BEING A WOMAN." He turned to Beau, who was swaying slightly and grinning, apparently unaware he was being insulted. Score one for feminism? "And . . . I dunno, don't do anything really stupid." Lamont laughed at himself. "Hey, you guys ready for another shot?"

I didn't look at Monique, in case she was. "Maybe later. Do you know where Kyle is? I said I'd meet up with him."

"Don't be *booooring*." Lamont slapped his mitt down on my shoulder. "It's still early. You have to catch up."

"I will, for sure," I said, trying to smile the way Monique had before. "I'll just get this out of the way then find you again."

"Okay, cool," Lamont said, nodding slowly.

"So . . ."

"You need something?" He smiled at me. Jesus, drunk people were the worst thing in the world when you weren't drunk.

"Do you know where Kyle is? Kyle Bonham?"

"He's . . ." He scrunched his face in thought. "I dunno, upstairs probably? I think I saw him going into Chad's room with . . ." He trailed off, confused. "Maybe upstairs-upstairs?"

Clearly Lamont was going to be incredibly informative.

"Thanks," I said. I turned to Monique. "Keep your phone on you, okay?"

"Okay," she said reluctantly. She kept glancing toward the far corner of the basement, where Sean Langford was hooking up someone's phone to speakers. He was a football player in our year, but he was in all Mo's advanced classes. She would never admit she had a crush—athletes were officially "not her type." But she'd also never had the chance to drink with him in a basement. She pulled her phone out. "I'll be here."

"All right," I said, running up the basement stairs before anyone sucked me into more drunk "conversation." "I'll find you. Soon."

Upstairs was more crowded, especially the kitchen, where the basement stairs let out. I squeezed around a knot of sophomore girls huddling into one another over their drinks and almost got clocked as I tried to edge around Scottie Tarlington, one of the football seniors, animatedly replaying some extremely elbow-centric story for the benefit of a couple of guys my year.

From what I could tell, Kyle wasn't in the kitchen. I wove my way into a dining room, occupied only by a couple making out against a wall, then wandered out into the massive, tiled foyer, a giant staircase leading up the center and splitting off into two half-flights to the hallway that ran around the entire second floor. Every couple of dozen feet white-painted doors led into what had to be bedrooms.

Upstairs-upstairs. Maybe Lamont wasn't as worthless as I'd thought.

I padded up the swirling floral carpet, turning left at the top on a whim.

The first door was partially open, the room inside illuminated only by the streetlamps pouring in the windows on the front side of the house. I pushed the door open just far enough to see a couple mauling each other on a bottom bunk . . . and a leg and arm sticking out over the edge of the top, dark silhouettes in the dim room.

I didn't go to a lot of ragers, but even I wouldn't be passed out *this* early.

I made my way to the second door. It was closed, but if I leaned my ear up to it, I could hear voices inside. It sounded like a girl was shouting.

I was just about to move to the last room on this side of the hallway when the door flew open and Emma Stashausen almost body-slammed me to the floor.

chapter twenty-eight

FRIDAY, 8:50 P.M.

I hadn't exactly expected my conversation with Emma to go well, but I'd thought if we talked in person I could make her understand. It's not like I'd wanted to ask Rachel instead of her. I was just going along with what the producers wanted. What Mom seemed intent on. It didn't mean anything. Emma would see that.

"What the hell do you want?" she spat the second the door to what must have been Beau's brother Chad's room clicked closed.

Me: maybe a little too optimistic about this one.

"I wanted to talk, Emma." I sat on the navy bedspread. I knew Chad was at college, but it was weird how empty his room felt. Just a couple trophies on the shelves, some decorations that didn't feel very personal (since when was Chad Anderson into duck decoys?) and dark-colored plaids on the lamps and for the curtains and throw pillows. It was like a catalog version of a guy's room. Carter's room still had all his high school stuff in it. All the lacrosse posters, and honors certificates, and pictures of him with various good-looking girls at various dances.

I patted the bed beside me. Emma raised an eyebrow and folded her arms across her chest. Oof.

"There's nothing to talk about. Obviously." She snorted. "Otherwise we would have talked already. *Before* you asked another girl to homecoming."

"Emma, you know that wasn't my choice. The producers said—"

"I know," she snapped, waving a hand at me. "For you to stay famous you had to agree to pretend I don't exist."

"It wasn't like that!" How could I make Emma understand? I *had* to do it. It was the first thing I'd done in years that Mom cared about. How could I disappoint her like that? And why would I? Being on TV more was a good thing, right? Plus, it had happened really fast. By the time I knew what was really going on, they were already getting me fitted for the tux. I would have had to let so many people down to say no.

I stood up and walked toward Emma. I needed her to at least look at me. She backed up until her butt was against the dark-wood desk and stared at her folded arms.

"It's just a dance. Anyway, you told me Rachel was getting a bunk deal."

"Yeah, but . . . I mean, why do you even want this? Just to be on TV?"

I frowned. It was like she was trying to miss the point. Kyle Bonham before this: nothing special, Carter's failed clone. With this: somebody. Right?

"I thought you were happy for me." My chest felt tight. I really thought Emma would come around. Faster. Not having her on my team made me nervous.

"I am, Kyle, but . . ." Emma rubbed her hands into her eyes, exhaling wearily. "You can't expect me to be okay with it right away."

"There's no *it*. There's just me filming some goofy segments for a TV show. That's all this is."

"You don't *know* that!" Emma shouted. For one second she looked at me, face twisted in pain. "You don't." She hurried to the door, banging it open . . . right into Rachel.

Oh jeez. The first thought I had was to hope she hadn't heard anything that would hurt her feelings. Which made me angry with myself: Rachel's feelings weren't the point, right?

"Sorry," Rachel mumbled, taking a few steps backward. Emma stared, frozen in place just outside the door, eyes wide. "I needed to talk to Kyle. But obviously this isn't a good time. I'll find him later, or . . . it doesn't matter, I'm sorry." Rachel retreated. I could see her face flushing red all the way to the tips of her ears. Any other time it would have made me laugh, the idea that someone's ears could blush.

"No, you don't have to go," Emma said. Her voice was tight and too high. Rachel stopped, turning to Emma with this half-confused, half-annoyed look on her face. It made me want to either laugh or go hug her. I wanted to hug both of them. Which would probably be the worst idea I'd ever had. "You and Kyle have important things to discuss. There's no reason for me to be here."

Emma strode past Rachel just as Jessie and Erin were starting to climb up, obviously looking for her. They met on the landing and clumped around Emma protectively, like they'd shield her with their bodies. Jessie lasered me with an angry stare, one that got even meaner when she looked at Rachel. Then she turned back to Emma. Clearly she'd heard some of my news already.

"I'll find you later," Rachel said. She still had that headache look. She squinted so hard her face seemed to temporarily fold in on itself. "It's important, though. I only came to this so I could tell you in person. So please don't leave without finding me, okay?"

She turned and started down the stairs, not looking back even when I called out, "Wait, Rachel, what's going on?" It was like she was fleeing the scene of a crime. It did sort of feel like one.

I guess that made me the villain.

Rachel didn't make it far, though. Before she hit the landing, Jessie squared off at her, so she couldn't get past.

"Who said you could leave?" She sneered at Rachel exaggeratedly.

Willow was climbing up to join her friends, looking confused about what was unfolding a few feet above her. Willow always looked a little confused.

"Listen, I'm going. There's nothing to—"

"I didn't tell you to talk either." Jessie took a step forward, pushing Rachel lightly on the shoulders.

Oh jeez. I was never going to get invited to Beau Anderson's house again.

chapter twenty-nine

RACHEL

FRIDAY, 9:03 P.M.

Jesus Christ, when did I get dropped into somebody else's cli-chéd soap opera? I wanted to spit back, "Seriously? Should I take out my earrings so we can go outside and claw each other with our acrylic nails?" But Jessie looked drunk. Mean and drunk. She'd probably have punched me if I said that. And she actually *had* acrylic nails.

Plus, I only had the guts to say something like that to anyone—especially Jessie, who actually knew me once—in my mind.

I had totally underestimated how many drinks I needed.

"So what, you think you'll take some pathetic fangirl pic-ture and suddenly Kyle's your friend?" Jessie cackled. "No one likes you. No one even *knows* you."

You do, Jessie. Something I also failed to say out loud.

"Jessie, you don't have to do this," Emma murmured, tugging at her arm.

Jessie wriggled it free without looking back.

"Why not? It's the truth. This reject stalks someone else's boyfriend and expects everyone to like her for it? Hell no."

I could see Emma shaking her head insistently at Erin Rothstein. She mumbled something like "not about her . . . not doing it for me," then ran down the stairs, leaving Erin looking undecided about whether she should go after Emma or stay for the annihilate-Rachel fest.

I thought Jessie had gotten this out of her system by posting that picture, and "decorating" my locker . . . and car. Apparently hiding out since Tuesday night wasn't enough to make this—her—go away. How long would be enough? The thought made my stomach curdle.

"What did you think was going to happen, anyway?" Jessie arched an eyebrow. Her eyes looked filmy, glass marbles smudged with fingerprints.

"Why are you doing this, Jessie? What did I do to you?"

Her eyes narrowed. Apparently acting as though we were allowed to exist in the same sentence was already a step too far.

"Did you really think he was going to *fall* for you?" She laughed harshly.

"Jessie, back off." Kyle's voice behind me was calm, but I

could hear a threat of something underneath it. I don't think Jessie could, though, or she didn't care; she rolled her eyes and snapped, "Stay out of it, Kyle."

I swallowed, trying to keep control of myself. She was just a mean drunk girl trying to prove a point, prove that she'd moved past me, that she was fully secure in the realms of Apple Prairie's popular elite. This wasn't really about me; what she was saying wasn't true. The fact that it sounded like a slurrier, louder version of the refrain running through my head since the picture blew up didn't make it true.

"I didn't mean to get in the middle of anything. I'll just go downstairs and—"

"I asked you a question," Jessie spat. "Did you think that? Did you think you'd be in a fairy tale?" She singsonged the last words, batting her eyelashes, clumpy with mascara, at the ceiling.

I could feel my body tensing all over with embarrassment. And something else: anger. What the hell was her problem? Didn't she know she—and all the popular girls she'd apparently appointed herself representative of—had already won? I was folding. I hadn't even played a single card and I was folding.

I fought to keep my voice calm.

"I didn't think anything. It was a stupid mistake."

"Stupid is right," Jessie laughed manically. "God, it's just *sad*." She pulled a blurry, mock-sad face and flailed a hand at me. "To be that unfortunate and not even be smart." She turned to Erin, who looked cornered on the landing.

Kyle put a hand on my shoulder. Even with Jessie saying all the things I was afraid he already believed, he was still here. And even with the vat of verbal acid she was hurling at me, I could still feel my skin going electric under his fingers. If only there were a way to get that—his touch, his nearness—without getting the rest of this. But there wasn't. I'd accepted that . . . or I would eventually.

"You should go, Jessie, you're drunk," he said. Now the edge in his voice was unmissable.

"Not until I hear what Dumptruck thought was so important that she had to crash our party to tell you." She looked at me, face suddenly open, like a deeply tipsy preschool teacher waiting for the kids to answer. "What was so important, honey?"

I wanted to smack the faux-sweet look off her sharp little face. I wanted to give in to the tears and run away and bury myself in my comforter until everyone had forgotten I existed. I wanted more than anything to have never taken that picture.

I wished I could prove Jessie wrong. But most of me was crumbling under the fear that she was right.

"It really is more sad than anything else." Jessie turned back to Erin, still looking shell-shocked, and Willow, frowning like she wasn't quite sure what she'd walked into. I was suddenly certain Jessie said stuff like this to Willow too. "You can't help but feel bad for someone who's got so little going for her."

Anger swelled through my lungs, hot and heavy. I was trying to think of a more coherent retort than shrieking when Kyle spoke up.

"Rachel didn't crash, she's here because I invited her. She's going to be on the show with me—didn't you hear? For weeks, probably." Kyle smiled an aw-shucks smile and threw an arm around my shoulder. I breathed in hard. He hadn't been this close since the hug, his whole body pressed up against mine. If it had been hard to think clearly before, it was impossible now. Half of me wished I were the kind of girl who could just fly at Jessie's face with my nails, and half of me was trying to melt into his side. "Didn't you know that part, Jessie? The homecoming invite was just the start. Rachel's going to get more airtime than I am, probably."

Jessie's eyes narrowed, and her thin lips pinched pale. She shook her head once.

I felt a surge of evil triumph seeing her so obviously off guard.

Then a surge of something else. Panic. This was not what I'd come to tell Kyle. It couldn't be further from what I had to say. I could feel the wave of rage I'd been riding crashing down, leaving me wet and shivery on the shore.

"That's what you wanted to talk about, right, Rachel?" Kyle turned toward me. I could feel his eyes on the side of my face, his breath warm against my cheek, the nearness of him radiating heat, like the sun. Or the burn it gives you.

I could hear the last bit of my willpower screaming

"ABORT, ABORT," but how could I? When he'd just defended me against Jessie's latest onslaught? She had been trying to force him to choose a side, and for some inexplicable reason, he'd chosen mine.

Slowly, unsure what else to do, I nodded. Jessie sniffed.

"Whatever. I'm not watching."

"That's too bad," Kyle said, smiling chummily. He sounded so calm, so in control. It was like a superpower. "Luckily, with millions of other people excited for the show, we probably won't even miss you."

Jessie whirled past Erin and Willow and stomped down the stairs. After a few seconds, they followed, looking slightly dazed.

Kyle pulled his arm off my shoulder, dimming me about fifty watts. It also made me realize how shaky I felt. Confrontation was terrible enough—I'd orchestrated most of my life thus far to avoid it, except for Mo, but usually I just gave in to Mo—but on top of that, Kyle had signed me up to do something that even thinking about made my stomach feel like a dish towel someone was wringing.

"You okay?" he asked, leaning down slightly to peer into my eyes. "Sorry about Jessie. Emma always says she's like her attack dog."

"I guess she got off-leash."

Kyle laughed, his lopsided smile like a flame in the dark.

"Anyway, what did you want to talk about?"

I could still tell him. I hadn't sent in the papers yet, hadn't started filming segments. I hadn't even told him this was something I wanted to do.

But he was looking at me like we were in this together. Like him standing up to Jessie wasn't totally unheard of, almost miraculous. Like I wasn't just another girl in one of his classes—like we actually shared something.

I'd be saying no to that too.

So in spite of the fact that the "ABORT" call was still sounding, faintly, somewhere deep inside me, I forced a smile and said, "Nothing really, I just didn't want to come to the party and not say hi. Apparently I need to work on my timing."

"Oh, cool. I'm glad you came."

"Me too," I said. Right at that moment, alone with Kyle, knowing he just stood up for me when he didn't have to, it didn't even feel like a lie.

## chapter thirty

FRIDAY, 9:10 P.M.

Rachel sighed heavily.

"You sure you're okay?" I asked. I almost tilted her chin up so she'd look at me before I realized how weird that would be. Being extra friendly to defuse Jessie in witch mode: fine. Getting all touchy: probably not fine.

She scrunched her forehead up and shook her head, then opened her eyes extra wide and looked at me with the kind of half-smile you give the coach who's just ordered you to run another lap. A smile holding back something you know you shouldn't say.

"I'm great, honest. But I think I've had enough of the party."

I deflated a little. I thought that with that over, we might finally get to have fun.

"You sure? We haven't even had a drink yet."

"Yeah, I'm sure. I don't think Jessie's gonna improve with more beer."

She sniffed and smiled. The smile: not quite sad, just really worn-out looking.

"Someone should probably tell her that 'drunk and jealous' isn't a good look for her."

"If you do, it's not my fault." Rachel raised an eyebrow. It pulled her cheek up with it in a tight, mischievous grin.

"Not your fault?"

"About you losing an eye."

I laughed.

"Anyway, talk to you soon." Rachel frowned and stared at her feet, suddenly awkward. "Or, you know, later. Whenever."

"Don't sound too excited, there."

"Not sure if you noticed, Kyle, but your friends aren't really fans of mine."

"Yeah, well, Jessie's not my friend."

Rachel barely smiled, like a secret, and ran down a couple stairs, stopping at the landing to look up at me.

"Either way, thank you. I'm too young to go to jail for murder." She ran down the rest of the stairs before I could come up with anything funny to say in response.

I headed down after her. Ollie was in the kitchen, watching

a couple guys from the team play quarters along the breakfast bar.

"Rachel just ran by if you were looking for her," he said, not looking at me.

"No, we talked."

"She looked like she was leaving."

"Yeah, well, Jessie reamed her out. I think she'd kind of had enough."

Ollie nodded, unsurprised.

"What, like you knew it was gonna happen?"

"Well, maybe not with Jessie specifically, but c'mon. Girls are crappy to each other. Someone was gonna get too drunk and lay into her."

I didn't know how to respond. He said it so matter-of-factly, it felt like I should have seen it coming too.

"What did you expect? You've seen what they've been saying about her online."

"I mean, I saw Jessie post that picture. But that died down pretty fast."

"Dude? I know you've been busy, but you're getting dangerously close to tool."

"What? I'm nowhere near caught up with my own notifications. Why would I look at hers?"

"Because I'm telling you that you need to."

I tried to think of something to say, but I had nothing. Probably because I had the sneaking suspicion Ollie was right.

"I'm gonna head," I said finally. Nothing about this party felt fun anymore.

"Always smart to get out before Lamont gets belligerent. You good to drive?"

"Yeah."

"Cool. Talk to you tomorrow." He turned back to the game.

# # #

I waited until I was home in bed to open Flit and search her handle.

There were thousands of mentions from the last couple of days. The most recent were mainly reflits and luvs, but it didn't take long before they turned nasty. Complete strangers called her a "disgusting slut." Someone said girls like her were "the reason we have anorexia." A couple: basically, like, death threats.

Holy crap.

I swallowed hard. My throat felt too tight. Why were people being like this to her? She still hadn't posted anything since the picture, so there was no answer there. No wonder she'd been so desperate to leave the party. I couldn't believe she'd agreed to do the show. Oof.

Wait. Had she? Or did I just kind of assume that was happening?

Crap, crap, crap.

Why hadn't it even crossed my mind that she might have wanted to say no? Just because my mom was ready for me to milk this for everything it was worth didn't mean Rachel was on board.

But she would have said something, right?

At the party? To Jessie?

Quadruple crap. I was a total jerk. And to Rachel of all people, this weird, funny girl who so clearly didn't play mean-girl games.

I scrolled through my phonebook until I found her.

(To Rachel): I just wanted to say I'm sorry

(From Rachel): What for?

She texted back almost right away. I wondered if she was lying in her bed too. The idea was kind of nice. Both of us in the dark, alone with each other. I wondered what her room was like. I looked around mine, lit only by the glowing phone screen. There were lacrosse posters, some trophies, my games, and a big-screen in the corner. It could have been anyone's room. Anyone who played lacrosse, at least. I bet hers was different. Maybe with whole scenes painted on the walls instead of just a color. Or poems written on the mirror in eyeliner. I bet Rachel's room screamed Rachel. I sighed. What would even scream Kyle? Kyle Bonham: just some kid who apparently plays lacrosse. I shook the thought out of my head. I must be getting weird and emo because of the night I'd just had.

(To Rachel): For tonight

> **(From Rachel):** None of that was your fault.

>> **(To Rachel):** Yeah, but I should have made sure we at least got to talk before all that BS happened.

I threw in a pouting emoji, a liquor bottle, and an explosion, so it wouldn't sound too serious. I didn't want to make it more awkward than it already was.

> **(From Rachel):** Seriously not your fault.

>> **(To Rachel):** And you're okay with doing the show? It's fine if you're not you know

There was no way to unawkward that one. It took her a minute or so to respond.

> **(From Rachel):** Of course I am. I can't wait to, if only to see the look on Jessie's face.

>> **(To Rachel):** What look? I thought you guys were BFFLs

> **(From Rachel):** Oh for sure. We braid each other's hair every night.

I smiled. I'd been so worried for a second, but Rachel seemed fine. She would have said something. Even if she hadn't said it to Jessie, she would have told me after. She so clearly took crap from no one. Plus, if she were legit broken up about it, she wouldn't have already been making jokes.

Still, we hadn't talked about what Ollie had said. About what I'd seen on Flit.

> **(To Rachel):** Are you okay otherwise?

She responded almost immediately.

> **(From Rachel):** Of course. Why do you ask?

> **(To Rachel):** No reason. It just seemed like people were being kinda crap to you since the picture and . . .

And what? Was I going to fix it or something? I deleted the "and."

> **(To Rachel):** . . . so I thought I'd ask.

> **(From Rachel):** I'm fine.

> **(From Rachel):** Trolls will be trolls, right?

I wanted to say something more. Tell her I understood. Or that she could talk to me if she needed to.

But it sorta felt like she was saying "back off." Even with texts making it hard to understand how people mean things.

Plus, I didn't really understand. And she hadn't told me about it herself. The room: suddenly feeling even darker.

(To Rachel): For sure. Anyway, txt me tomorrow about stuff for the show. We can plan our attack together.

(From Rachel): Will do. Tactical superiority will make us victorious!

I half laughed. Joking = okay, right? Maybe she really just didn't care about jerks on the internet.

(From Rachel): Later.

(To Rachel): Good night, Rachel.

I almost typed "sweet dreams," then I realized that was weird and stalkerish.

I rolled over, put the phone on the nightstand, and stared into the darkness of my bedroom for a long time, replaying our conversation, until I finally fell asleep.

chapter thirty-one

RACHEL

SATURDAY, 10:00 A.M.

I think I probably slept for a grand total of thirty-seven minutes.

I'd finally managed to pace off most of the nervous energy jangling through me after the confrontation with Jessie—I never get into real fights; Monique likes being in charge but she doesn't turn into some rabid animal when we disagree—and then Kyle had to text and start the whole thing up again.

I spent the entire night swapping the gut-heavy feeling that Jessie was right, everyone thought I was a pathetic "dumptruck," for the fluttery, fizzy anxiety of wondering what Kyle meant by checking up on me. *After* standing up for me. No one had ever done something like that for me, and he acted like it was just normal. To stick up for the weird kid. To be aggressively kind in the face of all that nastiness. Had he never seen a teen movie?

And when was I supposed to text him, exactly?

Around seven I gave up and went downstairs. Mom was up, sipping coffee at the kitchen island. She looked startled to see me.

"I'm going to do it," I said.

"Do what?"

"The show. I'm doing the show."

Immediately her face origamied into anxiety. "I thought we were on the same page. This kind of attention can be hard to handle. We weren't trying to pry, but after you left your dad wanted to see what you meant about the people on Flit, and . . ." Mom shuddered a little. Thank god Dad slept late on the weekends; Mom tried to fix things, even things she clearly had no control over, but Dad just got sad and hovery when he thought people were hurting me or Jonathan. It was suffocating.

"No, I want to. Mo was right, this could be the thing that gets us into Budding Playwrights. It's worth it just for that." I still didn't really believe that, and I was still pissed with Mo, but she'd laid that groundwork with Mom. "Besides, I already told Kyle." She kept staring at me, forehead corrugated with worry. I had to say something Momish to prove I was fine. "I've already had to deal with the mean-girl fallout, so I know I'm strong enough to handle that. All I'd be doing is throwing away an opportunity."

She nodded slowly. She was still frowning, but her shoulders dropped down, like some of the tension had gone out of her.

"We said it was your decision, and it is. You're sure?"

I nodded, swallowing against the nerves already creeping back up my throat.

"Okay, then. We'll support you. Without interfering, I promise. I didn't ever—" Mom frowned, searching for how to put it.

"I know you're trying to do what's best for me. I think this is what's best. For my future."

"Okay." She nodded, like she was trying to reassure herself. "Then we'll support you. We're so proud of the person you've become, Rachel, I hope you know that."

"Thanks, Mom. I'm gonna watch TV," I said, before she could really get going. The longer we talked about it, the more chances she'd have to see how completely not certain of this decision I was.

I hid all morning, bored by the Saturday TV I was flipping through, but unsure what else to do. I waited until I heard the floorboard sighs that meant Mom was heading upstairs to sneak into the kitchen for a cup of coffee and a bowl of cereal.

It was just me, in the basement, alone with my crazy.

I couldn't really text him, could I? First? What would I even say?

After all, I couldn't figure out what his standing up for me to Jessie even meant. Was it really as amazing as it seemed? It could have just been pity. Or did it not mean anything at all? Kyle always seemed so sure of himself, so confident. He might have stood up for *anyone* so obviously drowning in that tidal wave of evil.

And how did he do that, anyway? How could anyone face gale-force Jessie and not want to curl up into a little ball and disappear?

Halfway through the third episode of the home remodeling show I'd been zoning out to, the house phone rang. I heard Mom shuffle across the kitchen to pick it up. I don't know why we even still had a landline. Only telemarketers and Grandpa Parker called on it, and even Grandpa had a cell now, one the salesperson had programmed so the text appeared in one-thousand-point font.

"Rachel." My mom's voice floated down the basement stairs. "Telephone."

Oh for Christ's sake.

I ran up the stairs and grabbed the phone from Mom. She looked at me so hopefully, almost pleadingly. Something about it made me sad. She wanted so badly for me to have this—anything that would make me happy, really—and she had no idea I was lying to her.

"This is Rachel," I said.

"Rachel, hi, it's Mary." The producer sounded the same way she looked in person: like she was tending to multiple pots on multiple stoves, all of them a second from boiling over.

"Oh, hi."

I heard a shuffling sound and a behind-the-hand whisper. I wondered if Mary ever stopped multitasking people.

"Sorry, this place is falling to pieces. Anyway, your mom texted to let us know you're on board. Which is great. Fabulous. We are going to have an absolute blast with this series, I promise you."

"Oh. Um, great." Now I really couldn't back out. I was briefly pissed with Mom for cornering me, till I remembered I was the one who had just made such a huge effort to convince her this was what I wanted.

"I had an idea for your first segment on the flight back, and I wanted to see if you had any thoughts."

"All right." I couldn't imagine what kind of input I could possibly give a professional television producer. I'd never even taken a film class. It was flattering, though, even if Mary was just trying to butter me up.

"First off, where do girls near you buy homecoming dresses?"

"I mean, there are a few places by me . . ."

"Assume they had no spending limit and wanted the biggest selection possible."

I blinked a few times, then, still uncertain, pinched my arm.

It hurt more than I expected.

So this wasn't a dream . . . or a nightmare. It was really happening.

chapter thirty-two

SATURDAY, 9:45 A.M.

I'd gone to bed feeling kinda good.

I woke up remembering the look on Emma's face as she ran down the stairs. Hurt, and angry, and teary.

I did that.

Oof.

I headed downstairs. There was a note on the counter; apparently Mom was at some farmer's market downtown. Dad would still be asleep. He'd been pulling ridiculous hours lately, traveling at least once a week to meet clients whose portfolios he was managing. Saturday mornings, if he was in town, he usually stayed in bed till noon.

I was glad. He and I hadn't really talked yet about what had happened, except for one quick phone call when I was in L.A. and he was in Chicago. The idea of going through it in detail for him was kinda tiring. My ability to play the part Mom wanted (me: thrilled at this, totally on board, raring to go) was starting to wear thin. Emma was pissed, Rachel was getting attacked, and Ollie thought I was a tool. Being famous was supposed to be fun. Or at least less stressful. Was I really doing all this just to *maybe* get into a school I didn't want to go to?

I filled a soup bowl with Cap'n Crunch and headed back to my bedroom, plopping onto a gaming chair to eat.

I had to text her.

But I didn't really want to.

Maybe she wouldn't be up. I kind of hoped she wouldn't.

> **(To Emma):** Just wanted to check to see how you're holding up

She responded immediately.

> **(From Emma):** Why? It's not like you actually care how I'm feeling.

Awesome. This: why I'd been dreading talking to Emma.

> **(To Emma):** You know that's not true

(From Emma): I know you decided to defend her. Jessie told me what happened.

(From Emma): Maybe you're into her. Not the type I'd expect you to go for, but what do I know?

I hated when Emma did this. I'd never cheated. I'd never even looked at another girl since we'd gotten together, not seriously. Why would I? But every so often she'd get worked up over nothing as some sort of, like, power play. Usually I just gave in and said what she wanted me to: how could I be interested in anyone else when I have you?

I didn't want to do that, though. I'd played Emma's game for a year now, and where had it gotten me? We weren't together. She'd kicked me out of her house, then ignored me all day, then kissed me in the parking lot, then freaked out about a homecoming date she *knew* was just for TV. And now: fake jealousy. Was I really supposed to apologize for trying to keep Jessie from drawing blood?

(To Emma): Jessie was acting psycho. All I did was call her on it.

(To Emma): And I told you the producers set up the HC thing

(From Emma): Right. And you didn't even call me before you said yes. You just asked someone else and expected me to be fine.

(To Emma): What do you want me to do? Tell Rachel I messed up, I don't really want her to come?

(From Emma): Do whatever you want. Anything I say obviously won't make a difference.

I sighed. Apparently Emma had just gotten more pissed off overnight.

(To Emma): Rachel is just a friend. You know that. But if you're gonna be like this, there's nothing else to say.

(From Emma): You're right, there's not. Have fun with your pity date.

That was low. Emma was the one who told me about Rachel having a rough time of it in the first place, even before Ollie. For her to get all catty now was just . . . disappointing. It was bad enough she hung *out* with Jessie, she didn't have to be her.

I didn't respond.

But now I felt jacked up, sorta like I got before a game.

Nervous energy: pumping through my whole body with nowhere to go.

When I felt this way, video games just annoyed me. I needed someone to talk to. Or better yet, hang out with.

Emma was clearly pissed, and honestly, I was pissed at her too. That was weird. I'm not sure I'd ever let myself be pissed at Emma before. Either way, we probably shouldn't see each other in person today.

Ollie barely ever responded to texts, and I had a feeling if we met up he'd want to talk about what happened at the party. Ollie: loved acting like he was my other "big brother." Usually it was fine, if he didn't get patronizing. He'd only hinted so far, but I had the sense he didn't like Rachel. No, that wasn't it. But he didn't seem to approve of me asking her to homecoming, or her showing up at the party. Those trains: already left the station. I didn't really need Ollie getting judgy now that it was too late. I just wanted to do something *fun*.

I opened Flit and tapped out a quick message:

I've got the day off and no plans. What should I do for fun, fliends? **#weekend**

Within seconds it was getting luvs, reflits, responses. Awesome.

A girl whose photo was all duck face and sunglasses got to it first.

@ChichiGigi14: You could visit me?

Boring. But I should have expected that. I luvved the flit and looked at the next response.

@SurfSeaBree: If you came to SoCal we could
sunbathe together.

Whoa. The picture she attached made it pretty clear that she didn't have much of a dress code in mind. Or any dress code. That one I didn't luv. Girls who send pictures like that to randos probably go full stalker with any encouragement at all.

@SouthernBella499: follow me pleez I'll PF you
an AWESOME saturday plan

Jeez, they were all the same. Either girls wanted me to follow them or they just spouted some variation of "You should do *me* with your day off." But, like, not in a pervy way. Well, sometimes in a pervy way.

I don't know why, but I'd expected something . . . interesting. Or at least one person I'd want to respond to. Reading through them was actually making me antsier. I paced my bedroom, scrolling through the stream of flits, reading them slowly, then eventually skipping through dozens at a time and picking at random.

All the same.

I was about to whip my phone at my bed out of frustration when it pinged in the way that meant I had a text.

Probably Emma getting one last dig. It would be more real than my "fans," though.

> **(From Rachel):** Just sayin: Mary should come with a warning label. "May cause massive anxiety and an inability to get a word in edgewise. Use with caution, or better yet, tranquilizers."

I could feel myself grinning. Rachel's texts: definitely not boring.

I thought for a second before texting back. Rachel was always so funny, I had to up my game with her.

> **(To Rachel):** You must have had more to drink last night than I realized. A hangover is the only explanation for Mary-ing this early on a Saturday

> **(From Rachel):** I'm probably drinking right now and I don't even know it. Makes more sense than the call I just got.

Without really thinking I responded:

(To Rachel): Wanna meet up? If I stay here too long my dad will make me talk to him. Oof.

It took a minute for Rachel to answer. I stared at the phone in my hand, my nervous energy rising. She'd say *something*, right?

(From Rachel): I would've thought the famous TV star would be booked solid.

I exhaled. For a second, I thought I'd somehow messed up.

(To Rachel): I bumped some appointments

(From Rachel): Well I SUPPOSE I can squeeze you in. But only because I need you if I'm gonna reach the Laura big leagues.

(To Rachel): It's true: I've got you by the balls. Pick you up in 20?

(From Rachel): Sure—fair warning, though, that is nowhere near enough time to tame my hair. It may bite.

I still felt nervous walking out the door, but it was different. Like, good nervous.

chapter thirty-three

RACHEL

SATURDAY, 11:11 A.M.

Twenty minutes was *not* enough time to get ready. The girls Kyle hung out with probably spent that much time on eyeliner. I was going to look like a tornado. Or that cartoon guy that makes them, what's his name? The Tasmanian Devil. According to the internet, we shared a body type.

I figured the best option was to lower expectations from the start, so I'd texted that my hair would suck—most days, that was a given. As though he would even care what I looked like—I had to keep reminding myself that he wasn't into me, not that way. This was just friends hanging out on a Saturday. One incredibly gorgeous, sweet friend who stands up for girls he barely even knows, and one troll doll.

I ran upstairs to my room, almost knocking Jonathan and a stack of gaming cards across the landing.

"Sorry," I yelled, not looking back, veering into the bathroom, and slamming the door behind me.

What would help *most*?

I looked desperately at my makeup bag—it had a few weird-colored eye shadows I'd bought in middle school, sparkly fake eyelashes I wore for Halloween a couple of years back, when we'd all gone as *Midsummer* characters, a tube of mascara, random colors of eyeliner, and a handful of lipsticks I'd never liked, so they'd made their way out of purses and into the very bottom of my makeup bag.

This is what I get for never making any effort at girldom.

I grabbed the mascara and the eyeliner—the only things I ever really used—and jogged over to my parents' bathroom. Mom had an eyelash curler—that would probably make it look more professional and cover the spots where my eyeliner hand was less than surgical. That and some of the lip stain I wore on days when I remembered would have to be enough. Not only was I out of real options, I was still wearing an oversized T-shirt Mom had brought home from some Art Center event and a pair of flannels so old the bottoms were fraying. He might not notice my horror-show makeup; he wouldn't be able to ignore pajamas.

I swiped blackness around my eyes and headed back to my room, whipping open the top drawer of my dresser and pulling open the closet. I pulled out some T-shirts—stupid, and they made me look even stumpier than I was. A couple of blousey things hanging all the way to the left had seemed cool when I bought them—artsy—but now they just looked like something a kindergarten teacher would wear. I had a couple of good sweaters, but it was supposed to be in the sixties today, and I'd probably be sweating buckets already—why guarantee it?

Jesus, how is it possible to have so many clothes but have nothing at all you like?

Finally, overwhelmed, I grabbed an oversized tunic and a pair of leggings—the new ones I hadn't worn yet, since the other ones were "still good." Annoyed, I ripped all the tags off the new pair and balled up the old, saggy leggings and threw them into the Legend of Zelda tin garbage can I'd picked up at that garage sale.

Oh my god, why was I even bothering? I had a Zelda garbage can—my loserdom was clearly incurable, anyway.

I combed gingerly at my hair in the mirror over my dresser, trying not to electrocute it further. I could put on a hat?

No, I was not a hat girl. I would look ridiculous in a hat.

I was contemplating changing my entire outfit—maybe the blousey things actually *were* cool—when I heard a horn honk in the driveway.

Dammit.

I glanced at the mirror again, stuffed my phone into my purse, and ran downstairs.

Mom was peering out one of the long windows next to the

front door, looking almost ready to walk outside and actually talk to him.

"It's for me, Mom," I yelled from across the room.

She turned, obviously confused.

"Kyle wanted to hang out. We were gonna . . . talk about show stuff and . . . stuff."

Smooth, Rachel.

But Mom just smiled, like she'd completed some secret Mom mission.

"Oh, that's great. Tell him I say hi, would you?"

"Sure."

She looked like she had more thoughts on the topic, but I didn't want to hear them, so I kissed her fast on the cheek and ran out the door. Kyle was sitting in the driveway in an old Subaru wagon, obviously a parental hand-me-down. For some reason, I just assumed he'd have one of those big, aggressively new SUVs.

But I didn't have time to ponder the significance of my preconceived notions of Kyle's car; I had to focus all my energy on looking natural, normal, like a girl who makes last-minute plans with ridiculously attractive, a-little-bit-famous senior guys all the time.

Obviously not an easy job for a weirdo like me.

chapter thirty-four

KYLE

SATURDAY, 11:33 A.M.

Rachel slid into the front seat, smiling slightly, like she had a secret.

That's when I remembered we didn't know each other *at all*. Forget what she was thinking now, what did she think about ever?

Oh jeez, this had been a terrible idea.

"So . . . what do you wanna do?" I asked.

"Right now? Get out of my driveway." She stared through the windshield at her front door. I glanced over; you could see the outline of someone behind the pebbled glass panel on the right.

"Good place to start." I pulled out and arbitrarily turned

left at the bottom. "What's next?" I smiled, so she wouldn't know how awkward I suddenly felt. What *were* we going to do? What did girls like Rachel do? I really hoped she wouldn't suggest some art film or poetry reading. Poetry reading: impossible to pretend to like.

"I don't know. I figured you had a plan."

"That's where you vastly overestimated me." I smiled widely, but I felt like an idiot. I should have had a plan. Why didn't I have any plan?

"I mean, we could always go bowling," Rachel said.

"Bowling? Where would you even go, Funtown?" I was pretty sure Rachel wasn't serious about going to the kiddie birthday party spot. It was mostly an arcade, with a couple lanes of bumper bowling in back and a climbing wall that dominated the entire center of the building. Emma's brother, Nathan, had his birthday there last year. She and I were the oldest non-parent people in the room.

Rachel twisted her mouth up in a half smile. It made a little dimple pop out in just her left cheek. I'd never noticed it before. I almost reached over to poke my finger into it—would it feel different? Softer?—then remembered not to be a psycho.

"You know there are other bowling alleys in the world, right?"

"I mean . . ." I looked over. She was clearly trying to repress a laugh. I felt myself smile back. "Yes. Obviously I know that. I just don't know where any of them are. No one I know goes bowling."

"That's why bowling's so awesome," she said, looking out the window. "Get onto 169, I'll show you how to get to a real bowling alley. One without a giant cat mascot walking around, making children cry."

I worked my way to the highway, glancing at Rachel every few seconds. She was staring out the front window with the same half smile on her lips.

I still didn't know what private joke or secret she was holding on to, but I wanted to find out.

# # #

"I probably didn't explain this the first time. You actually want to *avoid* the gutters," Rachel said from behind me.

My ball rolled past the untouched pins. It was the third frame in a row where I'd hit nothing.

Sucking this bad at bowling: not reducing my antsiness. Usually I was good at new games, but I couldn't figure out how to get the flipping ball to stay in the middle. A couple times I'd randomly hit a few pins. One frame I even got a strike. But the next turn, I somehow overcompensated and the ball went straight into the left gutter.

I looked around the bowling alley. Maybe the atmosphere was making it harder for me to be good. The entire building was basically one big box that they'd forgotten to cut windows into. There were carpets everywhere. Threadbare, nasty-looking ones with blackened gum ground into them near the check-in desk and weird, nubbly brown ones climbing the walls by the lanes. They'd carpeted the *walls*. The screens hanging over each lane looked like computers in old movies, pixelated and out of focus and only in one color: neon blue. And everything else was dark. Ugly burgundy shelves for the balls. Brownish chairs turned grimy by years of butts. Two or three sad middle-aged men sucking the light out of the room a few lanes down.

This place: depression in a box. A concrete box.

I forced a smile. It was bad enough sucking, I didn't want Rachel to think I cared.

"It's all part of my master plan." I turned. She was standing behind me, hands on her hips.

"Really." She raised an eyebrow.

"I'm lulling you into complacency."

"You're doing an awesome job at that." Rachel pointed to the TV above our lane. KYLE was trailing TREX by a little over fifty points. He also sounded pretty boring, since he hadn't realized dino names were an option. I smiled. Of course Rachel wouldn't just use her real name. TREX was somehow way more Rachel than KYLE was me.

"I didn't want to say I was letting you win. That would have sounded mean."

"It would also sound ridiculous, since I'm clearly spanking you."

I gritted my teeth.

"Some of us play real sports."

"Oooh." Rachel put on a mock-impressed face.

"Yeah. Actually getting good at something that requires

real skill makes it hard to find time to play pointless games."

I sounded like a tool. But I also couldn't stop my jaw from clenching and I couldn't figure out how *not* to suck at this. Rachel grinned. It only pissed me off more.

"You've really never been bad at anything before, have you?"

I stared.

"Of course I have. I'm bad at tons of stuff."

"What's the last thing you tried that you were bad at?"

"I mean . . ." Ollie had crushed me at the most recent Grand Larceny game, but that definitely wasn't what Rachel meant. "I'm pretty miserable at creative writing."

"No you're not, your writing's good. At least it would be if you didn't always write about boring people." Oof. My last story had basically happened to Ollie and me after a game. "But you don't really care about creative writing, anyway. You *do* care about sports."

"I care." Rachel looked at me blankly. Did she really think I only cared about sports? That made me . . . not angry really, more like sad. Just because I was good at lacrosse didn't mean it was all I cared about. Jeez, I only played because Carter had first. Though that sounded even worse. . . . "Anyway, bowling is *not* a sport."

"Fair. Let me rephrase. You've never been bad at something you're truly trying to be good at. Especially something that is kind of *like* a sport, even if it isn't really a sport."

"I dunno," I muttered. I couldn't tell her the thought that

had just now burbled up from somewhere I couldn't see. Ugly, hyperdepressing thought: I only really tried at things I was good enough at to not *have* to care about.

"Of course if you were willing to admit you needed it, I *could* help you."

"Oh yeah?"

"Yup."

"What makes you such a bowling guru?"

"I've spent a *lot* of time here with Mark and Britta and Mo."

"Why?" It came out a little too fast. But seriously. The place still smelled like stale cigarettes. How long ago had they banned smoking?

"The atmosphere."

"Are you serious? I bet prison is more appealing than—" I looked at Rachel. She was failing to repress a grin. "Oh, ha-ha. Fine. You got me. But why, really?"

"I told you on the way over, no one ever comes here."

"So?"

"So you can get away from the hell that is Apple Prairie High if you hang out at places no one there is into."

chapter thirty-five

RACHEL

SATURDAY, 12:44 P.M.

Oh god, now I sounded utterly pathetic. Kyle would probably walk out so he wouldn't get tainted by my social outcast germs. Why had I teased him about being bad in the first place? We'd been laughing—even if he was doing it through gritted teeth—before I'd opened my big mouth.

So now I had to keep talking, try to bring it back around to normal with more words; I'd turned the moment into something weird, and unpleasant, and Ingmar Bergmany, but I could fix it, right? Jesus, Rachel, you don't have to prove your arts cred to everyone by going Nordic on a bowling date. Hangout. Not *even* a date.

"You really think it's hell?" He looked genuinely confused,

his eyebrows ridging together over his nose.

"Doesn't everyone?" I aimed for flippant. Pretty sure I missed.

"No. I mean, I don't think so."

"Even with girls like Jessie Florenzano polluting your friend group?"

"Yeah, Jessie's . . . a piece of work. But she's not a bad person, honestly. She's just . . . I dunno, insecure, I guess? When she's not trying to prove something she can be a lot of fun."

Jessie Florenzano? Were we talking about the same person? How could anyone see a good person underneath all that . . . Jessie?

"Probably only interesting people think that about high school." He smiled, but his eyes were still confused, still sad. I could feel my throat catch on itself. I almost felt . . . embarrassed. Mean and nasty, like I should live under a fairy-tale bridge. What the hell was up with that? I swallowed hard and faked a cough to buy myself time.

"Now I *know* you're just trying to butter me up so I'll share my bowling secrets."

I cocked my head to the side and put a hand on my hip. This had to work. Who would have thought saying "high school sucks" would have made the moment *more* tense? I always thought that was about as controversial as saying "oxygen is necessary."

"Luckily, I'm a sucker for flattery," I added. Kyle grinned— achievement unlocked. No more discussions of Rachel's profound square-pegness. I walked up to the lane.

"The trick is, you have to follow through." I started taking slow, exaggerated steps toward the line. "Put your arm back around here, then when you let go"—I swung my arm forward, releasing the imaginary ball—"you keep pointing it in the direction you want the ball to go, and your leg swings across behind you. It's like a counterbalance."

"So like this?" Kyle mirrored the motions, but swung his arm up too far, until it almost hit his other shoulder. Without thinking, I came up behind him and grabbed his hand to show him the right place. He jerked around to look at me. I could feel his eyes like a fire on the side of my face, but I couldn't look back. He'd see too much if I looked back. I was probably already purple from all the blood rushing to my cheeks.

"More like this." I forced myself to look only at his hand— it was just a hand, just fingers, not a car battery jump-starting every nerve in my body. Holding my breath, I moved his arm through the motion, letting go as soon as I could. "Smoother, see?"

"Yeah, I think so." He half-smiled at me as he went to grab a ball. "And I curtsy at the end?"

"More or less."

Kyle walked through the motions a couple of times with the ball in his hand, faking the backswing so he wouldn't accidentally throw the thing down the lane. Finally he let the ball go. Six or seven pins toppled over.

"See?" I couldn't keep the squeal out of my voice. Idiot. "That was way better!"

He laughed at me. "Not a high bar, Rach."

"Okay, fine, but next game you'll be better yet."

"I think I need a break." He smiled tightly. "Wanna grab some of those gourmet *nah-shows*?" He turned the word into some sort of terrible French, pointing at a sign over the snack bar, probably from about 1989, featuring globs of Cheez Whiz on bizarrely orange chips. I giggled. It was a dad joke, but we were joking again, thank all the gods.

"Yes. Definitely."

We ordered the chips and sat at one of the peeling plywood tables near the counter.

"It's nice, actually. Being in a place where no one knows you." Kyle looked around the room thoughtfully.

"Seriously?" I grabbed a Cheez Whizzy chip, then just held it. How do you gracefully eat a hockey puck of dripping goop? "I thought you were loving the attention."

"Meh, for a little." Kyle tossed a chip in his mouth. Because this wasn't a date, so who cares how we eat. Jesus, Rachel, get it together. "It's cool to have that many people notice you, obviously, but it's also kinda insanely stressful."

"You don't seem stressed." I frowned. Seriously? Thirty seconds with Laura, and I thought he'd been born on talk shows.

"Yeah, well, the inside isn't matching the outside there."

He raised an eyebrow, grinned, and grabbed another chip.

"How do you do that?"

"Do what?"

"Seem so . . . normal?"

"I mean . . . I dunno." Kyle blushed slightly. It was quite possibly the most adorable thing a human face has ever done. "It's like when I'm about to go on the field. I'm nervous, but it's like all the nerves are making me sharper, you know?"

"No. I literally have no idea what you're talking about." It sometimes took me multiple in-head rehearsals to give an answer in class. One that I knew.

"I mean, I'm nervous. Like, super nervous. But it's this rush too. I don't know how to describe it."

"Why don't you do theater?"

"Weirdos do theater," he said automatically, then squeezed his eyes tight and shook his head.

I knew it. He *did* just think of me as the weird girl. The pity girl.

"I don't mean that, just that . . . my parents always pushed me and Carter, my brother, to be a certain way. We never . . . theater is cool, honestly, it's just not my thing."

"No, for sure. It's not for everyone." I could hear how tight my voice sounded, but I couldn't change it.

"Rachel, I really didn't mean—"

"Do you wanna get going? I think my mom wants me to watch Jonathan; I should get home." Hopefully he hadn't seen Jonathan when we were all talking with Mary. Then he'd think my whole family was weird, expecting me to babysit an almost-teenager. What did it matter, though? Today hadn't been real. The fact that I'd started to believe that was just embarrassing. Jesus, he probably already regretted this whole thing: the show, and homecoming, having to see me more than never. Me, the weirdo.

"Sure, we can go." Kyle winced, then stood up, forcing a huge smile on his face. "This was really fun. Thanks for showing me this place."

"Sure, yeah." I tried to get my face to mirror his, but I don't think it worked very well. After all, theater kid or no, Kyle was the one who could act.

chapter thirty-six

KYLE

SATURDAY, 1:07 P.M.

That foot in my mouth: not tasting so hot.

"Do you even . . ." We hadn't spoken since we got in the car. My voice sounded too loud, too bright. "I mean, you don't act, right?"

"I write plays," Rachel said quietly. "But no, I don't act. I'll be terrible at the show."

"You won't. You'll forget the cameras are even there."

Rachel raised an eyebrow and stared out the window for a second.

"Either way," she said to her reflection. I could see her breathe in deep, try to smile. "You should give me some tips. I've never been on TV before, so with what, two appearances now?

No, three—okay, you're *definitely* the expert on this topic."

We kept talking about the show, and Rachel kept smiling, but things felt different.

Maybe because I'm a complete tool with no filter between my brain and my mouth. I didn't even think theater kids were weird; that was the kind of thing Carter and his friends would say. Or Dave. It was like I'd channeled someone else for just long enough to be a total jerk to Rachel.

We pulled into her driveway. Rachel tugged at the door like she couldn't get out fast enough.

"Hey, Rachel?"

Last chance, Bonham. She turned and looked at me expectantly.

"I know I'm pretty square, but I *like* weirdos, you know."

She stared for a second, then smirked. Her dimple popped in to say hi.

"Good. Because I'm probably not going to be able to change that before I shoot Monday."

Then she laughed, just for a second, and slammed the door before I could really say good-bye.

I almost opened the door to run after her. But that was dumb. What did I even have to say? At least she didn't still hate me, that was all I'd wanted, right? Or did she? She might have just been acting nice to smooth things over. What was she doing right now, with her brother?

Probably not thinking about me. But me: still thinking about her. The way she smiled with one side of her face, like she knew some joke you didn't. And the way she stuck out her tongue at the corner of her mouth when she was concentrating, and clearly had no idea she was doing it. Even the way she gave me crap about my bowling game. I didn't know anyone else who would have done that with someone they barely knew.

I had to take my mind off all that. What did it matter as long as we ended friendly? When I got home I played video games for a few hours. When that got boring I went on Flit and asked my followers what I should do with my hair. "Nothing, it's perfect" was the consensus, which I should have expected, but I was still annoyed by how boring that was. When this thing hit: couldn't get enough of knowing so many people thought I was something special. Now: already starting to feel pointless.

When I was little, really little, we had this DVD of some random kids' show, with puppets that, like, turned into cartoons to have adventures. I think Mom bought it for Carter originally, but we were so close in age that it wound up being mine too. At the end of every adventure, the team would sing the same song: "Smile, laugh, be happy! You're the best you that you can be!"

That's what I had on Flit. A chorus of puppet-cartoons telling me I was already perfect. It felt much less satisfying now than it had at age four.

Finally, around dinnertime, I couldn't take it anymore.

(To Rachel): We were so focused on how

terrible I was at bowling, and speaking, that I never got to hear about what torture Mary's planning.

She wrote back immediately:

(From Rachel): Dress shopping, part filmed in advance, part back and forth with Laura.

(From Rachel): Mary said I'll have to try on dozens. It'll be like Pretty Woman but without Julia Roberts's figure, or looks, or charm. And hopefully better sleeves.

I had no idea what she was talking about. Who the heck was Julia Roberts? Whatever, it didn't matter.

(To Rachel): Sounds like it could be fun. Though I think you're right to be worried about the sleeves. Sleeves these days . . . oof.

(From Rachel): You are a total connoisseur of sleeve fashion.

I could imagine her face while she typed it: secret smile, dimple on one cheek, dark-brown eyes shining a little brighter, sparkly with laughter.

If I hadn't messed things up, she might have been here with me. The thought made my insides twist. We could have been watching a movie in the basement. Something weird she'd choose and I'd try to get. And she'd make some joke about whatever was happening onscreen, and she'd have that look on her face, and I would throw my arm around her and pull her closer, squeezing her so she'd giggle.

And then . . .

I shook my head back and forth, trying to erase the image. Why was I thinking about that? With Rachel? I was trying to work things out with Emma. That must be it, I must still be screwed up over last night's fight.

I should send her another text, see if she'd cooled down.

But I didn't want to. I was always going first with Emma, always begging for forgiveness. Rachel was so different. So one hundred percent herself all the time. She didn't play the games Emma did. Talking to her didn't feel like a minefield, it felt fun. Natural.

There was no reason to overthink this. Rachel was a friend, one I wanted to get to know better. That's why I wanted to make her laugh, and why I wanted to spend more time with her. I'd been the same way with Ollie when we first started hanging out, and I definitely didn't want to get with him.

That was all there was to it.

I grabbed my phone and tried to figure out something clever to say. Something that would make Rachel smile that way, even if it was only in my head.

chapter thirty-seven

RACHEL

MONDAY, 12:28 P.M.

"Whoa. Nope. Just . . . nope."

I could see Monique's grimace over my shoulder in the mirror. She was right; the dress she'd just zipped me into was flat-out hideous. Everywhere I looked was an explosion of tulle—even my boobs looked like chiffony clouds—it barely covered my butt, and the lemon-yellow color made my skin look like I'd contracted some kind of plague.

"Are you ready?" a soft, girlish voice called from outside the dressing-room door. Anastasia worked for the local television affiliate and was running the ground operations while Mary puppet-mastered us all from L.A. The two women couldn't have been more different. Anastasia was tiny, with wispy blond hair pulled back into a neat ponytail, crisp khaki pants, and a navy polka-dot oxford that had clearly been starched. She was so quiet and unassuming it was hard to believe she was in charge. Especially since the cameraman she'd brought along was even beefier than Eddie. I couldn't remember this one's name; apparently never speaking was a cameraman thing.

Mom had excused me from Monday classes, and Monique had strong-armed her parents into a mental health day by promising to bring homework and threatening to skip if they didn't let her take it. Part of me still wanted to be mad, but I was too grateful to have her there; I told her she was still on my list on the ride over, then dropped it.

Together with the small crew Anastasia had brought, we'd taken over the entire "salon" section of the store, where the dressing rooms were bigger than my bedroom, each with real wooden doors and brocade-covered furniture inside. They emptied out—little tributaries of expensive clothing and ornate moldings—onto a circular ocean of fluffy, spotless cream carpeting, a small dark-wood platform in the center for you to stand on, and floor-to-ceiling mirrors with gilded scrollwork edges on every wall, angled to show you yourself from all sides at once. All the items in this section of the store had price tags with multiple zeroes. Usually you weren't allowed into these dressing rooms unless you were the kind of person who bought them.

"This is awful," I said, turning to Monique. It was the

eleventh dress I'd tried on so far, none of which I would ever wear. Mary wanted me to put them on one by one, then emerge from the dressing room to "vamp for the camera." Apparently they were going to edit this part into a montage, then later I'd get back into normal clothes and talk with Laura for the intro, then change again, into a dress that actually looked good— I was starting to doubt that I'd find one—and talk with her again. It would be edited so the montage sort of flowed into it. Luckily, after the first dress—shiny silver, made me look like a beached tuna—it stopped being so nerve-wracking. I didn't have to talk, or do anything special, I just had to exist. In hideous clothing.

"It's definitely the worst so far." Mo's nose curled up.

"It's like someone turned Big Bird into a skin suit."

"I was going to say a disco ball and a yellow piñata had a baby, but yours works."

"I don't mean to rush you, Rachel, but I want us to stay on schedule," Anastasia whispered through the door.

"This one's not a keeper," I called back. "Let me change?"

"No, come out!" Her voice was a little stronger. "We chose these dresses specifically, so there would be variety."

I looked at Monique, sitting on the padded piano bench in the corner. She was trying to repress a laugh.

"Go on, Rachel," she said, giggling a little. "This is what it's like to be a star!"

I flipped her the finger.

"You're a terrible sidekick."

My phone screen lit up on the side table.

(From Kyle): How's it going? Dare I ask about the sleeve situation?

I couldn't help but grin.

(To Kyle): This dress is all sleeves. That's how bad it is.

(From Kyle): I'm praying for you

I snorted and put the phone down. Somehow, his goofy texts were helping calm me down even more than the repetition of trying on dress after dress. He was always so at ease, so comfortable with himself. His pep talk of the night before: "If people make fun of you, screw them, they're jealous." Coming from him it didn't sound like denial, it sounded . . . true. I could feel the tiniest bit of that rubbing off on me, a little surface dusting of not giving two craps whether I looked ridiculous.

"Kyle again?" Monique asked. She was trying to sound nonchalant, but her eyes were narrowed slightly and she was leaning forward.

"Yeah." I glanced at the door. Monique hadn't been too loud, had she? There were no cameras in the dressing room—I was too close to naked in here—but if Anastasia knew Kyle was texting, I had a feeling it would become part of the show somehow.

"You guys have been texting a lot in the last few days."

"Yeah. There's a lot of show stuff to talk about."

"Really." Her voice was flat. "*That's* why he's messaged ten times since we got here."

"Yes, really." I couldn't smile. If I smiled, Mo would want to analyze things, and then the air would get let out, and somehow it would become clear that it didn't mean anything. Better to just pretend I already thought that. Best of all to try to think that; Kyle might claim he liked weirdos, but he still dated Wolfettes.

"All right. Whatever you say."

I put my hand on the doorknob.

"Wish me luck."

"Vamp it up, girl." Mo leaned back against the wall, eyebrow raised.

I walked out of the dressing room, tugging at the bottom of the skirt to make sure my butt was staying covered—not an easy task, since the hem looked like the haircut I gave myself in kindergarten.

"Step on the platform," Anastasia said quietly.

I glanced at one of the stationary cameras set up behind me, then at Eddie 2, Anastasia standing just to his right and nodding at me encouragingly. Sighing, trying to keep my legs glued together so nothing would show—which only made them look fatter—I stepped up.

Dear god. All the reflections circling me were just . . . hideous. I could almost hear the trolls grumbling underground. I had muffin top and muffin bottom. The color was like a safety vest someone rejected for being too over-the-top. And somehow my boobs managed to look like one big loaf of lumpy bread. I could feel all the Kyle dust falling off me. What had I been thinking? Jealous or no, I was begging people to destroy me.

"Rachel, could you show off the dress a little? Maybe twirl around, or give us a kissy face?"

I folded my arms across my chest and turned my most withering look on Anastasia, raising an eyebrow at the end for emphasis.

"Yes, perfect." Anastasia's smile was barely there, but her eyes were widening hungrily, like she'd just spotted prey . . . me. Maybe there was a reason Mary had been willing to assign her as proxy.

"I haven't done anything."

"You've done plenty. You can change."

I shrugged and headed back to my dressing room, where an assistant had deposited a new dress. Mary had explained, just before we started filming, that I couldn't see them in advance, it would ruin my reactions. That was also the explanation Anastasia gave for setting Mom and Dad up in another dressing room with a monitor and a camera on them for "reaction shots" after dress number three, though I think she was just tired of Mom starting full-on conversations about every ruffle, walking into frame to snap cell phone photos, and generally distracting me and slowing things down.

I glanced hopefully at my phone, but Kyle hadn't texted.

"I should never have agreed to this." I held up my thicket of hair so Monique could work zippers and hooks and eyes.

"Why? That was funny."

"Yeah, 'cause I looked hideous."

"Anyone would look hideous in that."

My phone pinged. I leaned toward it hungrily, pulling the dress out of Monique's hands. It was just Mom sending tongue-out emojis. If even your mother thinks it looked bad, it looked *bad*.

"Expecting somebody?"

"No." I tugged the dress to the floor and started unzipping the one on the wall so I wouldn't have to look at her. It was longish, a sort of a shimmery gray color, with sheer lacework over the top half winding its way up to cap sleeves and a high, scalloped neckline. It probably made anyone without a perfect-waif figure—i.e., me—look like someone's aunt at a wedding.

"Rachel, I know how you feel about Kyle."

"Yeah, and you know it's pointless, so let's not."

"Why are you like that?"

"Like what?" I pulled the dress off the hanger and stepped in.

"So down on yourself."

"Um, you've seen me, yeah? Met me? You know we hang out with the weirdos, right?" Even though he'd been nice, even though he'd said that he liked weird, it still made me cringe imagining the word coming out of Kyle's mouth. Knowing that was how he saw me.

"Yeah, but I also know you're awesome."

I snorted.

"Yeah, well, no offense, but I don't want to jump *your* bones, so your opinion isn't really the issue." I wriggled the dress up to my hips.

I stared at them in the mirror, wide, round, with a layer of pudge everywhere that Mom generously called "contouring." I wondered what Emma's hips looked like. Probably like something out of a Victoria's Secret catalog. And I thought Kyle would fall for me? For *this*?

"I should never have done this," I muttered.

"Then pull the plug."

I turned to Monique. She was staring at me, arms folded across her waist, eyebrow arched in a challenge.

"I can't just . . . stop."

"Why not?"

"Because . . . what about our application?" Monique's lips twitched; she was definitely aware of how straw-grasping it seemed for *me* to be worrying about that.

"I want to get into that program as much as you do. Maybe more. But I don't want to force you to become some kind of martyr to talk shows to do it."

"Come on, you're the one who tricked my mom into having me do this."

"I'm gonna ignore that, since we called a truce. But yes, obviously I thought this was the best move. I also thought you'd come around. That you'd agree with me once you started doing it. I mean, Jesus, you're my best friend. I don't want you to be miserable all the time just to get us into a summer program. We'll get in anyway." Mo cocked her head to the side defiantly.

"So you really think I should just . . . quit?"

"I think you should try to change your attitude about this whole thing. But if you really can't, then yes, you should quit."

"But then . . . I wouldn't have . . ."

"What, Rachel?"

I hated her for making me say it.

"Kyle wouldn't talk to me anymore."

"Yup." Mo nodded. "You're probably right. Quitting means losing things—lots of things. And if you stay, maybe nothing happens with you and Kyle. That's a real possibility too. But at least you'll have *tried*."

"Are you ready?" Anastasia's voice came through the door.

"Almost!" I yelled.

I stared at Monique. Her face softened.

"I know it's scary putting yourself out there, Rach, especially for you. I don't know if I could do it. But think about what you could be missing. Do this, and you're risking something. Some pain, some embarrassment, possibly even breaking your own stupid heart." I rolled my eyes. "But don't you get it? Going home and doing nothing is a risk too. You can't lose that way, but you can't win."

"Thanks, Coach."

"Shut up."

"So basically your advice is put up or shut up?"

"Well, yeah, but I was way more eloquent than that."

I sighed. This is what I got for having smart friends: they were right about things.

"Fine, then zip me up. I might as well get a free dress, right?"

"Exactly what I was gonna say."

I could hear Anastasia tapping at the door again, so I didn't bother to give myself the once-over before heading out to the mirror gauntlet; there would be plenty of time to assess my numerous flaws from every angle.

I stepped onto the platform. Maybe I'd do an ironic hair twirl, or one of those can-can moves where you swish the skirt back; it was long enough.

I looked up to see what I was working with.

Who the hell was that?

The girl in the mirrors looked delicate, the gray of the dress turning her skin ivory pale. The cut of the dress emphasized her curves; even under the tulle skirt, you could see the outline of a rounded hip, and the lacy cover only made the swell of her chest more obvious, but her waist looked tiny in between. She looked like some celebrity on a red carpet, expensive and sexy and totally in control.

She couldn't actually be me.

My mouth literally dropped open. I could hear Mom's "oh!" through the door of her dressing room.

"This . . . I look so . . ."

"Let me guess," Anastasia said from her place at Eddie 2's shoulder. "We've found our dress."

I nodded mutely.

"Then get into your street clothes and I'll check about getting the live feed to Laura up and running." I stepped off the podium, reluctantly tearing my eyes away from the Rachels in the mirrors. "Great job," she added, not looking up from her phone. "You're a natural at this."

## chapter thirty-eight

MONDAY, 1:15 P.M.

"The hero's journey isn't just limited to fantasy or adventure stories, though." Mr. Jenkins started scribbling on the whiteboard. "How many of you have read *To Kill a Mockingbird*? And if you haven't, this would be a good time to lie, since I know you were assigned it in Freshman English."

I raised my hand with everyone else, not really listening to Jenkins blathering on about Scout and "moral trials instead of physical ones." It was hard to focus on anything he was saying. I kept looking at the empty desk in the front corner and wondering how Rachel was doing with the film crew. Not like I was worried about her or anything. She'd just been so nervous when we filmed on Friday. How was she holding up on her own? Maybe she needed a little moral support? That was normal. After all, we were doing this together.

> **(To Rachel):** The key to dealing with Laura is to never, ever imagine her in her underwear. You'll start wondering about laws of gravity, and biological processes, and soon you'll be too wrapped up in science to answer quickly.

"Dude," Ollie hissed. I glanced up, dropping the phone onto my lap at the same time. I grabbed the handout Mr. Jenkins was passing out, trying to act nonchalant, like I'd just been soaking it all in with my hands in my lap. Jenkins smirked but didn't say anything. He was one of those teachers who'd rather not make a scene. Once he was halfway up the next row I pressed send with my thumb.

"You texting Rachel?" Ollie whispered once Jenkins was safely out of range.

"Yeah."

"What do you guys even have to talk about? It's not like you know any of the same people." Ollie's voice: normal, low-key. His subtext: judgy.

"I dunno. The show mostly."

"Where are things with Emma?"

"We haven't talked since Saturday." I clicked my phone to light up the screen. I knew Rachel hadn't texted back. But it was something to do with my hands. "She's still pissed. I already apologized. There's nothing else I can do."

"Mmm." Ollie scribbled a few notes on the bottom of the handout. Either he was really interested in the hero's journey or he didn't want to make eye contact. "So you guys aren't together?"

"Definitely not."

"But you'll make up, right?"

I thought about it. I still liked Emma. She was still fun to hang out with, most of the time.

But I was sick of it. Sick of getting the silent treatment whenever she was pissed. Sick of being expected to grovel. Sick of getting broken up with, then having her "want me back" a week later. Sick of Emma being jealous of girls she didn't even know. Girls I didn't even know.

"I dunno."

"Mmm." Ollie nodded, still not looking at me. "Gonna play the field? You could probably hook up with a new girl every night. You'd be living Dave's wet dreams."

"Yeah . . ." That sounded cool in theory, until I thought of the freshmen that first day in the hall. And the girls on Flit telling me how perfect I was. It was suffocating. Worse: boring. Worst: Ollie was right, it screamed Dave. Who wanted to scream Dave? "Probably not. It's not really about that. I just need a break from the drama."

"Emma can be drama, sure. But—"

Ollie looked like he wanted to say something else. Something especially big brothery.

"Gentlemen." Jenkins was staring straight at us, one eyebrow raised in annoyance. "Unless you're discussing the stunning brilliance of the handout I gave you, save it for passing time."

Ollie and I nodded. His lips were pursed and his cheeks were a little red. Ollie hated getting in trouble.

My phone buzzed in my lap. I waited until Jenkins had turned to the board to click the screen on.

> **(From Rachel):** Thank god I didn't see this before I filmed the Laura segments, because seriously, the old-lady-undies mental images will. Not. Disappear.

I typed back quickly with one thumb.

> **(To Rachel):** How'd it go?

> **(From Rachel):** Okay. People will see how brutally awkward I am and they'll take pity. Total step up from where I'm standing.

I looked up at Jenkins. He was writing something about mentors. I copied it down before texting back. It was good to look like I was paying some attention, in case Jenkins was still keeping an eye.

(To Rachel): Why don't you come by later to watch today's show? Seeing how dumb I look with that fry bouquet will make you feel better

(From Rachel): It's a date.

I smiled a little. She'd probably have some hilarious stories about dress shopping. Plus, it would be nice to have someone to watch with. And Rachel would be an easy critic. If she laughed at the segment it wouldn't feel like she was laughing *at* me. It would have with anyone else.

Somehow a lot of things were different with Rachel.

chapter thirty-nine

RACHEL

MONDAY, 1:10 P.M.

"Okay, so you took the picture for your friend."

"Kind of. We flit pictures back and forth sometimes to make each other laugh. It's this dumb game we have." I adjusted the earbud so I could hear Laura better, doing my best to follow Monique's instruction to "keep smiling whenever you're not talking" in the general direction of the camera. It felt as natural as if someone had glued a pair of gummy lips to my face.

"And you thought she'd get a kick out of a picture of Kyle? Did someone have a crush?" The audience *wooooed* in the background.

"No, she's just really into modernist burger art. This was

my riff on Edward Hopper." I gulped against the surge of renewed, throat-noosing nerves. Jesus, Rachel, can you not play it straight for *five fricking minutes*? But Laura laughed.

"Me too. I find it very tasteful. Okay, so the picture blew up, obviously. We know all about that, so I'll ask the question I think we all *really* need an answer to." She looked out at what must have been the audience, wiggling her eyebrows suggestively. I could hear some laughs and whoops coming through the feed. "You ready for this one?"

"Maybe?" Was I smiling, or did I look trapped inside my own eyes? Please don't make me talk about the trolls. I'd be stiff and stupid and possibly also cry on national television.

"How. Do you get. Your hair that way?"

I frowned. What?

"Because seriously, it is *awesome*. It's like a sculpture you get to live inside. I was so jealous that I tried to steal your style before today's show, and . . . well, who wants to see how it turned out?" Everyone cheered wildly, and Laura nodded, smiling ruefully.

"This was attempt number one." A picture flashed onscreen of her with fat, sausagey poodle curls all around her head. She looked like some Victorian child, but old. Everyone laughed uproariously. "But that seemed too tame, so I decided to try something a little edgier." The picture showed a super-teased, eighties-looking Laura. More chuckles. "But that still didn't have the depth I needed, so I tried one more time." The orange fro wig she wore next had to be at least a foot deep in every direction. The audience loved that. Laura waited a solid fifteen seconds so the camera crew could get audience shots before she quieted them down.

"Obviously none of them came close. So what's your secret?"

"Um . . . I guess shampoo? And not cutting it too short. Then I look like that last picture."

"Mmm. Shampoo. Should've known. Thanks for the tip. Now that that's out of the way, we have something fun planned for Rachel today . . ."

Laura launched into an explanation of how I was shopping for the perfect dress for the homecoming dance I'd be going to with Kyle, and I nodded and smiled and uh-huhed through the rest.

"And . . . cut." Anastasia strode forward to help me remove the mic pack. "Great job, Rachel."

"Am I done?"

"For today! You did great, though, so I'm sure Laura will want at least one more segment before the dance." Was she just humoring me? But thinking over the interaction, I couldn't point to a place where I'd really screwed up. Except for occasionally grimacing like someone was torturing me just off-screen to get me to deliver their manifesto.

"Okay." I unclenched my fists. I hadn't realized how hard I'd been squeezing them until right that second.

"You can get your things together and head home. We'll get things squared away with the dress."

"Great. Thank you."

"No, thank you." Anastasia turned to one of the crew and started rapidly issuing directives. Mary in sheep's clothing, that one.

When I got back to the dressing room, Monique was failing to repress her grin, my phone in her hand.

"You have a message."

I tried to frown at her for looking at my phone, but I couldn't pull it off. I was still pulsing with anxiety—it was like the camera turning off released a brand-new flood of stomach-twistingness—but it felt different . . . almost good. Knowing Kyle had texted was too much to stifle.

I sent a couple of messages.

Then he asked me to come over and watch the show.

"Mo." I blinked a few times. Was he serious? Saturday's bowling fiasco was one thing. The party had been such a rain of flaming crap, he probably felt like he had to check in on me to make sure I hadn't curled up into a ball and died. Plus, we had to get to know each other a *little* before the dance.

But after how that ended I'd sorta figured he'd keep his distance. And he could have asked anyone to watch him on TV—like his stunning maybe-girlfriend, Emma. But he hadn't. This didn't feel like due diligence for the show, it felt like he just wanted to hang out with me. Maybe that girl in the gray dress wasn't only a trick of the lighting. . . .

I passed Mo the phone.

"I thought you were watching with me," she said, looking at me expectantly.

"Oh. I mean, that's . . . okay." I stuck my hand forward robotically. I'd never had to think about girl code before, because there had been no one to break it for, but I *had* promised.

"Jesus, Rachel, I'm *kidding*." Mo laughed.

"Oh." I laughed, relieved. Maybe studio lighting fries your brain briefly. "Okay, cool." I typed in a quick response. "I'm really doing this?"

"Absolutely."

I hit send.

## chapter forty

MONDAY, 3:30 P.M.

Okay, I had fifteen minutes to get everything together before Rachel got here. That was plenty of time, right?

Mom had a deposition she couldn't move, so she'd made me promise to DVR the show. Which took care of one obstacle: we could watch in the main living room without Mom drilling her.

Should I make snacks? It seemed like something you were supposed to do when people came over, at least new people. I poured a bag of chips into a bowl and put it on the coffee table. It looked kind of pathetic on its own, so I threw some popcorn in the microwave and grabbed the Tupperware of fruit salad Mom always had in the fridge and set it next to the chips. Girls liked fruit salad.

I turned the TV on, made sure the *Laura Show* was still scheduled to air at four. Check. What else should I do? I could change shirts. Rachel hadn't been at school. She wouldn't know I'd done it.

Besides, Rachel's clothes always looked like they'd been made just for her, like no one else could have come up with them, or pulled them off. Other girls at school all tried to wear the same things at the same time, like they'd all walked off the same catalog page, but Rachel dressed like someone . . . interesting.

But I liked this shirt. It was one Carter left behind over the summer. He's more built than I am, but I'm taller. The shirt was faded in a cool way. You could tell someone had worn it forever, not bought it that way. And it was a little too tight across the chest, which made me look less skinny. It seemed like the kind of shirt Rachel would think looked cool. Plus, I wasn't really sure what other shirts were clean.

I looked around, wondering what else I should be doing. What would Mom do? I realized I was bouncing up and down on the balls of my feet. Jeez, dude, it's just Rachel. You're just friends, right? I forced myself to stay flat on the floor. I could still feel anxious energy pulsing around my body. Trying to get me to move.

The microwave pinged, and I threw the popcorn into a bowl. I set it on the coffee table seconds before the doorbell rang.

"Hey, Rachel." I leaned up against the entryway wall like I'd seen Carter do when girls came over. Carter doing it: cool, casual. Me doing it: the creep in a bad movie. I stood back up. Oof.

"Hey." She looked behind me. "Nice place."

"Oh, um, thanks. My dad's a banker." *Oooooof.* C'mon, man, really? That sounded so flipping weak. Thank goodness Ollie wasn't here to see my total lack of game. And why was I trying to have game? Jeez, I was a mess.

I swept my arm back, trying to pretend I hadn't just said that. "Right this way."

Rachel stepped inside, slipping her shoes off at the door. They weren't high; they were some kind of sneakers. But without them on it was even more obvious how tiny she was. Like, not even up to my shoulder. It was weird to realize. She had the kind of personality that seemed ten feet tall.

I walked us into the living room and pointed Rachel to the couch.

"Do you want anything to drink? Pop or something? We've got Sprite and root beer. And my mom probably has Diet Coke."

"Do you have coffee?"

"Uh, maybe?" I opened a cupboard. Mom drank coffee, but I wasn't sure how she made it.

"Don't worry about it. Water's probably better anyway." She settled into the corner of the couch, hugging one knee to her chest and setting her chin on top. "I'm going to need it if you expect me to eat four thousand chips."

"Sorry. I thought maybe you'd want snacks."

"No, snacks are good. I just can't promise to eat my weight in them within the next hour."

I laughed. I could feel my shoulders relaxing. Why had I been so worried about Rachel, again? Talking to her was always so easy. Like, natural. I grabbed a Sprite and Rachel's water and headed to the couch, flipping on the TV as I sat. She scooted a little farther into the corner so she wouldn't slide into me. My chest tightened watching her move away. Whatever, though. I had no reason to care, right?

"We have a little while before the segment's gonna air," I said. The "up next" commercials were on the screen. "Tell me about the dresses."

Rachel dug her forehead into her knee. When she tilted her face toward me, her cheeks were red. Man, those eyelashes. Suddenly I wanted nothing more than to feel them on my face, fluttering against my cheek. I blinked. Stop staring, Bonham. Jeez.

"Let's just say I'm glad that's not what we're watching today." Rachel smirked. I looked for the dimple on her cheek. It was there, a perfect pinpoint. "They didn't let me pick the dresses, and I only realized way too late that Mary clearly *wanted* some to be hideous, I guess for comic relief. As though I need help looking like a joke, right?"

I frowned. I knew Rachel was kidding, but I didn't like it. "I bet you looked great."

"Thanks, Mom."

"Okay, so they were ugly."

"Yeah. Well, most of them. The one at the end was . . ." Rachel's eyes went sparkly. I bet that's how they looked when she saw an amazing painting or play. Like fireflies were exploding inside her. How could someone say so much with her eyes? "Let's put it this way, you won't have to be *totally* embarrassed to have me as your date."

"I wouldn't be embarrassed anyway."

Rachel raised an eyebrow, mouth tight. She didn't say anything, turning to look at the TV instead. I kept looking at her for a second, hoping she'd turn back. Did she know I meant it? I wasn't just being polite. Me: filterless. Ollie reminded me all the time. I'd have probably told her I *would* be embarrassed if that were the truth. But she just kept staring at the TV. Sighing, I sat back. Laura was just finishing up her monologue.

". . . and then we'll be talking with the cast of Cirque du Soleil. Which reminds me, audience members, beware of falling acrobats, okay?"

People laughed. I glanced at Rachel. She was still staring intently at the screen, her jaw twitching.

"Before we get to that, though, you remember Kyle Bonham, right? We had him on the show last week after he pretty much broke the internet."

The picture of me in my uniform flashed onscreen. My stomach flipped for a second, but I was starting to get used to seeing myself places. Rachel's mouth came open a little, like she was breathing in the show.

"And we got to thinking, 'a kid this cool needs to go to homecoming in style,' am I right?" The audience cheered their approval. I grinned. If the *Laura* audience was any gauge, people were liking Mary's plan. It felt good. Like I'd achieved something major. "We thought we'd help out. Here, take a look for yourself."

There I was, in a tux, in the back of the van, clutching the fries. "Are you nervous?" someone asked off-camera. "Yeah, mainly because I smell like a fryolator." The audience laughed.

The camera was trailing me up to the door. I knocked. Rachel opened it. Then closed it. I laughed. They couldn't have scripted a better moment. Real-life Rachel stared at me, eyes huge and round, then turned back to the TV.

The door opened again, and I did my down-on-one-knee bit. She said yes, we hugged, and they cut back to the studio. The whole thing was three minutes, tops.

I turned to say something about being relieved it was over, even though I was kind of bummed. The more I did this, the more I craved that moment, the intensity spiking through me when I knew people were watching.

But Rachel wasn't there. Well, she was, but she'd totally collapsed into herself, both knees drawn up, face buried deep between them.

"Rachel?"

She didn't say anything.

"Hey, Rachel, are you okay?" I put my hand on her back. I could feel her muscles tensing beneath it.

"How do you *do* it?" She was talking into her legs, so it came out echoing and fuzzy.

"Do what? The show? I mean, you saw me, I wasn't exactly smooth."

"No, not the show." She turned her head my way. Half her face was still in the shadow of her legs. It made her look mysterious, and a little wild, like some old-timey movie star. "Well, yeah, the show too, but more . . . how do you watch yourself doing it?"

"I mean, it's embarrassing for sure." I actually hadn't thought about it until that moment, but it seemed like the right thing to say. Rachel blinked rapidly, her forehead scrunching up in disbelief. I had to stop myself from reaching out and touching her cheek. Touching her face: weird, not what she wanted. Right? "But it's only a few minutes, how bad can it be?"

"I guess." She exhaled and straightened out a little. She looked frustrated, almost angry. I wanted her to look at me again.

"But Rachel, you were awesome just now."

"Were you watching the same show I was?"

"The one where you were funny, like always, even though you didn't know we'd be showing up? And the audience obviously loved you? 'Cause that's what I saw."

She turned to look at me full-on. Her looking at me: an

electric shock. Suddenly I was really aware of my hand on her back, of the warmth of her skin through her shirt. I could even feel her breathing. She forced half a smile on.

"Well, at least the trolls will probably have something new to say. Should be fun peering under the bridge now, right?" Cheeks: stretching farther, but looking more and more grimacey.

"But who cares? I mean, they're just angry jerks with nothing better to do."

"I know. Totally." Her face looked like it had frozen that way.

"You know what, I bet you're wrong anyway." I squeezed her arm. She inhaled rapidly, like I'd surprised her, but didn't move away. That was fine. We were friends now and that was friendly. "I bet you're gonna get all kinds of love for how awesome you just were."

"How much of that burger money are you looking to lose, Kyle?"

"I'm good for twenty dollars if you are. After all, we'll probably both have, like, endorsement deals soon, so why not live a little, right?"

Rachel grinned. Not a full-on laugh, but a lot better than the pained, fake smile.

"When you sing, do little birds come and do your hair for you? I swear, Kyle, you're the most sunshiney person I've ever met."

"Naw, I'm just confident I got this one."

"You're confident about *everything*." Rachel actually laughed. Score.

"Here." I grabbed my phone and clicked on Flit, ignoring the several thousand notifications from the last twenty minutes. "I'll prove it."

"Oh god. Don't say I didn't warn you." Rachel buried her face in her knees again, blushing. I scooted closer on the couch, so she'd be able to see the phone too. We were so close now I could smell her. Milky sweetness, roses, and some kind of herb. Focus, Bonham. All girls smell good.

"Apparently the show has an official hashtag, #FriesWith-Homecoming." I scrolled down until I saw her handle. "Look, here's one about you. Zero trolling. Pay up." I put the phone between us, right next to her leg. She moved her head slightly. I could feel her breath on my wrist, shallow and rapid.

@Bella18943: I love that @attackoftherach_face
slammed the door in @YourBoyKyle_B's
face. At least bring burgers, amirite?
#FriesWithHomecoming

"That doesn't count, it's not really about me." She was still partially curled up, but I could see her grinning a little. "Though a girl *does* like a burger, Kyle."

"Fine, but only 'cause I like you." I scrolled farther. Rachel leaned over the phone. Her hair brushed against my jaw. It tickled, but I didn't want to brush it away. "Here."

Rachel sighed elaborately. "I'd accuse you of cherry-picking to win the bet, but I didn't lay down ground rules. I'll get my wallet."

She leaned forward to stand. I grabbed her wrist, wanting to keep her here. She turned, obviously startled, and stared at me with those huge brown eyes. Rachel's eyes: so deep and dark you could drown in them.

"I'll let you get by with an IOU on one condition."

"What's your condition?" She wasn't smirking anymore. Without it, she looked . . . closer. Like a door had opened. I could feel my heart beating faster.

"You have to admit I'm right."

"Right about what?"

"How awesome you were. How awesome you *are*."

Rachel smiled so slowly, her lips parting a little. She wasn't wearing any makeup, and they looked soft, like peach skin. Like something you'd want to taste.

"You drive a hard bargain, Kyle."

"I'm a tough man, but fair." I could feel myself leaning closer. Her eyes, lips, the skin of her cheek: magnetized.

"All right. Just this once. I guess I was kinda . . ." She rolled her eyes, grinning embarrassedly. "Awesome?"

"Not just this once. Always."

She looked down, smiling but shaking her head, like she was humoring me. Like she didn't believe me.

How could she not know I was telling the truth? She was funny, and smart, and just . . . different from other girls. And lately, the more time I spent with her, the more I looked at her right now, her curls tumbling over her cheeks, hiding just enough of her face that you couldn't help but want to see more . . . she was beautiful. How had I never known before that Rachel was so beautiful?

I leaned in and kissed her. At first she was motionless, barely kissing me back. Then I felt her unfold, pressing her body along mine. Her tongue slipped into my mouth, and I wound my hand into her hair, pulling her closer, kissing her harder.

I didn't hear the garage door open so much as feel it jolt through Rachel, the sound tensing her up. She pulled away, staring, eyes wide and a little scared. Her cheeks were redder than usual, and her hair was everywhere, a wild dark tangle. I could still taste her on my lips, she was still so close. . . .

A key started rattling in the back-door lock.

"I should go," she said.

"It's just my mom. I could introduce you."

Rachel grabbed her phone off the table, looked around frantically for her bag.

"Kyle, are you in here? Whose car is that in the driveway?" Mom's voice drifted out from the mud room.

Before I could think of anything good to say, she ran off down the hall.

chapter forty-one

RACHEL

MONDAY, 4:52 P.M.

Had that really happened? That couldn't have happened.

I pulled out of Kyle's driveway fast, absurdly worried about being followed, then pulled over a couple of blocks away, leaning my forehead on the steering wheel and waiting for the electrical current coursing through my entire body to settle down enough for my hands to stop shaking.

I looked around. In every direction, orderly driveways led up to semi-attached garages. Carefully pruned trees waved overhead, their leaves orange and yellow. Lawn after lawn was trimmed short, and the sidewalks were empty, like they were only there for show.

I was solidly in suburbia—far too boring for me to be

dreaming. So we had to have really, truly kissed.

What did that mean?

More important, why in all the gods' names had I run away?

I flipped through radio stations, but everything sounded annoying, so I turned it off. Had he made a mistake? Or maybe it was a pity thing. It was the only explanation. There's no way he meant to kiss me. He was Kyle Bonham. He could have had any girl in our school before this all happened; now he could have any girl in the continental United States. With all that, there's no way he'd choose *me*.

And yet . . . even without the kiss, he'd gone out of his way to try to make me feel better—even to make me feel good about myself. I'd never had anyone do that before, besides Mo. Definitely no guy had ever done that. It should have felt cheesy, but it didn't. It was weird realizing someone I already had a crush on was *better* than I expected. I always assumed the more you knew of someone, the more they let you down.

Once I could breathe normally, I drove home, checking my phone at every stop sign to see if he'd texted.

He hadn't.

Mom was waiting inside the door, like a froed-out lion ready to pounce.

"Honey, you were fantastic!" Behind her glasses, her eyes looked about a foot wide. She pulled me into a big hug. Good, this way she couldn't see my face. "You were so funny. And you looked adorable! I'm so proud of you."

"Thanks, Mom," I mumbled into her shoulder. "It could have been worse."

"I don't think it could have been *better*." She pushed me to arm's length. "I really feel much more confident about this decision. Don't you?"

She was squinting at me like she'd be able to see any lingering mental issues if she just found the right level of focus.

"No, I'm happy, definitely." I forced a smile. "It's just weird seeing yourself on TV, you know?"

Mom leaned back, apparently satisfied. "Of course."

"I'm gonna head upstairs and do some homework," I lied. I couldn't stand talking about this any longer.

"Good girl. Dinner will be in an hour or so—I made homemade split pea soup for the TV star." Mom grinned widely, like she was so proud of remembering what I liked to eat. I smiled back.

"Thanks, Mom. Yell at me when it's dinner."

She nodded, and I ran upstairs.

I didn't even wait to get into my room to check my phone again.

No new texts.

He must think it was a mistake. Why else wouldn't he say anything? It made more sense than the alternative—that he actually liked me—but it made my lungs feel like a nature video of flower petals folding shut. It hurt now in a way it hadn't yesterday. Or even a couple of hours ago.

Oh Jesus, maybe he was radio silent because he was still

with Emma. How had that not occurred to me until now?

I did have a few hundred Flit notifications, though. Bored, and too antsy to focus on anything real, I opened them. I already felt like a tangle of frayed nerve endings; now was as good a time as any to get destroyed by the internet.

@PugLifeNYC: I can already tell @attackoftherach_face will keep @YourBoyKyle_B on his toes. Pass the popcorn. **#FriesWithHomecoming**

@BunheadJoJo: Wish @YourBoyKyle_B had shown up at my door. @attackoftherach_face is soooo lucky. :(

@LindyBoBindy2: @attackoftherach_face kinda makes the Bozo hair look hot. **#hairenvy** **#FriesWithHomecoming**

Laura had been right in our interview; a lot of people were weirdly into my hair.

I kept going. There were questions about my outfit, screenshots of me frowning at him down on one knee that people were turning into memes, even a few that said we made a "really cute couple." Like people believed we were on the same level.

No one seemed to think I was a waste of valuable oxygen.

Nobody thought I was pathetic—if anything, people were openly jealous. No one even called me fat. One girl said I was curvy, but that's *good* fat.

Kyle was right. There wasn't a single mean thought in the bunch. Even if there had been, I felt like I could have handled it. It felt less important.

It was dumb that I still cared so much; it's not like I didn't know the people last week were trolls. But it still felt good that people were saying I was good enough—to be seen, and with Kyle no less.

I thought back to the kiss. The way he'd looked at me right before, like I was something really special, something beautiful even. And the feel of his lips pressing into mine, insistent, almost hungry. His arms snaking around my back, pulling me closer . . .

It made me start to wonder if maybe it hadn't been a mistake at all.

chapter forty-two

KYLE

MONDAY, 6:15 P.M.

I picked up the phone for, like, the fifth time, and opened a text to Rachel.

But I couldn't figure out what to say. Probably because I wasn't sure how I felt. On the one hand, I wanted her here now. I wanted the smell of her and her crazy hair tangling through my fingers and her lips against mine. I wanted things to go further . . . though probably not in the living room, now that Mom was home.

But I also felt guilty, and just . . . confused. I wasn't with Emma. If we'd been almost together after the picture dropped, Beau's party and her texts since meant we definitely weren't now. Still, didn't I owe her something?

The whole thing made me feel like punching Mom's stupid throw pillows.

Rachel didn't text all through dinner.

I went on Flit. She'd finally posted something new. It didn't even have my name in it.

@attackoftherach_face: For everyone looking
for the secret to my hair, let me suggest
standing too close to strong electrical currents.

It was funny, but the idea that she was talking to all these strangers made my stomach muscles clench. Why hadn't she texted me? Had I screwed something up with her already? None of those Flit randos even cared about her.

Then I remembered I was sitting here worrying about Emma and tried to stop being such a jealous tool. My brain today: apparently locked in caveman mode.

By the time I'd finished nodding at my parents through dinner, I couldn't take it anymore. Before I could think too hard, I pressed send.

(To Rachel): Are you okay? You're not freaked out, are you?

The phone hadn't even gone dark when her text came in.

(From Rachel): Not freaked out. I just couldn't imagine talking to your mom right then. Sometimes I lose a little brain-processing power when things are good.

So she thought it was good. Immediately I imagined kissing her again. Taking off her shirt, then her bra. It would be lacy, maybe black. Artsy girls would totally wear black bras. She'd be shy at first, but then into it. . . .

Dude: focus. Thinking about Rachel's bra was *not* making it easier to think of something normal to respond.

(To Rachel): Wanna try round two on Wednesday? That's when they're airing your dress thing. My mom has a partners meeting, so no need to plan a speech

Oh man, that sounded kinda . . . like I meant something else. Did I?

(From Rachel): Absolutely.

(To Rachel): Cool. Meet me at my place after school?

(From Rachel): Can't wait.

Most of me couldn't wait either.

But I couldn't get rid of that feeling in the pit of my stomach. Like I didn't really deserve this. Like it was just a matter of time until I got caught.

chapter forty-three

RACHEL

TUESDAY, 7:48 A.M.

"What do you think it'll be like?"

Mo and I were sitting in her car in the junior lot. We'd already been here for about five minutes while I made ridiculous, contorted faces in the passenger-side mirror in an attempt to settle my nerves.

"I have no clue."

"Well that's reassuring."

"Sorry, I could lie, but who knows? People online were cool, so that's good. Plus you gained how many followers last night? By the time our application is due we'll be shoo-ins. But the internet doesn't care about high school politics, or have loyalties to Kyle's exes." Mo shrugged, tapping her foot in the seat well impatiently.

"Thanks for the pep talk."

"Okay, yes, but if it's terrible, just imagine us in New York, writing plays. Or think about the fact that you made out with Kyle less than twenty-four hours ago." Mo grinned mischievously.

I could feel a shivery tingle flow through my entire body. I could still imagine the moment almost physically—him leaning in, his lips on mine, him drawing me closer. And he wanted to see me again. It was really happening.

"Fine, I'm fortified. Let's go."

I forced myself to keep my head up—for once, don't look at the ground, Rachel—as we walked to the front door.

But no one said anything. A couple of girls stared in the math hallway, but we made it all the way to my locker without a single word from anyone.

Great. So much for everything being different. It was dumb, but this small part of me had thought maybe people wouldn't just be not-crap, they'd actually be cool. Actively cool.

I'd also secretly thought my locker might be decorated with "Go, Rachel!" stuff, like they sometimes did for new members of girls' sports, but I'd *known* that was dumb, so I was only the tiniest bit disappointed that it was just a plain locker. It's not like there was a Varsity Social Acceptance Team.

I turned to Mo, frowning a little. She shrugged.

"No one being evil is *not* a bad outcome."

I nodded, trying to be okay with that.

I was grabbing my French stuff when Sarah Frederics walked up. She was my year, tall, fit, with white-blond hair and a perpetual tan. She was definitely popular with the athletes and band kids she ran with. She'd always been kind of self-important, and she didn't really get sarcasm, but she was nice enough. We'd just never had much to say to each other.

"Oh my *gah*, Rachel, can I tell you that I saw the show last night?"

I looked at her expectantly. Sarah had this way of talking where it sounded like she was done with a thought when she wasn't.

"You were totally awesome. When you slammed the door in his face? I was laughing. So. Hard." Sarah put a hand on her hip and gave me a close-lipped smile.

"Thanks, Sarah. That's nice of you to say."

"Seriously, I'm so glad he asked you. Kyle's cool, but you'll be, like, funny."

I nodded, smiling. I wasn't really sure what else to do.

"Anyway, that's all. I just wanted to tell you we all thought you were awesome."

"Thanks."

Sarah smiled in a self-satisfied way and strode off down the hall. I turned to Monique. She was frown-smiling, shaking her head at Sarah's retreating form.

"That was nice. Not like Sarah was being mean before, but

at least I have someone on my side."

Mo narrowed her eyes.

"I think you have a *lot* of people on your side. Sarah wanted to win."

"Win?"

"Be the first to tell you they'd all switched over. So she's the most loyal subject."

I laughed.

"You make it sound so weighty. Like one of your medieval courts from Euro."

"Rachel, high school is *exactly* like a medieval court. Just without swords."

# # #

Monique was right about one thing: Sarah was only the first of many who wanted to make sure I knew they were on Team Rachel.

By lunch, at least a dozen people I'd never spoken to had addressed me by name—like they'd actually known it two days ago—and told me how good I was on TV, or how happy they were for me, or how excited they were for Wednesday's segment. One of them was even on the Wolfettes with Emma (she was only a sophomore, so she probably didn't realize she was supposed to hate me).

In Creative Writing Kyle and Ollie talked to me for a couple of minutes before the bell rang, and whenever I'd glance back at Kyle's desk, he'd be looking at me hard, eyes narrowed, like I was something he needed to sear into his memory. I couldn't help but smile. Maybe Kyle's optimism was like mono, and you caught it through kissing.

I wanted to text him after school, but I didn't. There was something kind of delicious about waiting.

The next day things were almost embarrassing. Random people smiled at me in the halls or waved hello. Alisa Gutierrez and Rosemary Montague sat down with Mo, Mark, Britta, and me at lunch, and we had to try to talk to them, even though they were basically strangers. Mo and I "remembered" a book we'd left in her car toward the end just so we could escape to the parking lot.

I sat-leaned on the bumper of Mo's car, staring at the school.

"So . . . Alisa and Rosemary, huh?" I smirked. Both girls were on cheer squad, which everyone knew was Wolfettes for wannabes. Alisa talked superfast, staring up over your head and pulling on a strand of straightened, bleached hair while she went on about stuff that was *way* more personal than you wanted to hear. Rosemary had this laugh like a donkey braying. And apparently she thought Alisa was fricking hilarious.

"If this is what it's like to be popular, I'm starting to understand why so many popular girls are *meeean*." Mo rolled her eyes. The entire meal she'd been squeezing my knee when things got extra annoying. "If they try to sit with us again, I'm faking a wasting disease. Something contagious."

I grinned. They were annoying, Mo was right, but they were harmless. And it was nice to have people like me this much. Embarrassing and awkward—they definitely couldn't keep sitting with us—but thrilling too. I'd never been someone people wanted to rub off on them before.

Someone emerged from the door between the middle school and the high school, walking fast. It was a girl with dark curly hair, her head down. It wasn't until she was almost across from us that I recognized her.

Oh Jesus, this was going to be awkward. Better to say something than nothing, though.

"Hey, Emma." I waved a little, trying to smile as pleasantly as I could. She clearly wasn't a fan of Kyle taking me to homecoming, but she'd been so nice that first day. The only person who had been, actually. It made me feel super guilty, suddenly, about the kiss. They weren't together, right? I tried to focus on keeping the smile as normal as possible, even though my stomach suddenly felt snake-pitty.

She stared, recognition flitting across her face for just a second, then disappearing as her eyes narrowed and her dark eyebrows lowered, like thunderclouds coming down over a sunny day. She nodded at me once and kept walking toward the woods even faster, not looking back.

"See what I'm saying?" Mo pointed her foot a few times in the air, miming dance steps. "Mean."

"This can't be easy for her," I murmured as we headed in for fifth hour.

Kyle slipped into his seat right before class started, and I couldn't seem to catch his eye all period. He kept frowning at his handout like it was an incredibly difficult puzzle he wanted to murder. When Mr. Jenkins was writing on the board, I slipped my phone out.

> **(To Kyle):** Everything okay? You seem . . . intense.

I pressed send and looked back at him. He pulled out his phone, frowned, glanced at me, then pasted on an obviously fake smile, pointing at the handout like it was the problem. He slipped the phone back into his pocket.

Okay, that was weird. I swallowed hard. My throat felt tight, like it was getting stuck on itself.

But he didn't text anything back, so I tried not to worry about it too much.

I waited for about ten minutes after school, putting on eyeliner in the bathroom mirror, then rubbing it off, since I couldn't seem to make it *not* look like some cartoon goth—how did other girls do this without looking like idiots?—before heading to my car. I didn't want to seem too eager; it might make him realize that I was a ridiculous puppy dog, not a legitimate option. Plus, it would be super embarrassing to get to his house before he did.

The text came in just as I was pulling out of the school parking lot.

> **(From Kyle):** Can we rain-check tonight?
> Something came up. I'll text later.

I skidded the car to a stop, staring at my phone incredulously, before I realized that I was in the middle of the street in front of our school, and frankly lucky that no one had rear-ended me. I pulled off to the side.

Had he known before that he was going to cancel? He'd been so weird in Creative Writing, I should have known something was really wrong then. But why would he wait until now to tell me? Unless, of course, he didn't give a rat's ass how I felt about it. Stomach revolting, throat feeling like someone was sucking all the air out of it until it went flat, I forced my thumbs to type out:

> **(To Kyle):** Sure, no worries. Talk to you soon.

Then I texted Mo to come over, SOS.

I left my phone out the entire drive home, the whole time Monique and I sat on the couch together watching me twirl in dresses—why had I been so embarrassed about this? It didn't matter at all. I even left it on in my lap through dinner, clicking it to life occasionally, not even caring if my parents noticed.

He didn't text back.

## chapter forty-four

KYLE

WEDNESDAY, 3:40 P.M.

I pulled out my phone to stare at the text again.

> **(From Emma):** My dad just told me he's marrying Lindsay NEXT MONTH, and he wants me to be her fricking maid of honor. Can I come over after school? I need to be around someone sane.

I'd written out the "no" text a dozen different ways at lunch. I spent most of fifth hour trying to figure out how to make "I have plans" sound true. Even though it was, it looked like I was just trying to avoid her. Emma had said, in so many words, that she needed somebody now. Today. And she wasn't the kind of person who had an easy time asking for that stuff. How could I say no when she was so clearly in a bad place? Wouldn't that just be cruel?

But I tapped out "I have a thing tonight, what about tomorrow?" half hating myself, half relieved to not have to take on Emma's problem. I didn't want to let her down, but I didn't want to be with her anymore, either. Wouldn't it be confusing to do all the boyfriend legwork if I didn't want the position?

Still, I felt like a piece of warmed-over crap all through sixth hour. Even Señora commented that I looked "muy irritado."

I had to push it out of my mind. Rachel would be here any minute, and I didn't want to be a drag, especially when this was almost like a first date. Or a second date? Was this a date? I could feel myself starting to smile, almost like a reflex. It reminded me, I needed to focus on Rachel now. She'd be able to tell if I was still turning this thing over in my head, and it might hurt her feelings. That was the last thing I wanted.

I threw my backpack in the front hall, then set the DVR to record the episode of *Laura*, in case we got busy doing . . . other things.

I'd barely managed to grab a Sprite out of the fridge when the doorbell rang. My stomach flipped. I had been so worried about Emma I'd forgotten how excited I was to see Rachel again. And how nervous. She better not have realized she wasn't into doofy lacrosse players in the last twenty-four hours. . . .

I padded down the hallway to let her in, focusing on keeping my face calm. Be cool, Bonham. Channel Carter. I pulled open the door.

"Hey . . ."

But it wasn't Rachel.

It was Emma.

This wasn't right.

No, no, no, this absolutely could not happen.

"Hey, Kyle." She looked up at me, eyes wide and lower lip trembling slightly, then quickly looked away, into the corner, almost like she was embarrassed, or scared. I forced my jaw closed.

"Hey, Emma," I started, searching for words. How could I get her out of here? Like, now? "Sorry I had to bail on tonight, but I have a thing later . . . with Ollie." The lie tasted bad on my tongue, but I forced myself not to make a face. She smiled sadly.

"Totally, I'm sorry, I just was driving by, and I saw your car in the driveway, and I couldn't help it. I'm so . . ." She frowned deeply, shaking her head like she was embarrassed of herself. "I don't want to keep you, I'll just . . . go." Her voice broke a little.

"No, it's okay," I said automatically. Flipping idiot, what is wrong with you? But I could see the tears in her eyes. "I'll text to let him know I'll be late."

"Oh, thanks, Kyle," Emma said, voice almost embarrassingly grateful. I forced a smile. She needed me more than

Rachel did right now, that much was obvious. And they couldn't run into each other, not when Emma was like this. It would be Anderson's party all over again. Besides, Rachel would be fine, of course she would. Rachel was so sure of herself, she probably wouldn't even care. Emma was the one who needed people to prop her up. The fact that she came over when things were so weird between us, even after I'd said no, just showed how bad this must have been for her. Not that I could blame her. I wouldn't have wanted to go through this with Jessie Florenzano either.

There was no reason Rachel even had to know that Emma was the reason I was rain-checking.

That thought made me feel even dirtier, so I typed out the text as quickly as possible, hit send, and dropped the phone into my pocket before I could be tempted to wait on her response.

Emma walked down the hall to the kitchen, perching on one of the stools at the breakfast bar.

"You want something to drink?" I headed over to the fridge. If this was happening, I might as well try to be nice.

"Sure, do you have a—"

I put a Diet Coke in front of her, grinning a little. She smiled back.

"Thanks."

"So, uh . . ." It was weird to feel this awkward around Emma. She was still Emma, obviously, the same girl I'd gone to dances with, and made out with in her musty-smelling basement, and whispered secrets to, lying in the backyard at Erin Rothstein's house, staring at the stars. But something had changed. I didn't know what to say to her. I didn't know how to be . . . *normal*. "Your dad, huh?"

"Yeah." She smiled bitterly. "I knew this was coming, but I guess I thought he'd give me a longer engagement to get used to the idea. They started dating what, like, a year ago? It would be like you and me getting married."

I gave an awkward laugh. "I guess so." Emma rushed on.

"She's barely older than me. And, like, why doesn't she have any of her own friends in her wedding?"

"Mm-hmm." I nodded. My role right now: sympathetic human wall to vent to.

"They could have waited until I was at college. Then I wouldn't have to care what he did, or who he was lining up for his next divorce." Emma took a big gulp of Diet Coke, sputtering a little, like a bubble had caught in her throat. Her cheeks were bright red with leftover rage. No dimple, though.

Dude, thinking about Rachel right now: *not helping.*

Emma turned to me, eyes narrowed like she was looking for something, then shook her head and looked at the gray granite speckles of the countertop.

"I'm sorry, I shouldn't even be bugging you with this stuff, I just didn't know who else to talk to." Her eyes got a little filmy again.

"No, I don't mind," I said automatically. Please don't actually start crying. This would be even harder if she started crying.

"Really?" She looked up at me. My heart squeezed a little. Suddenly I knew, like, deep down knew, that I didn't want this anymore. Didn't want to deal with the games, and the anger coming out of nowhere, and the drama. I'd been telling myself that earlier, but I think I'd still doubted it, just a little.

Not anymore. Emma and I really were over. Like, over-over.

Knowing it for sure didn't feel liberating, though, it just felt like a loss. A big empty space opening up in a part of me that used to be filled with Emma.

So I lied. Again.

"Really."

"Thanks, Kyle." She smiled softly. "You've always been so good to me."

That just made me feel worse. I turned to the fridge and started rooting around.

"You want something to eat? We've got fruit salad, obviously. And . . . I think this is quinoa?" I leaned out, holding a bowl. Emma was holding her phone in front of her face, looking at the screen intently and tapping at the bottom. "Em?"

"Sorry, my mom just texted. Um. . ." She looked up. "No, no thanks. The only thing I want right now is, like, an entire gallon of cookies and cream."

"We might have rice-cream?" I opened the freezer. Since Carter left, Dad and I were basically in thrall to Mom's need to stay "trim." Any foods she had "weaknesses" for were replaced with crappy versions.

"Don't worry about it, I'm really not even hungry." Emma looked up at me, eyes big and sad. She was so beautiful, and so fragile, like she needed someone to protect her from the world. It made something twinge. Like some part of me wanted to keep her safe even though the rest of me didn't necessarily want her around anymore.

We both sipped our pop in silence. The silence: more and more awkward.

"I should go," she finally said, pushing the can across the counter. "Nathan's afterschool program ends soon, I should be home."

I nodded. My chest felt tight. I almost felt like I should hug her. But I knew I couldn't.

"Will you be okay?"

Emma smiled sadly. "Not really. But yeah. You know me, I'm the rubber girl. Bounce back from anything. Shoot, I even have a homecoming date, so I've got everything covered." She smiled again, but I felt that knife twisting. Classic Emma.

I still felt sad for her, still wanted to help. But I'd never been more certain this was the right decision. Rachel would never try to dig into me just to . . . Jeez, it was getting harder and harder to pretend to myself that things with Rachel were still just casual. Emma showing up like this: apparently the thunk on the head I needed to realize what should have been obvious, like, ages ago.

"Good." I swallowed. Hopefully I wasn't blushing. "That's good."

"Okay, I'm going now. For real."

I walked her to the door.

"Thanks for letting me come over." She sounded so small it made my throat tight. She slipped her spindly ankles into the tall boots she'd left on the bright-white tiles of the foyer.

"It's really no big deal." It felt less like a lie now. Maybe because I finally felt sure of what I wanted . . . and it wasn't Emma. A shoulder to cry on: I'm there. The rest of me: not Emma's anymore.

I pulled her into a hug. It didn't seem dangerous now. You hugged people when you said good-bye.

She folded into me, sighing into my chest, until I pulled my arms away.

Emma blinked at me rapidly, then seemed to make some sort of decision. She forced a smile and started down the walkway.

She was halfway to her car when she turned to look over her shoulder.

"Kyle?" Her voice was lower, a little ragged.

"Yeah?"

"I miss you."

Then she ran out to her car, slamming the door behind her, leaving me alone.

chapter forty-five

RACHEL

WEDNESDAY, 6:48 P.M.

Nothing.

I clicked on my messages to make sure the phone hadn't somehow fried itself and forgotten to tell me about the new one from Kyle.

But there weren't any. Whatever had come up, it had wiped me from his mind. The idea was like a hole in my middle, raw and black and painful.

Why had I let myself get my hopes up? It was only a matter of time before he realized I'd just been a bout of temporary insanity. Though he'd be too nice to ever put it that way. I'd never known someone as nice as Kyle. As determined to see the good in people. Even crappy, bitter people like Jessie . . .

. . . and me?

The thought made the hole a little bigger.

I rolled onto my back, scooting up the bed to find a cool spot on the pillow, and opened Flit. I searched the hashtag from the show. When I'd looked earlier with Mo, people had been saying nice things about the segment. And they hadn't even shown me in the last dress; they were saving the "reveal" for the dance. Maybe seeing some of them would cheer me up a little. Or at least distract me.

@DancerLolo918: OMG @attackoftherach_face's FACE in that yellow dress! **#laughing #ugly #FriesWithHomecoming**

@NeedaThneedHQ: where's that third dress from it looked hot **#dressenvy #FriesWithHomecoming**

@Hadleytron: It's official. I'm more in love with @attackoftherach_face than @YourBoyKyle_B now. **#FriesWithHomecoming**

Apparently flits were still coming in, but already I was bored. None of them were enough to distract me from the nervous need to constantly refresh my texts.

Then, miraculously, one came in. But the number wasn't familiar . . .

> **(From 781 . . .):** Rachel? It's Emma, I got yr number from Gabi Ruiz.

My stomach turned to jelly and slid around my insides gelatinously. Why would she text me? Unless she knew about the kiss. Cautiously, unsure what to do, I texted back.

> **(To Emma):** Hi. Yeah, I'm . . . me.

> **(From Emma):** Cool. I don't know how to say this, but I didn't want you to get hurt. I know the show is gonna try to push you guys together

> **(From Emma):** Kyle and I are hanging out again

> **(From Emma):** We agreed it made more sense not to let anyone know, coz of the show. But I wanted to tell you. It wld be so unfair if YOU didn't know.

Seriously? I'd been starting to think Emma was better than the company she kept—after all, she gave me a pep talk in the parking lot, instead of a locker makeover—but this kind of mean-girl head game BS was as pathetic as anything Jessie had pulled, just on the opposite side of the passive-aggressive continuum. I almost laughed out loud in relief—I'd been legitimately worried for a second. But this just felt desperate. And it meant I definitely didn't have to feel at all guilty about anything *I'd* done—

. . . then another text came in.

> **(From Emma):** <img loading . . . >

There was a picture of Kyle, smiling and holding a Tupperware toward the camera. He was wearing the same outfit he'd had on at school. So it was definitely from today. That had to mean Emma was the something that came up . . . the reason he'd canceled on me . . . the girl he was actually into.

> **(To Emma):** Thanks for the heads-up. Don't worry, we're just playing along for the show.

> **(From Emma):** Cool. He kinda implied that. I just wanted to make sure you knew so you didn't get hurt. He is pretty cute after all.

> **(To Emma):** Ha ha.

(From Emma): Obviously don't talk about it at school, we can't have anyone know, in case they leak on Flit. Maybe don't even talk about it. He already feels so bad that he can't be honest about us, reminding him would just make him feel worse. The producers are really pressuring him to "sell it" with you.

(To Emma): Sure. I get that.

It still seemed weird how insistent she was about me not saying anything, like maybe she was lying about something. But what would she be lying about? That picture proved she'd been there this afternoon—she might even be there right now. Mary had made my family sign dozens of documents—releases, nondisclosures, contract stipulations. Why shouldn't she have made Kyle sign a few that I hadn't seen? Maybe one about who he was allowed to appear with in public, say—or who he wasn't?

I could feel my body sinking into the bed painfully, like all my limbs had been weighted with stones. How could I have been so stupid? Of course he wasn't into me—we'd only spoken because producers thought I could be their reject Cinderella. For all I knew, the kiss was something Mary came up with. "Make her think you actually like her so we get some good shots of her looking enamored at the dance." I couldn't even blame her; I'd watch that show too.

Worse, it had worked. I'd believed in it. Believed in him.

God, I had been so *wrong* about everything. The idea made me so frustrated I wanted to scream.

I stared at my phone screen, eyes half glazing over. A new Flit notification had popped up.

@EHSSoccerFan: @attackoftherach_face if
things don't work out with @YourBoyKyle_B,
would you go out with me?
❤❤❤ **#FriesWithHomecoming**

You know what the great thing is about Flit? No one can tell what you're actually thinking or feeling, they only know what you decide to tell them.

@attackoftherach_face: @EHSSoccerFan only
if you like bowling. I have a strict policy against
anyone who doesn't understand the beauty of
bowling.

I bit my lip to keep the stupid, angry tears from spilling out of my eyes. I could put on a show too.

chapter forty-six

THURSDAY, 1:03 P.M.

It was already three minutes into passing time before fifth hour and she wasn't here. Where was she? I tapped my foot against the floor, trying not to stare at her empty desk. Ollie: pretending not to watch me. Me: pretending not to notice.

Finally Rachel walked through the door. Her hair was the only thing I could see over people's heads. Annika Parker and Eleanor Chang called her name. She turned to them, smiling pleasantly.

She still hadn't looked at me.

They were talking at her rapidly, and Rachel was nodding. Whenever she spoke her hands moved through the air, weaving words together in front of her.

Cam Eaton yelled something at the three of them, and Rachel smirked and shot something back. I couldn't hear what she said; everyone in the room was talking. Cam grabbed at his chest theatrically, and made ridiculous googly eyes at Rachel.

Class was going to start any second. I looked at Ollie. He was drawing something on the cover of his notebook, but he glanced at Rachel every few seconds, then at me.

Maybe he thought he could keep me from liking her with the force of his eyes.

I walked up to the group. Rachel didn't look over, she seemed absorbed in something Eleanor was saying.

"Hey, Rachel."

She turned. She seemed surprised.

"Oh, hey, Kyle." She smiled and turned back to Eleanor.

"I wanted to say, about last night—"

"You watched too, right?" Eleanor turned toward me, eyes wide. "Wait, were you there? Do you film all these together?" I shook my head no. "Oh. Well then, we'll both be surprised! Oh my god, I hope they pick a good dress. One of the not-slutty ones."

Rachel's smile looked mischievous, but she didn't say anything.

"I haven't even seen the segment. Rachel was supposed to watch with me, but something came up." I tried to catch Rachel's eye. "Rachel, can I—"

"Oh my god. Are you guys, like, a real couple now?

Because that is so. *Cute.*" Eleanor's eyes flitted between us, like we were competing puppy videos or something.

"Well, it's comp—"

"No, we're not," Rachel said, smile never faltering. "Just friends. I'm gonna go settle in—El, Annika, find me after class?"

"Um, *totally.*"

Since when did Rachel want to see Eleanor and Annika? They seemed like the kind of people she went to dingy bowling alleys specifically to avoid. But she was walking away, waving at them and grinning hard. I followed, leaning over her shoulder to whisper in her ear.

"Hey, sorry, I shouldn't have brought it up in front of other people."

She set her bag on the floor and turned to me, face totally blank.

"Shouldn't have brought what up?"

Rachel's expression didn't move at all. It was like trying to figure out what a brick wall was thinking.

"Last night. I know I canceled kinda last minute, and—"

"It's fine. Stuff comes up." Rachel sat down and leaned over to look through her messenger bag.

"If you want to rain check tonight, I DVRed it."

"That's nice, but actually I'm busy. A few girls were gonna help me pick shoes now that I have a dress. I texted Mary, and she said the show isn't going to run a segment on that. Plus, I watched it already with Mo."

"Oh. Okay."

She looked up at me, same bland smile pasted on. It was like she'd pulled curtains over her eyes. That smile: a locked door. And I didn't know what words were the key.

"I've gotta get ready for class." Rachel gestured at the pile of papers she'd dug out.

"Sure, yeah, totally." I leaned back and forth from one foot to the other, feeling awkward. "We're cool, though?"

"Of course," Rachel said. "Still friends."

"Oh. Uh, cool." I took a couple steps back. "Catch you later."

"Mm-hmm."

Friends.

Oof.

# # #

The next day I filmed a tux-fitting segment. Somehow they managed to find a burger-themed tux, a fry-box outfit, and Burger Barn orange everything to force me into. I sent Rachel pictures. She just replied with "haha" every time.

Over the weekend they took Rachel to a salon to do crazy things with her hair and makeup. Flit: loved her hair. That's where I found a teaser picture. On her feed.

I'd text her, and she'd always text back. But nothing ever, like, *real*. It was like I was running up a hill and never reaching the top.

And as the dance got closer, and people got more excited about the show coming to our school, Rachel just got farther away. Every day more girls from school would be around her, asking about Laura, about what she was wearing, about when we'd film next. It made it impossible to ever talk. I couldn't help but notice more guys started hanging off her too. Which made it impossible to focus on whoever I was talking to, or really anything but the red color taking over my field of vision.

Every day that went by I felt more and more annoyed. With her, with the show, with everyone. This was not what was supposed to happen. This whole thing was supposed to be *fun*.

"It's like she's trying to avoid me," I said, grabbing the bag of Doritos off the coffee table. Ollie was over to watch Rachel's latest segment. They'd run my tux thing Tuesday, they were running Rachel's hair today, then they'd film the dance over the weekend and air it next week.

"Maybe." He grabbed a chip. "Probably."

"At least you're happy, right?"

"Why would I be happy?"

"You made it pretty clear that you wanted me to get back together with Emma."

Ollie frowned. His tongue: moving around in his mouth like it was trying to dig words out of his cheeks. Could've just been Doritos, though.

"What I wanted was for the whole Flit thing not to change you."

"What?"

"Okay, Rachel: she's a nice girl, right?"

"Yeah." I said it grudgingly. It was true, she hadn't been mean about anything. She just seemed . . . distant. New Rachel: nice, but farther away. Less nice to *me*.

"But you never talked to her before this. None of our friends knew her. And she posted that picture of you, so obviously she had a crush."

"Not that obviously," I muttered.

"Kyle, I don't care who you hook up with, I just didn't want you to become some massive tool. Like Dave, if Dave were ever able to close the deal."

"What are you talking about?"

Ollie dug his fist into his forehead.

"I thought maybe you were using her. Like, just to make yourself feel better."

"Dude, what the—"

"I know. I should have known you better. It just seemed so . . . random. I didn't get it. But I do now. She's different and . . ."

"What?" If he said something crappy about Rachel, I didn't care how good a friend he was. I'd punch him.

"You're different with her."

"What's that mean?"

"I dunno. Just . . . you seem more . . . like, okay, last week you were talking about *theater*."

"So? What's wrong with theater?" I could feel myself

bristling. Kyle Bonham: human porcupine.

"Nothing. Theater's cool, you just never cared about it before."

"Yeah, well—"

"Maybe you should, though. Like, maybe that's your thing."

"So theater's not for weirdos anymore?"

"Dude, Dave said that, not me. And only guys like Dave care who's a weirdo, anyway." I exhaled. He was right. I'd always known it deep down, but I'd still been afraid Ollie would agree with the Daves of the world.

He frowned again, trying to gather his thoughts.

"It's like this. I've known you for what, six years now?" I nodded. "I feel like in the last couple weeks, you've been more . . . *happy* than you were the entire time before. At first I thought that was the show, and you getting attention, but it's not. I think it's Rachel. Emma is fine, but Rachel makes you, like, more . . . you?"

"When'd you get so deep?"

Ollie shrugged, grinning a little. I felt something loosen that had been all knotted up inside me. I'd been worried he didn't like Rachel, and all along, he'd just wanted to make sure I wasn't becoming a tool. Wasn't becoming the kind of guy who would play around with a girl just to make himself feel important. I felt a surge of love for Ollie. Ollie: quiet, kinda superior sometimes, but he actually *cared* about people.

"Yeah, well, too bad she's obviously not into me. Maybe

she's the one ready to play the field." I laughed. The laugh: hollow.

"I don't think so."

"She's been avoiding me for, like, a week."

"Yeah, but I think that's 'cause she *is* into you."

"That doesn't even make sense."

"Yeah, well, girls don't make sense."

He leaned back, turning up the volume on the television. I grabbed a handful of Doritos and stuffed them into my mouth, barely tasting them.

"So how do I fix it?"

I really, really hoped Ollie had some more surprise wisdom, because I had no idea how to make Rachel even look at me again. *Really* look at me.

"You really care about her?"

"I mean, I think so. Yeah."

"Just . . . make her see that."

"How do I do that?"

Ollie chewed thoughtfully. "I don't know, man. But you'd probably better figure it out fast."

chapter forty-seven

RACHEL

SATURDAY, 3:02 P.M.

"I thought of another pro." I blinked rapidly. My eyelid itched, but I didn't want to touch it. It would smear the makeup the *Laura* people had so carefully applied an hour ago. So of course every part of my face kept alternating where to itch.

"A pro?" Monique fiddled with her hair in the hallway mirror. The crew had started my hair and makeup around noon; now we were just waiting at my house for the limo to pick me up. Setting up at each of the predance locations—pictures in the rose garden downtown, dinner for two at some fancy restaurant I wasn't allowed to know the name of, the grand entrance at the school—meant our "evening" would start around 3:30. Mom and Dad had already been carted off to the garden, possibly so Mary wouldn't have to deal with them getting in her shots here. Once the crew picked me up, Monique would leave to get ready.

"Of being totally wrong about Kyle. Namely that I'll be way less likely to make a fool of myself on national television knowing there's no chance."

"Rach."

"Otherwise who knows? I might faint when he puts on my corsage."

Monique sighed.

"Don't give me that. You know I'm right."

"Actually, no, I don't." Mo turned to face me. "From what I've seen, Kyle has been making a huge effort to be cool to you and you've totally shut him down."

"It's just for show."

"Why text on a Saturday night for show?"

I sniffed.

"It's better this way. Since when am I into jocks?"

"Seriously, Rachel, you're so full of it." Mo turned back toward the mirror. "Stand up, you'll wrinkle the dress."

I pinched my lips, annoyed, then stood. She was right about that part.

"Why?"

"You obviously care about Kyle, and trying to convince yourself you don't on the night you're going to homecoming with him is just . . . pathetic."

"It's not pathetic." I clenched my hands into fists. It was

the only thing I could do that wouldn't wreck something professionals had spent hours coaxing into position. "I was wrong about him, that's all. And I'm being realistic. I'll play nice for the cameras, don't worry." I smiled a Disney-princess-among-her-animal-friends smile for Mo.

"I'm not worried about that. Although playing nice for the cameras is boring."

"Jesus, why are we friends?"

"Seriously, Rach, what are you so afraid of?"

"I'm not afraid." My stomach went slithery. I pressed one of my fist-balls into it.

"Prove it."

"I have." I could hear my voice getting wavery. I tried to breathe. "I have proved it. I'm doing this, aren't I? Putting myself out there in front of literally *millions* of people?"

"Rachel. You know we're not talking about that. But even that Kyle convinced you to do. He's the first person I've seen get you to open up in I don't know how long."

I sighed.

Obviously I'd told Mo what Emma had said, but she didn't know the thing I really *was* afraid of: how hard I'd fallen for Kyle. Somewhere between bowling and the texts and the kiss—god, the kiss—he'd become more than just the cute guy I had a crush on. He was so positive, and so genuinely nice to people, and being around him actually made me feel . . . happier. Before I'd just assumed most people sucked. But the more time I spent with Kyle, the more I started to wonder if maybe I was wrong, and then . . . I wasn't. It felt like learning that Santa wasn't real, like someone had deliberately tricked me about something magical and wonderful.

I assume. We weren't particularly religious, but my parents weren't such bad Jews that they'd let me believe in Santa.

"This is simpler."

"Maybe." Mo screwed her mouth up, considering. "Since when has that ever been a pro, though?"

My phone buzzed in the tiny purse I was carrying. It was Mary: they were five minutes away.

"I think I have to go," I murmured.

"Good luck."

I thought about what Mo had said.

"It's not going to work the way you think it is."

"You don't know that. I think how it works out is up to you."

"Jesus, Mo." I came over to stand behind her, giving myself one last check in the mirror. "Does it ever get boring being such a know-it-all?"

"Not yet."

#

I peeked through the pebbled glass panel next to the door. Mary's "five minutes" had stretched to thirty while they set things up in my driveway. I couldn't see anything from this angle—just a few burly guys hiding lights between our bushes—and Mary had absolutely forbidden me from opening the door, since it would "ruin my reaction shot."

I tapped my toe against the wood floor, the sound appealingly sharp.

Finally my phone buzzed.

> **(From Mary, Laura Show):** This is it.

I breathed in as deep as the dress would let me, trying to smooth out my face. Just be pleasant. Pretend he's like guys who asked you to dances in the past. Like Mark: just a friend. Someone you like, but don't *like.*

The doorbell rang. Like I wouldn't hear a knock from two feet away. I counted to five slowly, picked up my purse and the boutonniere Mary had sent over, exhaled, and opened the door.

Kyle stood there, tall and slim in an expensive-looking black tux, like something you'd see on a movie star. The stylists had swept his hair back, which only made it easier to see his stupid-beautiful green eyes. He was smiling slightly, shyly, like he didn't know what to do next.

Resolve would be easier if he could be even slightly less adorable.

"Hey, Rachel," he said softly, staring at me. "You look . . . beautiful."

Hearing him say it out loud, I suddenly felt beautiful. Sophisticated, in my designer dress, with my hair pinned back loosely like some kind of fairy princess.

Breathe, Rachel. Just a friend.

"Thanks. You clean up pretty nice yourself."

"I have something for you." He pulled a Burger Barn box from behind his back. I couldn't help but roll my eyes. I looked around; they'd spread fries along the edges of the entire walkway, like the most downmarket rose petal path that ever existed. Apparently that joke never got old.

He pulled open the cardboard top and pulled out a soft, orangey-yellow corsage.

"Daffodils?" I frowned, confused. "How did you know I liked . . . ? Wait, how did you even *get* daffodils in October?"

He smiled, his mouth pinched closed like he was working to keep it from going full-teeth.

"I have my sources." He bent down slightly, catching my eye. "Do you like them?"

"I love them." I was too stunned to play it cool.

"Good." He reached for my fingers, gently drawing my hand up. I could feel the warmth of him pressing into my fingertips, but it was hard to focus on that, since his touch was rapidly shivering around my entire body. I willed myself not to get visible goose bumps. Slowly, ever so slowly, he slipped the flowers—the perfect, beautiful, totally out-of-season flowers—onto my wrist.

"Ready?" He swept his arm out over the fry-lined path grandly. I laughed. "Original *and* high-end."

"Sure. Let's go embarrass ourselves."

I put my arm out to link with his, but he reached his hand around me, setting it lightly on the small of my back.

Breathe, Rachel. He's playing a game for the cameras.

We made it into the limo, and he sat down next to me as they closed the doors, his hand ferreting between the layers of tulle until it found mine.

There were no cameras on us now.

How would I be able to remember it was just pretend when it felt so real?

chapter forty-eight

KYLE

SATURDAY, 3:49 P.M.

So far everything was going according to plan. The daffodils had been hard to swing. Apparently they don't grow in fall. Good thing Monique knew about Mrs. Ettinger's greenhouse at the Arts Center. When I told her I wanted her help making a corsage of Rachel's favorite flower, she actually squealed, like some middle-aged middle schooler.

Ollie had said the flowers would be clutch, and he was right. It was almost like I could see a layer of ice melting off Rachel as I put them on her wrist.

And she was letting me hold her hand.

I grabbed the remote for the sound system and clicked it on. Monique better have been right about this one. I'd never heard of this guy, and the picture on the "Best Of" album looked old. Like, history class old.

Cupid, draw back your bow-oh.
And let your arrow go-oh.

"Oh, Sam Cooke! I love Sam Cooke." Rachel turned to me, eyes shining. One strand of hair was falling across her face, begging me to touch it, to stroke it away from her cheek. I swallowed. Take it slow. That had been Ollie's advice. And he had three older sisters.

"Yeah."

Rachel smirked.

"Do you even like him?"

"I mean, this song is pretty cool." She raised an eyebrow. I laughed awkwardly. "Honestly, I've never heard of him till today."

The door opened, and Mary escorted the cameraman inside.

"What were you guys talking about?"

"Just the music," Rachel said. She drew away from me a bit on the bench seat.

"How about you talk about the dance? Just be natural."

Rachel: face like she'd swallowed rotten milk. I laughed. She turned to me, frowning, then grinned.

"Okay, ready? I'm closing the door, so listen to Charlie on

this." Mary drew away. "Start chatting!" Slam.

Rachel stared at me, then the camera, frozen.

"Are you excited for tonight?" I asked, looking at her until she locked in on me. Her eyes: even deeper and darker and more mysterious than usual. Maybe just because I hadn't seen them in days.

"Yes, definitely," she chirped. She looked happy but closed. Like when she was talking to other people in class.

"I hope they play good songs," I said. "Maybe some Motown. That's great to dance to." I felt awkward saying it, not sure how to deliver the line. But Monique had said: Sam Cooke and Motown and some guy named Otis something, who I couldn't find because I forgot his last name.

"Yeah, that'd be good," Rachel said. She smiled just the littlest bit, her dimple winking hello for a second. She really looked at me then. Defenses: briefly down. "It'd be like they planned it just for me."

# # #

At first it was hard to figure out how to talk to Rachel while the cameras were on. But then it got to be like a game, me making sure she noticed the things I planned, her accepting them, warily at first, then more and more happily.

AT THE ROSE GARDEN:

ME: Too bad there aren't any daffodils. They'd match Rachel's corsage.

MARY: (absently, yelling at her assistant) Is that what we ordered? Find some orange roses to put them against, I guess. They'll complement each other.

RACHEL: (smirks at me)

# # #

AT DINNER:

WAITER: Split pea for the lady, Caesar salad for the gentleman.

MARY: No, no soup! Soup is slurpy. Jesus, I called ahead, this isn't that hard.

RACHEL: (sneaks one bite while Mary's running around finding another salad so we can eat the dinner we pretended to order) It's exactly like my mom's.

ME: I wonder how that happened.

RACHEL: trying not to grin) What a strange coincidence.

# # #

IN THE LIMO NOW:

ME: Did you leave something under the seat?

RACHEL: No. Is it for a segment? They'd tell me about it if I needed it, right?

She looks worried. Mary and crew have gone on ahead to set up at the high school entrance.

ME: I dunno, I can just see something sticking out. You should check.

RACHEL: (pulls out a box of cupcakes from Sweet Tooth

and can't even hide her groan of pleasure)

ME: You like them, right?

RACHEL: I would film an extra three hours for one of these. With Mary watching. And the whole school in the bleachers.

ME: So . . . yes, then.

RACHEL: Don't get smug.

"I'm going to explode all over the dance floor in a rain of frosting. It'll be grisly." Rachel swiped the frosting off a cupcake and stuck her finger in her mouth. Watching her pull it out slowly, sucking off all the chocolate: torture. Good torture.

"That's definitely covered by the show. I checked our contracts."

"We should split this double-fudge, just in case." Rachel grabbed the plastic knife next to the box and cut the cupcake in half. "Why go to all the trouble? When did you even sneak these in here?"

I could feel my cheeks getting warm.

"I just . . . wanted to make sure you had a good night. Not just for the cameras, like, *actually*." I looked at the floor of the limo. "Also, Mo helped. There were big stretches of time when the limo was parked."

She smiled at me for real, dimples and eyes like lakes of velvet and all. It was like someone opened a cage I hadn't known was padlocked around my chest. It felt . . . easier.

Someone knocked at the window as the door to the limo opened.

"We're ready," the woman said quietly, smiling blandly at me and Rachel.

I think her name was Annie? Even though I'd met her, like, four times already, she was so unassuming she was hard to remember. But she was Mary's right-hand woman in Apple Prairie, so she must be memorable to someone.

"Kyle, get out first, then hand Rachel out, okay?"

"Mm-hmm." My stomach went jittery. I was starting to like these jolts of nerves, how alive they made me feel. If I could get this way for lacrosse, I'd be all-state.

"Rachel, take his hand, and the cameras will follow you down the carpet and into the school, okay? Once you're indoors, we're done for an hour or two. We'll bring a couple cameras inside for action shots, but you can just have fun. We'll probably set up one last shot toward the end, but we'll find you for that."

"Okay," she said, her voice small and tight. I reached out and grabbed her hand, squeezing her fingers in mine. My skin: buzzing, like someone had dialed up the power even higher. She turned to me, trying to smile. Her eyes were nervous, though, and she was breathing fast and shallow, chest heaving up and down. Stop looking at her boobs, Bonham. Staring at girls' boobs: never a smooth move.

"Okay, Kyle, we're ready for you. Count off ten, then start."

"Okay." I nodded, breathing deep.

The assistant closed the door, and I started counting.

Ten . . . nine . . . eight . . .

I gave Rachel's hand one last squeeze.

Seven . . . six . . . five . . .

Reluctantly, I let go. I could still feel where her hand had been, like I was missing a part there. I scooted over to the door, ready to spring. Was this going to work?

Four . . . three . . . two . . .

Here goes.

One.

I opened the door.

chapter forty-nine

RACHEL

SATURDAY, 8:47 P.M.

I was glad I was looking down as I got out of the limo; now
that it was legitimately dark out, all the lights the camera people had set up to capture our "grand entrance" were blinding.

I blinked a few times, trying to get my bearings, but there
was no time; Kyle had grabbed my hand and was leading me
down a red carpet—literally, a red carpet—into the main
entrance of the high school.

The cameramen dropped off at the doors, but just past
the ticket table—a fake-wood cafeteria model with bunting
around the edge; I wonder what Mary thought of that—
another one was waiting.

Also, we were thronged.

The commons had been taken over by the pictures people, a lot of velvet rope organizing everyone into lines, effectively barring anyone *not* buying photos from spreading into the wide-open space in front of the auditorium, so we had nowhere to turn. Sea-green lockers on the left wall, people making another on the right. Guys from Kyle's lacrosse team were high-fiving him and slapping him on the back, like they were best friends. Their dates pressed close, fingering the fabric of my dress, commenting on my hair. Once they'd edged away, a new rush of people showed up—acquaintances from a single class, popular girls from other grades who had never spoken to me *without* a camera hovering, even one of the chaperones, a new math teacher a lot of girls had a crush on, 'cause he was just out of college. The only relief was knowing the cameraman probably couldn't catch what I was saying— or more like sputtering awkwardly.

Kyle got pulled into a kind of bro huddle almost immediately. He gave me a helpless look and dropped my hand, looking at me even though I could see guys talking at him. I tried to smile, like I didn't care, but it felt like a physical absence, like someone had disappeared a few of my fingers. He couldn't know that, though.

Just friends, just friends: it was the mantra I'd had to keep repeating to myself the entire afternoon.

But if he only wanted a friend, why go out of his way to find out things about me—my favorite flower, songs to play in the car, even a special dessert? The show had set everything up; he didn't need to. Still, Emma had told me they were on again, keeping it secret. She had photo evidence. Couldn't this just be all for the cameras?

But would Kyle really do that? Was he really that kind of person? Or had Emma lied to me?

My brain told me to believe the bad version, so it wouldn't hurt as much when the truth came out. But my heart and my gut and my fingers and that spot on the small of my back wanted to bet the house.

I turned a fake smile on everyone around me and nodded, pretending to hear—and care about—whatever they were saying.

After what felt like an eternity we made it to the top of the stairs that led to the cafeteria. Sparkly fish cutouts had been taped onto the tiles of the wall, swimming downstairs to the "Enchantment Under the Sea." Pulses of dance music drifted up. I turned back to Kyle, but he was nodding pleasantly at Sarah Frederics, who was pinning him against the wall with the force of her conversation, hand on satin-clad hip.

Finally I caught his eye.

"I'm finding Mo," I mouthed.

He scrunched his forehead.

"Mo-Neeeque," I mouthed, going hard on the *e* sound. He nodded, smiled, then gave me a fake panicked look before turning back to Sarah. I laughed, running down the stairs.

My eyes had barely adjusted to the disco-ball darkness

when Mo found me.

"So?" She stared eagerly, eyes already smiling.

"So what?"

"Shut up, Rachel, tell me about the afternoon. The limo, and . . . all of it, I want to hear all of it."

I raised an eyebrow.

"Why? You're the one who planned it."

Monique gave me a confused frown. Well played, but I could see through that.

"Oh, come on, he came up with my favorite flowers, and Sweet Tooth cupcakes, and *Sam Cooke* on his own? I know you told him what to do."

"Swear to god, I didn't."

I raised my eyebrow.

"I mean, yeah, I told him what you liked when he asked. But he called with, like, a checklist. And I didn't know your favorite flowers, I don't know where he got that one."

I stared at her for a second. I could feel a little balloon of excitement starting to puff up in my chest, expanding faster and faster.

"Really?"

"Swear on everything holy."

"He held my hand. Not just when we were getting out of the car."

"Ooh, slutty." Monique grinned.

"Shut up. It was . . ." I wanted to explain how it had made

my whole body feel alive, like it could sense him just inches away, but it felt like I'd break something. "It was nice. Sweet."

"So things are going well? How are you feeling?"

"I'm feeling . . . hopeful." The smile took over my face almost without me realizing it. "I shouldn't be, probably, but I am."

chapter fifty

SATURDAY, 9:17 P.M.

"Also, everyone thinks it's *totally* adorable that you're a couple now?"

"That we're . . . sorry, what?" It sounded like Sarah was asking a question, but I couldn't translate fast enough. I looked down the stairs. Rachel had found Monique, and she looked so happy. Like she was lit up from the inside. I pulled my eyes back to Sarah's tanned face.

"You and Rachel? Aren't you guys, like, together?"

"Um . . . not exactly. Not yet."

"Well you should be." Sarah tilted her head to the side as though she'd taught me some important lesson.

"I'm working on it."

"Work fast." She nodded exaggeratedly down the stairs. Lamont Davis was hulking over Monique and Rachel, blocking the stairs with a massive arm.

"Uh, thanks," I mumbled, starting toward them. Halfway down I caught a glimpse of familiar movement out on the dance floor.

Emma was twirling in a tiny dress that showed off her long legs. It was red or pink, I couldn't tell in the dark. She was laughing, falling onto a guy's chest . . . Dave.

I should have been annoyed. Dave: finally getting to act on all his creeper fantasies. But all I felt was relief. She was here, having fun, and Dave would *definitely* make her feel wanted. She could be fine without me.

"C'mon, Sarah isn't that bad," Monique said teasingly as I walked up. I forced the frown off my face.

"Just stretching out after all the smiling for the cameras."

"Your life is really hard, huh, Kyle?" Rachel put on a look of mock concern. Lamont frowned at her. He was kinda literal.

"Extremely." I grinned.

"Speaking of, I think we're supposed to have some scheduled fun." Rachel pointed over my shoulder at the cameraman approaching. "Would you like to spontaneously dance with me?"

"Sure." I grabbed her hand and pulled her onto the dance

floor, ignoring Monique watching us.

I tried to stay as far away from Emma and Dave as possible, but I kept seeing them out of the corner of my eye.

It was hard not to look at them. I could have been wrong, the light wasn't good, but it seemed like Emma was watching me.

chapter fifty-one

SATURDAY, 10:22 P.M.

I was actually panting, tongue half out like a dog.

I like dancing as much as the next girl, but the cameras following us around the floor meant everyone wanted to pull us into their group. Girls I'd never met were faux-karaokeing with me, bros who hadn't known my name a few weeks ago were picking me up and twirling me in the air, and every song was someone's "favorite *EVER*."

It was kind of awesome at first—I'd never felt in-demand like that—but it was also exhausting.

I grabbed Kyle's hand impulsively, pulling his ear down to my level.

"Do you want a break?"

He turned, a leftover smile stretched across his face.

"Yeah, for sure. Let's get a drink."

I pointed at the cameraman. Currently he was aimed at the walls, getting more scenery shots of the blue paper covering every square inch, glittery seaweed, mermaids, and tumorous octopi suspended on its surface.

We crept off, slightly bent over, toward the vending machine alcove, where tables crepe-papered in different blues held huge icy buckets of water and pop. Kyle grabbed two dripping bottles in one hand and my hand in the other, then started running, pulling me after him into one of the half-lit hallways that spidered away from the cafeteria. I laughed, gasping as we turned left past the history classrooms, then left again down the narrow hall where Speech, Econ, and Sociology lived in an ugly, low-ceilinged little outpost of misfits. Kyle didn't stop until we were all the way at the end, near the narrow glass fire-exit door overlooking the loading docks.

"Charming scenery." I stared at him, deadpan.

"I liked the contrast of grim industrial landscape against the frenetic energy of the preceding action."

"Jesus, you really *are* starting to sound like one of the weirdos."

"I told you. I like weirdos." He passed me a bottle, suddenly unable to meet my eyes. I breathed in sharply. Now I couldn't look at him either.

"Are you having a good time?" He busied himself with the top of his bottle.

"I'm having an amazing time."

He smiled shyly.

"You deserve it," he said, finally looking up. "All the attention I mean, the cameras. Like, I'm just some random guy. But you have so many ideas. You actually *do* things."

I shook my head, too overwhelmed to respond to that. Is that what Kyle thought? It sounded so much more impressive than I actually was. But hearing him say it made it sound real. Like this so-much-better version of me wasn't just a figment of his imagination. I took a drink of soda to steady myself. It was too fizzy and the bubbles tickled my nose. I set it down on the floor carefully, not making eye contact.

"That's not why I'm having a good time."

"What do you mean?"

A wave of nerves rippled through my body. Don't risk it, Rachel. What are you thinking?

But why was I avoiding it? To make sure nothing painful happened? It was too late for that. I felt like Kyle had cracked something open in me and shined so much light inside, and now I couldn't shut the door again. I'd never known anyone like that, able to see the good in everyone, to bring out the good in everyone. Telling him was risky, but saying nothing—resigning myself to sitting alone in the dark again—felt scarier somehow. I wanted his light.

"I mean, the reason I'm having a good time . . ." I swallowed hard. Suddenly it felt like I couldn't breathe, couldn't speak. "It's you. You're the reason."

I could feel blood pounding through my head, rushing into my cheeks and neck and chest and ears—I probably had flame-red ears right now, like some kind of Willy Wonka experiment gone wrong.

Then I felt his hand find mine, his fingers weaving in and out and over my skin, and all the worry washed away like writing on beach sand.

"For me too," he said softly.

"Really? I thought you were with Emma." Good one, Rachel. How about you remind him about the extremely gorgeous girl the *moment* he says he's into you. I barely kept myself from rolling my eyes.

"Emma?" He looked genuinely confused. "No. She's still a friend, I think, but we're done. We've been done for a while." Was this an act? He couldn't have gotten that good that fast, could he? He'd never even taken a drama class.

Emma's words rattled around in my head, whispering that I was making a fool of myself, she was the one he wanted.

Screw that. I wasn't listening to that voice right now.

"So tonight wasn't for the cameras?"

"Tonight was for you. I think this entire thing has been about you, at least since that first time we hung out." Kyle shook his head, smiling. "I've never met someone who's so . . ."

"Strange?"

"Sure of herself." Kyle leaned in closer, just inches away now. I could sense his breathing—his chest was almost touching mine—alternating with my own, you in, me out, you out, me in. "You know exactly what you want. Exactly who you are. You don't care what anyone thinks about you."

"I care what everyone thinks."

"No you don't. Or at least, you don't let it change you. I feel like I've spent the last four years auditioning to be my brother, and it wasn't until I met you that I realized I didn't want the part."

"Well, good," I said. "No one remembers an understudy."

Kyle laughed. Then he shook his head, staring at me. His eyes were still sparkling, happy, but he wasn't laughing anymore. He was intent. I saw his gaze drift lower, linger on my mouth . . .

Then he leaned in to kiss me.

It felt like something had exploded in my chest, burst open like a flower toward the sun. I wrapped my hands around his neck, and he pushed me backward against the wall, leaning into me with his whole body, like any space between us would hurt.

Thank god the cameras hadn't found us yet.

chapter fifty-two

SATURDAY, 10:31 P.M.

Rachel heard it before I did. She pulled away. Rachel: flushed this beautiful shade of pink, blinking fast, stupid-long lashes fluttering up and down like a fan, smiling in that private way, like she couldn't not. I leaned back into her.

She nodded toward the other end of the hall.

Shoes clacked sharply against the speckled stone floors of this corner of Apple Prairie High. Rachel raised an eyebrow.

"I'll go see what's up," I whispered. "Or we could both go?"

"No, you go. I need a second. I'll be right behind you."

"Okay."

I stared at her for a second, every part of me wanting to

forget whoever was at the other end of the hall and just grab her again. She raised an eyebrow.

"Go." Dimple: out. "If it's one of the camera guys I'd rather not have them find us first, all right?"

I sighed dramatically. Rachel laughed, and I walked off. It wasn't until I was just a few feet away that I realized who it was.

chapter fifty-three

RACHEL

SATURDAY, 10:33 P.M.

I waited until Kyle walked away from whoever he was talking to to stride down the hallway, focusing on every step. Confident strides! Nothing to see here! This girl not only belongs in this off-limits area, she definitely wears heels regularly!

I tried not to giggle out loud. I felt so fizzy and light, it was like laughter was preloaded in my mouth. Like Kyle had left some of his there as a parting gift.

I turned the corner back toward the cafeteria.

Dave Rouquiaux was standing there.

"Hey, Rach," he said. We'd never spoken before. It was weird trying to figure out who knew my name before the show and just never bothered using it, and who had only learned about my existence from TV.

"Hey, Dave." I could feel my cheeks going hot. Could he see it on me? Did I even care? "What's going on?"

"Hey. I told her I'd wait here for you." He squint-leered. Dave was a little . . . weird. "I guess they're setting up, like, confessional footage? You know, away from the dance floor, actually talking."

"Oh, okay." I nodded rapidly. Mary must have sent Dave out to find us. "Where should I go?" I felt so buoyant still, the idea of talking straight to a camera didn't even scare me. At least not too much. Maybe Kyle was right, maybe things *could* be good scary.

"They set up in Ms. Laurila's room. But they won't need you yet. If you wanna, you know . . ." Dave made a circling gesture around his face. "Clean up or whatever."

I raised a hand to my face, suddenly self-conscious. What did I look like for *Dave* to be telling me to fix myself? But it hadn't stopped Kyle. . . .

Still, this was national television. Kyle's not your audience, Rach.

"Sure. Will you tell them I'll just be a few minutes? I have to find my purse."

"Yup." Dave nodded, not looking at me. Was he blushing?

I checked to make sure a boob hadn't fallen out. We hadn't even made it that far, but it would be just my luck to be talking to Dave Rouquiaux half-topless.

But I was decent. So just mottled and unpresentable, then.

"Thanks," I yelled over my shoulder, running around the cafeteria to the tables where we'd left our things.

I thought Dave would already have headed off toward the producers, but he just stood there, watching, tapping something into a phone.

## chapter fifty-four

KYLE

SATURDAY, 10:34 P.M.

I opened the door to Ms. Laurila's room. That's where Dave said the camera would be.

The camera: there. Also there: Emma, staring at her phone screen.

"Uh, hey," I said. "Maybe I'm not in the right place. Dave said they wanted Rachel and me to do some talking to the camera stuff?"

"Yeah, they do." Emma smiled. "When I told Jimmy about you and me, he thought it would be interesting for us to do one together. I guess Mary agreed, so . . ."

"What do you mean, you and me?" I looked over at the cameraman. Jimmy, apparently. "Is he recording?"

"No, that's just the power light."

"Well, either way, there's nothing to talk about." I turned toward the door. Emma grabbed at my hand. I shook it off. She looked like I'd slapped her. "I'm not trying to be mean, Em, just . . . there's no us anymore."

"But why? We were so good until all this happened."

"You dumped me *before* this happened."

"I know, but I was wrong." Her voice broke a little, and she looked down. When she looked back up, her eyes were liquid with tears. "And then you were getting so much attention, and I didn't know how to make you want me again, and I got so *jealous*. All those girls were so much prettier and smarter. And now all the stuff with my dad's happening and I just . . . I *need* you, Kyle."

"Emma, they're not prettier. That's not it at all. And it's not that I don't like you, but I don't think we're really—"

"No, I get it, you don't have to say it." Emma gulped noisily. "You don't think I'm good enough for you anymore. Now that you're famous."

Emma buried her face in her hands and started crying.

I walked over and put an arm around her shoulder. I felt bad for her. But that aching need to be the one to make her happy again, like a hook pulling through my guts: gone now. And not just because we were over. I was starting to realize she'd never actually feel better until she worked this stuff out for herself.

She buried her face in my shoulder, shaking softly for a

while. Then she turned to look up at me, eyes glistening, tears still caught in her lashes.

"Kyle," she said, her voice soft. "I miss you so much."

I didn't want to lie to her, so I just smiled. Then I felt her arm wrap around my waist . . .

chapter fifty-five

RACHEL

SATURDAY, 10:42 P.M.

Well, it sure as hell wasn't a professional job, but at least I'd cleared up the smears under my eyes and pinned back a few of the craziest flyaways. It was . . . artfully disheveled?

I honestly couldn't make myself care. What was it Kyle had said? Other people's opinions couldn't change me? He was right. Anyone who wanted to take me down because my hair wasn't perfect wasn't someone whose opinion I needed.

I strode around the outside of the cafeteria, staying on the outer perimeter so I couldn't get caught up in the dance craziness. Ms. Laurila's room was on the hall that snaked out from the vending machine nook. Light from the doorway spilled out into the dim, empty hallway like a beacon in a nighttime sea of flat green lockers and ghostly reflections on tiled walls.

I stopped a couple of feet from the door, baring my teeth for the glass. I'd been in such a rush I hadn't even checked to make sure they were lipstick free—that would be kind of embarrassing—then took a step forward to open it up.

Then I froze.

He was in there with her.

And his arm was around her.

And now she was gazing up at his face with a look made for some romance novel cover, saying something to him, and he wasn't pulling away . . .

. . . and they were kissing.

I ran away down the hall.

I didn't need to see more. But I really needed for the camera not to see me.

chapter fifty-six

SATURDAY, 10:44 P.M.

I pulled away, jerking up off the desk.

"Emma, what the hell?" I wiped at my mouth. Emma frowned.

"Don't you see, Kyle? We're supposed to be together."

"I told you, this is over. We're over."

"Why? Because of *Rach-el*?" She singsonged the name viciously. "Come on."

"You don't even know her."

"Neither do you." She laughed tightly, a too-high tinkling of bells. "Do you honestly think she's into you? The big man on campus *jock*?"

I frowned. Saying yes somehow seemed dense.

"Kyle, think about it. She's in this for the same reason you are. For that." She pointed at the camera. "For the attention. For the chance to be on TV. For everyone on the internet telling her how awesome she is. I mean, come on, three weeks ago she was social kryptonite. And now she's everyone's favorite person? Who *wouldn't* take that deal? I don't even blame her."

"That's not true." It didn't even make sense; Rachel actively *disliked* everyone knowing her.

"Textbook Kyle. The nice guy to the end."

I should have been mad, but suddenly I just felt sad. It didn't have to go this way.

"I just don't believe you. You're bitter, and you're getting mean, but—"

Emma's face twisted up in a mix of rage and pain.

"She's *using you*, Kyle, don't you see that? As soon as this is over, she'll leave you behind, and you'll have thrown away the one real thing you could have had. You'll have thrown me away."

"No, Emma. You threw us away. Over and over."

"Kyle, I—"

"And I honestly don't care what you say about Rachel. I *do* know her. That's not who she is."

"What if you're wrong?"

Emma was staring at me. Face: perfectly still. Eyes: desperate. I shrugged.

"That's a risk I'm willing to take."

Then I walked out the door to find Rachel.

chapter fifty-seven

RACHEL

SATURDAY, 10:44 P.M.

Stupid, stupid, STUPID.

I ran down the hall, turning at random, barely able to see where I was going through the film of tears pouring out of my eyes.

So much for cleaning up. I barked out a bitter laugh.

Finally, panting, I stopped, leaning against a locker for support. It couldn't keep my legs from feeling like beached octopi, though, so I sort of slid down the side of it until I hit the floor.

I'd been so wrong. Believing that all that sunshine he gave off could be real. He was a sunlamp, just some fake version anyone could have for the right price. Shining on me was all just part of some game, some manipulation to get . . . what, a random makeout session? It didn't make sense, except I'd seen what I'd seen.

I buried my face in my hands and let out a sob that sounded like an injured seagull.

I sat there, ugly-crying on the floor, for what felt like hours, but was probably only a few minutes.

"Hey." A familiar voice a few feet overhead. I didn't look up.

"H-h-hey," I choked out snottily. I was suddenly very aware of the fact that I didn't have a tissue. "How'd you find me?"

"You ran past the cafeteria bathrooms. I just followed the general direction. Though I will say, managing to weave your way to the Latin hallway when the building's only half-lit is pretty impressive. In heels, no less."

I half laughed. It also came out snotty.

"You wanna go home?"

"I want to curl up in a ball and disintegrate."

"All right. Well, home is as close to that as I can offer right now."

I let Monique pull me up and lead me out the door, into the night.

## chapter fifty-eight

SUNDAY, 4:42 P.M.

My phone buzzed against the top of my nightstand.

Finally. I dropped the controller midgame, ignoring Ollie's shouts of annoyance, and dove on it.

But it wasn't Rachel. It was Mary.

I picked up the phone.

"Kyle, we've seen the footage."

"Oh, so they *were* filming." I laughed bitterly. "Of course."

"First off, let me apologize. I thought you were made aware of the situation. Our cameraman shouldn't have filmed you and Ms. Stashausen without your knowledge."

Mary coughed.

"But you got your drama, right?"

That one: ignored.

"We can pull together a cut that doesn't use that footage. If Rachel's not on board anymore we'll have to figure out a workaround for the live chat with Laura, but—"

"Use it."

"Sorry?"

"Use the footage."

"Kyle, that's not the story we're—"

"And neither of us is coming on the chat." I actually had no idea what Rachel would do. She wouldn't respond to a single text, or call, or the stupid-expensive daffodils I'd sent to her house. But judging from Monique's texts, I was probably right.

"Kyle, we always planned to end this with—"

"I mean, if you want me to tell the audience I'm contractually obligated to be there, fine. Maybe I'll mention how all the grown-up producers tricked me so they could get a reality-show ending."

The silence: thick as tar.

"We're still not using the footage." Mary's voice didn't sound harried anymore, it sounded cold. Good. Clearly I was getting through.

"Use it or I'm going nuclear on Flit." Would she call that bluff? How did people even have Flit breakdowns? Shave head, smoke things, swear a lot?

"All right."

"Thanks for calling."

I hung up.

Five minutes: all the time it took Mary to get to my mom.

"What are you *thinking*?" She burst into my room without even knocking. Very un-Mom.

"Honestly? I was thinking that callbacks for the play get posted Monday. I really hope I got one."

"What are you talking about?" She squinted at me like I was some foreign object. The body snatcher who took her son. She had the timing all wrong, though. I was only now waking up.

"The school play. They had auditions during lunch last week, and I think I really have a shot, even with all the *Laura Show* crap."

"So you're planning to throw away the best opportunity you've ever been given in order to . . . play pretend?"

I sighed. Ollie: staring at the screen so hard it looked like he might be attached to it through his eyes.

"Mom, the show was great. It was fun. But I'm not going to keep milking this thing while it hurts everyone around me."

"Who are you hurting? This is about your chance to—"

"Rachel, for one. She'll probably *never* forgive me."

Mom frowned. It clearly hadn't occurred to her that some other child might have different feelings about all this. Or any feelings.

"Fine, I understand that, but if you want Princeton as an option, you have to—"

"But I *don't*. I'm not Carter, Mom. I don't want to keep pretending I am."

"Kyle..." She looked stricken. Rachel would like that. Stage direction: stricken. "I thought this was what you wanted."

"I'm glad I did it, really. I would have never known *what* I wanted if I hadn't. But I'm done."

She sat down on the bed. She looked tired but not mad. It was a start.

"Theater? Really?"

"I actually think I'll be good. Or at least I want to be good." I could have tried to explain about how alive I felt when I was about to perform, how every nerve ending felt like a blaze of light, but instead I just smiled. Mom: barely processing what I'd already told her.

"I suppose I'll have to tell the Burger Barn people we're not interested," she said to herself, squinting up at the ceiling.

"What are you talking about?"

"Oh, I was planning to tell you today. They called about some kind of partnership. You'd run their social media, I think? We hadn't worked out details."

"Do you have their number?"

Mom's face brightened a little.

"You want to do it?"

"No." I smiled at her apologetically. "But I know someone who might."

chapter fifty-nine

SUNDAY, 5:15 P.M.

The screen of my phone lit up, a little bluish beacon in the darkened basement.

I ignored it. It would just be Kyle again, trying to explain why he'd been kissing Emma, trying to trick me into trusting him again so I'd play nice for TV tomorrow. Not happening.

Of course it could have been one of the thousand new "besties" I'd sprouted overnight feigning pity over whatever version of the rumor they'd heard, but eff. That. How they even got my number was beyond me.

The phone lit up again. Monique leaned across the table to grab it, looking at me questioningly. Even though we'd both seen *What Ever Happened to Baby Jane?* a million times, we didn't talk through movies.

I shook my head no. She stared at the screen for a second, then typed in my password, which should have been annoying, but whatever, at least the notification wouldn't scream at me once she left and I was alone in my bedroom.

Monique clicked the controller.

"Rachel, you need to look at this one."

"I don't *need* to do anything."

"Okay, let me rephrase. I would like you to look at this one, then we can go back to the movie."

"Yeah, well I'd like—"

"And if you disagree, I'll keep pestering you until you do, and you'll have to fight me for the remote, and we both know my crane style beats your tiger style."

"I'm scrappy."

"I'm serious."

I rolled my eyes and grabbed the phone out of her hand.

"Kyle. What a surprise."

"Just read them, Rachel, seriously."

(From Kyle): I know you're mad, and I get that you don't want to talk to me, but could you watch the show tomorrow?

(From Kyle): If you never want to speak to me again after that I promise I'll leave you alone.

> **(From Kyle):** I told them you're not gonna do the live chat, so don't worry about that

> **(From Kyle):** But please watch? I swear I'll leave you alone if you say you will

"Well?"

"Who cares what he wants. Why should I watch his stupid show anyway?"

"You know there's more to this, Rachel. If you just let him—"

"I know what I saw."

"So do I." Monique sounded annoyed, which was weirdly reassuring; Monique usually got to annoyed much sooner. "I saw him looking at you like you were the most beautiful thing he'd ever seen. And I saw your face when you came by to tell me you guys had kissed. I know you always have to believe the worst, but why not at least hear him out?"

I frowned. I wasn't being unfair, I was just right. Why wouldn't Mo accept that?

"There's nothing they can show that will change what happened."

"Okay. So watch and you get an ironclad guarantee that Kyle loses your number."

The idea that I wanted that still felt like a physical ache. Like a light turning out.

But of course, as usual, Monique was right.

"Fine."

I typed in a text.

"You press send." I flipped the phone at Monique's lap. She sighed exasperatedly but picked it up.

(To Kyle): Yes.

True to his promise, Kyle didn't respond.

## chapter sixty

KYLE

MONDAY, 4:31 P.M.

My legs were starting to cramp up. There really hadn't been any point to getting here twenty minutes before the show even aired, but I was so nervous of screwing up the timing that staying home hadn't been an option.

I looked out the car window at the front of Rachel's house. The house: totally unremarkable. White siding, neatly trimmed hedges under the windows facing the street, blocky two-car garage sticking out to the right, like an afterthought. The only thing that stood out were the flower beds lining the pathway up to the door, filled with strange, spidery red flowers and furry fronds and a bunch of other weird things I'd never seen in any other garden.

Still, that didn't tell me anything about what was going on inside. It just meant Mrs. Ettinger had the same flower aesthetic at home as she did at her shop.

I moved my phone closer to my face, peering at the tiny live stream of the show. I couldn't make my next move until I was sure she'd seen it.

I heard my name. Finally, Laura was getting around to our segment. I wonder if opening with the Halloween makeup artist had been some sort of punishment from Mary. Fine, you can leave, but we'll bury you.

There we were in the limo, Rachel laughing at something with her whole body, like it was the funniest thing in the world. At the rose garden, Rachel plucking a flower and putting it in her teeth and making her fingers into those little clicky things. Castanets? Then in the crowd, Rachel's face lit up by the circling lights, but more from the inside, her smile a thousand watts huge as she turned to the people around her, letting them pull her into a twirl or a dip.

And me: watching Rachel. In every one. Like there was no one else in the room.

Ms. Laurila's room appeared on my screen. I could feel my heart start to race.

Emma: crying. Me: comforting. Emma: kissing. Me: pushing away. They edited out her cattiest comments, but they left me saying I was ready to risk it for Rachel.

The screen cut back to Laura with a big bin of popcorn. The audience was in an uproar.

"I can't wait to know what happens next. We thought today would be the end of Kyle and Rachel's story, but we'll all just have to stay tuned." Laura started stuffing more popcorn in and turned back to the screen, where I was once again pushing away from Emma, making my speech.

They cut to commercial. I got out of the car and walked up the driveway. It felt like I was stepping out in front of my biggest audience yet.

chapter sixty-one

RACHEL

MONDAY, 4:40 P.M.

Monique sat on the couch, watching me from the corner of her eye.

The doorbell rang.

"Really?" I turned to stare at Monique. If she'd set me up again . . .

"It's not what you think."

"Then my dad can answer it."

"I already told him you would."

Classic Monique.

"I said I'd watch, not that I'd talk to him."

Monique blinked rapidly, trying to recalibrate. I forced myself not to smile. I so rarely got to make *her* squirm.

"You saw; it definitely was *not* mutual. And he told me he had to threaten Mary to even get them to use the footage. He's putting *everything* on the line, Rachel, it's—"

I stood.

"But I will."

She rolled her eyes exaggeratedly, then shooed me upstairs.

I ran to the door. Kyle was there, staring at his feet, kicking at the concrete.

"Hey," I said, unable to meet his eyes. "No cameras?"

"I wouldn't do that, not now." He frowned. "Anyway, I think I'm done with all that."

"But it's been so utterly positive for both of us," I deadpanned.

He smiled at the ground.

"So you saw?"

"Yeah." I looked up at him. He was suddenly staring at my face so intently it immediately made me blush.

"I had no idea. I didn't want that to happen at all. I didn't even know they were recording. Though I guess I'm glad they were. Otherwise you might've thought . . ." He shook his head. "Anyway, I'm sorry. That you had to see that. That I hurt you. I never wanted to hurt you, Rachel." His face was one big plea, all lowered eyebrows and wavering lips and beautiful, sad eyes.

"I know." I smiled a little. For the first time I wasn't second-guessing this, or him, or me. He was telling me the truth. He had been all along.

Neither of us said anything for a minute. I could feel his stare on my forehead, laser-intense, heating me from the inside. It felt amazing and terrifying at the same time, because I knew I would let him in. That I already had.

I had to change the subject.

"So you're pulling the plug? I thought you liked performing."

"Yeah, I do. But I thought I should, you know, perfect my craft." He grinned goofily. "I got a callback for *Rosencrantz and Guildenstern*."

"Whoa. Even weirdos know that's a play for weirdos."

"Had to make up for lost time. Oh, also, that reminds me, Burger Barn is gonna be calling you. You can tell them no if you want, I just thought—"

"Burger Barn?"

"They wanted to do a social media thing. Where, like, you take over their Flit accounts for the day? I told them you might want to write some sketches, or, like, mini plays? They seemed really into that; they might do a whole series of webisodes."

"But you're the Burger Barn guy. Why would they call . . ." I'm such an idiot. "Wait, you turned them down?"

"You're the one whose flit got all the attention. You're the writer. And just think, everyone will notice you, but you won't even have to be onscreen. Monique said you guys had this application . . ."

"You'd do that for me?"

"Well, I mean . . . yeah." Kyle looked confused, then grinned mischievously. "Besides, you're gonna need someone to star in the stuff you write, won't you?"

I grinned back. Kyle leaned forward and grabbed my hands, setting off thousands of tiny explosions in my fingertips, and my arms, and the pit of my stomach. . . .

"So are we . . . okay?" He leaned in a little closer. Standing on the door frame I was right at his eye level, my outline silhouetted in the green of his eyes.

I smirked a little.

"I *guess* I'll give you a second chance. Just this once. You better not waste it, though. I'm not a very forgiving woman."

"But you have to be, at least for a couple hours," he said, lips curling into a smile.

"Why?"

"I thought we could go bowling."

ACKNOWLEDGMENTS

I was going to try to be sparklingly clever in my acknowledgments, but I have far too much sincere gratitude to waste time with that, so here goes, from the heart:

Thank you more than I can possibly say to Melissa Miller, without whom this book wouldn't have been possible. I absolutely won the editor lottery with you, which more than makes up for the fact that I never win real-life raffles.

To Heather Alexander, the most amazing agent a girl has ever known. When I grow up, I want to have your hair. In the meantime, fantastic conversation and the occasional rooftop cocktail are very good substitutes.

To Anica Rissi and Katherine Tegen, for taking a chance on me, and Kelsey Horton, whose keen editing eyes are very much appreciated. To Bethany Reis and Jill Amack for fixing my myriad mistakes. To the HarperCollins subrights team for championing *#famous* overseas. And to the entire team at Katherine Tegen Books, whose brilliance is unparalleled.

To E. Jean Carroll: without your ceaseless support for me when I was still just an unformed Jilly-shaped lump, I would never have had the courage to keep writing.

To Laurel Snyder, for propping up my self-confidence when I most needed it; Jesse Andrews, for pointing me in a new direction; and Amitav Ghosh, for helping me realize the value in the voice I have, not the one I thought I ought to have.

To Jen Russ, the most patient, thoughtful, and brilliant critique partner in the world: I cannot wait until I see your amazing words in print.

To my fantastic writing group, especially Carrie-Anne DeDeo, Ken Marden, Jillian Melnyk, and Ben Miller, who helped me make this book the best it could be.

To the many brilliant editors who took a chance on me over the years, especially Nicole Cliffe at The Toast, whose matchmaking prowess is no less impressive for being unintentional.

To my family. Mom, you cheered me on every step of the way on a crazy long-shot dream. Claire, Janie, Nicole, Camille, and Jeff: you were my support system and the stand-ins for the therapist I really need to start seeing. Dad, I miss you more than you know. I wish you could be here to see that I listened, and never stopped doing the thing I loved.

To all the friends who have kept me smiling even when I thought this could never happen. I can't possibly list you all by name, but I love you, even if I generally express that through sarcasm.

To coffee for making anything possible. To *Witcher III* for providing a much-needed rabbit hole.

And to Zelda and Captain Gentleman, the best colleagues a girl could ever hope for.